A Stalker. A Secret. A Syndicate.
And No Where to Hide

ABILENE

NO PLACE TO HIDE

B. A. Mealer

Abilene: No Place to Hide

B. A. Mealer

BAM Publishing.
https://www.bamelaer.com
ISBN 978-1-970130-00-3 (mobi)
ISBN 978-1-970130-01-0 (paperback)
ISBN 978-1-970130-02-7 (hardcover)
ISBN 978-1-970130-03-4 (e-pub)
PRINTED IN THE UNITED STATES OF AMERICA

Dedication

This book is dedicated to all the women who persevere through thick and thin to achieve their dreams.

Chapter 1

Wade turned into the parking lot of the grocery story, scanning the lot for a parking space. He gritted his teeth and cursed his younger brother Chad for not telling him he was coming to town. The last thing he wanted to do today was grocery shopping. He preferred staying at the ranch. Not only did he have a lot of work to complete, but he was very aware of perils of being in town alone meant.

An empty spot beside a old model jeep appeared on his right. He put the truck into park before taking a deep breath and blowing it out, hating the thought of going into the grocery store. His gaze went to the jeep. It wasn't one he recognized as belonging to one of the locals. Other than a few small dents, a fine covering of dust and dirt and needing new tires, it was is great shape. Whoever owned it had taken good care of the vehicle.

"Quit stalling," he muttered, steeling himself to enter the store. It didn't pay to be a bachelor, a widower or divorced in this area if you had money, owned a big spread or had decent looks. The looks were optional if the man had money. If all three were present, Wade knew from experience what to expect.

Over the past eighteen years he had been the objective for many of the eligible females in and around the town. Unlike Chad, he never learned to flirt and play. With being the oldest, he had been given the responsibility of learning how to run the large ranch. Other than a short foray into marriage, which didn't work, he avoided the females. It had hurt when his wife left after seven years of marriage, saying she didn't love him and was moving to the city. She had left their six-year-old son with him, saying she wanted to have fun while she could. He didn't try to keep her since he had learned how being in lust was totally different from being in love.

With the news of his divorce, he became the center of attention of the women who were looking for marriage. He had dated over the years, but the women would push for marriage too early for him to continue dating them. As the years passed, he found fewer and fewer women interested him, while they did what they could to get his attention. Of those who chased him, few wanted him, only what he would have when his father retired. Being the heir to the ranch had made his social life more difficult.

He released a breath, cursing Chad again as he stepped out of the truck and strode toward the store. "I might as well get this over then I can get back to work." he grumbled to himself.

Wade pulled a shopping cart out of the line before removing the list of things he needed to get from his shirt pocket before entering the store. Mentally he derided his father's decision to give their housekeeper the same two weeks off he was to be in the capital. That left him and Chad to fend for themselves while completing the work he wanted done before he returned.

He noticed Linda at the service counter brighten with a smile when he entered the store. With a nod, he made his way to the far side of the store, hoping to get to the dairy section without being stopped by Missy Gentry who was eyeing him. She was nice enough but not someone he wanted to date. Now the pretty redhead at the bank was another story. From the time she moved her, he had been attempting to figure out how to ask her out without asking Chad for advice as he would tease him unmercifully for at least a month or more.

When he rounded the corner of the deli, Chad was standing in line, flirting with one of the women. Wade, his mouth in a grim line, wended his way through the waiting customers to his brother.

His gaze locked on his brother, eyes narrowed, not noticing the glances the women sent his way.

"Chad, what are you doing here?" Wade's voice was stern, startling his brother, who turned to face him, grinning.

"Lunch. I'm starving and figured a sub would be better than hotdogs. Wanna share one?"

Expelling a breath and his anger, Wade nodded. "Sure. Why not? When you're done here, I could use your help in getting the things on this list before you leave." He glanced at the woman Chad had been talking with, who was eyeing them before asking, "You get the parts Sam needs?"

"Yep. They're in the truck." Chad happily said, "You hear that the renter for the Haskell place showed up last night?"

Wade glared at him. "No. I didn't." His eyes flicked to the woman who was listening to them, then back to Chad. "What was the name of the renter? I forgot." He hadn't forgotten, but there was no reason to broadcast he knew more than the place was rented.

Chad chuckled and shook his head. His quick wink indicated he knew Wade hadn't forgotten the name. "An A. Brown. No one has seen the person, but Sally said someone pulled in last night, as there were light on at the house. Wonder what the person plans on doing with the place?"

Wade grimaced. "Who knows. It isn't suitable for farming and doesn't have enough land to put cattle on it. Hopefully they'll be a good neighbor this time."

The number for the next customer for the Deli was called. Chad checked the ticket in his hand. It apparently wasn't his number. Wade was glad Chad picked up on things making it easier to keep a low profile on their side job.

"I agree. The last renter was a total nut job," Chad said rolling his eyes and shaking his head.

Wade's stomach growled when the next number was called. It was Chad's, cutting off whatever else he planned on saying. Wade leaned against the post where his brother had been standing, crossing his arms, while ignoring the other customers. A surreptitious glance at those around him made him want to leave the list with Chad and head back to the ranch. He was uncomfortable with the attention he was garnering as he studied the shopping list.

Chad returned in less than three minutes with the sub and two packages of chips which he placed in the seat of the basket to keep it from getting crushed. Wade tore the list in half, giving Chad the bottom portion. They strolled down the dairy isle, ignoring the stares they were getting, intent on what they needed to get in groceries.

The two brothers stood out in the store where most of the shoppers were women. They were considered the most elusive eligible bachelors in the county. The striking duo had short thick black hair with silver at the temples. While wade had bright blue eyes, Chad's were hazel. If the women who knew them were to be believed, they were a mix of Randolph Scott, Clint Eastwood and Sean Connery with Paul Newman's eyes. The overall effect was one of rugged good looks which went from the range to high society with a change of clothes. Both were lean and muscular from the hard work on the ranch, but that was where the similarities ended.

Wade was the taller of the two and fit the description of tall, dark and handsome with a hint of danger about him. Meanwhile, Chad was the good-looking playboy with an easy smile and laugh whom everyone knew and liked. When together, the pair drew stares like iron to a magnet, but it was Wade most women were after. He was the one who would inherit one of the biggest and most profitable ranches in the area.

"Let me get started on this list," Chad said, not the least perturbed with being in the store. When he took off, it left Wade to make his way through the aisle feeling like he stuck out like an elephant in a china shop. With the two of them working together, it wouldn't take long to finish and get out of the store.

In the aisle with the paper goods, Wade noticed a woman comparing paper towels. She was tall, about five eight with enough weight to give her noticeable curves. The mahogany brown hair fell in waves and soft curls to the middle of her back. The profile was that of a cameo with a peaches and cream complexion. Her shirt and jeans accentuated her buxom figure. From what he could see, he guessed her to be around thirty-five, give or take a few years.

He stopped to get the aluminum foil the needed before glancing back at the woman, wondering who she was. He hadn't seen her around town before today. The woman turned toward him and flashed a shy smile before putting her choice in the shopping care and moving away down the aisle. He was older than he first thought, most likely in her forties. Her face reminded him of Maureen O'Hara with the classic oval and beautiful eyes.

Returning to the task at hand, Wade turned up his lips in a slight smile. She was on female he wouldn't be averse to meeting. Again, he wondered who she was and where she was staying. Knowing Chad, he'd have the information soon enough. Chad was privy to all the gossip in town through the men and women he had a friends.

Wade picked up several more items from the aisle before heading into the next one. The woman was halfway down the aisle putting laundry soap into her cart. Chad came up behind him with an armful of items from his portion of the list. Wade kept his face blank when Chad noticed the woman.

"Hey. Check that out. She's one sexy female." Chad kept his voice low while staring at the woman.

Wade lifted his eyes from his list to glance at the appealing lady. "I noticed. Saw her in the last aisle. I wonder who she is."

Chad chuckled. "I want to know how long she plans on being here."

Wade grinned at Chad who had turned to him with a big grin creasing his face. "Take it easy, kid. From what she's buying, you'll get your chance to meet her." With a quick glance back at the intriguing female, he said, "Go get the rest of the stuff on your list. Sam needs those parts and we need to get back to work. Dad wants that stallion ready to ride by the time he gets back and you have that filly to finish breaking."

"Yeah, yeah. Meet you in the veggies," Chad grumped, the grin still in place. He gave the woman another once-over before leaving.

Feigning disinterest, Wade moved closer to the mysterious woman, who was not comparing dish soaps. He reached around her and grabbed a bottle of dish soap, which was on his list.

"Excuse me," he mumbled with an apologetic smile.

The woman peered up at him with widely spaced green eyes under arching eyebrows. Her lips turned up in a smile when their eyes met. "No problem," she said in a throaty musical voice, enticing him in to getting her to say more.

He gave the enchanting woman a quick smile and nod before moving to the next aisle. He let out the lungful of air he'd been holding before taking a deep breath. She was a damn good-looking woman with a voice he wanted to hear again. Maybe it was time he began to socialize again. She had gotten his complete attention with her captivating voice and those green eyes.

Wade pulled himself back to the job at hand, finishing his list before joining Chad in the produce section. After loading the cart with the rest of the items Chad picked up, they headed to the checkout lanes. Wade watched and listened to Chad flirting with Jenny, but his thoughts were on the woman in the aisle, attempting to come up with a plan to meet her. He envied Chad's easy manner as he joked around and chatted with Jenny. It was a skill he'd never developed leaving him to be classified as the strong silent type.

While Wade was paying the bill, Chad elbowed him and indicated with his head to look over at the checkout lane beyond them. The woman was putting her things on the conveyor belt.

Wade watched for only a few second before nudging Chad toward the door. He wasn't about to tell him he had spoken to her. It would only result in multiple questions he didn't want to answer.

As they put the groceries into Wade's truck, Mrs. Collins, the town gossip, interrupted them. "Have you heard that the person who rented the Haskell place is a woman?"

Chad glanced at the elderly lady. "Juts heard the person came in last night. Didn't know it was a woman."

Puffing up with importance, Mrs. Collins said, "Well, Mr. Gentry told Bob that he saw her this morning outside as he was driving by. Said she was a real looker and there didn't appear to be anyone else with her."

"Really?" Chad commented, sending a quick glance to Wade, encouraging the woman to tell them more.

"Yes. He said she was something else. He's planning on having Missy go over later today to welcome her and invite her to the dance tomorrow night. You two will be there, won't you?"

The brother exchanged a glance, well aware of how she thought of herself as a match maker.

"Maybe. Depends on our day," Wade responded with his usual way out if he decided not to attend the dance.

"Oh, you two have to come. Everyone will be there, and what would a party be without you boys to liven it up?" she said, eyes wide.

Not wanting to commit to something he didn't normally attend, Wade stated, "I'll think about it. Chad should be there. He never misses a chance to dance."

Accepting his response with a big smile, the elderly gossip heading into the store to impart her news to anyone who would listen. She was better, more accurate and timelier than the social section of the paper.

Chad's voice drew Wade's attention. "Big brother, you really need to get out more often. You're turning into an old fart." Chad moved out of Wade's reach when he lunged for him.

Wade glared at Chad. "Like I said, I'll think about it. Unlike you, I have work to do and it isn't just working with the horses."

After moving the shopping care out of the way, Wade unlocked the truck.

"You're coming with me to this dance if I have to drag you this time," Chad said, not smiling.

Wade rotated back to his brother, quirking an eyebrow. "You and who else?"

Chad, with merry eyes and a big grin said, "I'll have help if needed. Plan on being ready right after supper. I need some backup this time. Like old lady Collins said, everyone will be there."

Not rising to the veiled threat, Wade slid into the driver's seat, started the truck and put it in gear. He would think about it. It might be worth all the hassle to attend if the woman in the store might be there. There was only the slightest resemblance of the woman to the picture he had seen of one Abilene Brown. It might be an interesting six month if she was the Mrs. Brown they were expecting.

Chapter 2

The brothers spent most of Saturday in connecting corrals by the big barn working with the horses they were training. It was close to four then they quit and took the horses to the barn to groom them. After putting the horse he'd been training into its stall, Wade drew in a deep breath and blew it out, the smell of manure and horses permeating the air. He believed what Chad said about having help to get him into town this evening. There was no way to get out of it this time. He might as well suck it up and go.

No matter how he looked at it, it was going to be a long evening. Chad and the others wouldn't want to leave until late. With being the designated driver whenever they went out, he wouldn't be able to leave early. If worse came to worse, he could sleep in the trunk until they were ready to leave. Then again, if the fascinating new lady was there, he might stick around.

After giving the stallion he had been working with a last pat, Wade ambled toward the house to get ready for the evening only to see Chad bounding down the steps toward him as excited as a kid with a new toy.

"Hey, Wade. You know that lady we saw yesterday at the store?"

"Yeah. What about her?"

"She's the A. Brown who rented the Haskell place, and guess what? She's attending the dance tonight!"

Wade studied his brother, keeping his face neutral. The evening promised to be a more interesting. "Who told you that?"

"Missy. She just called. Her dad sent her over with a casserole to welcome the new neighbor, and there's this lady there. She described our woman in the store to a T. Cane you believe it? Six month of one hell of a good looker close by."

Wade shook his head, keeping the urge to grin under control. "Down boy before you scare her half to death with your enthusiasm."

Chad was correct. She was good looking. The photographs of her didn't come close to the actual woman. It was no wonder he hadn't recognized her in the store.

Chad stopped, grabbing Wade's arm. "Do I hear some interest in her, big brother?"

He flicked a glance at Chad, who had sobered. With a nonchalant shrug, he said, "Maybe."

Chad quieted, keeping pace with him as he resumed his walk to the house. After several steps, Chad grinned. "Hey, you saw here first, so you get first dibs." He punched Wade on his shoulder. "You'd better make it good, big brother, or I'll take her from you.

Wade reached up and rubbed his nose, keeping his gaze on the house. "I'll admit she got in interest, but let's see how she handles all the attention she'll get this evening. Who knows, she might see someone else she'll be more interested in."

Chad laughed. They both knew most would gravitate to them. Dropping the topic of the woman, they saw in the store, they moved onto what they were wearing and when they were leaving for the dance. Wade knew his brother would give him a chance. Once chance only. Not that it made any difference. If he wanted her, he would do whatever it took to get her and keep her. He could still see her green eyes meeting his. And the voice. It had drawn him in like the Pied Piper. Oh yeah. He was interested in the new lady.

Wearing the requisite dress jeans, fancy shirt with string tie, fancy boots and Stetson hat, Wade joined his brother and the two other men who were waiting for him by the truck. Chad ran his eyes over Wade with a smirk.

"You clean up nice, big brother," he teased. Chad remained behind Jamie, the eldest of the four of them, out of Wade's reach.

If Wade could have reached his brother, he would have cuffed him sharply.

Jamie, with twinkling eyes and a stern face, said calmly, "Enough. Time to go." He proceeded to take the front passenger seat in the extended cab truck.

Wade glared at Chad before going to the driver's side. Chad and the ranch hand, the fourth member of their group, joked around on the way into town to the large community center. Wade and Jamie remained silent. Maybe he was turning into an old fart after all.

He pulled into an empty parking spot beside the jeep he had noticed at the store, hoping it was the new lady's vehicle. After turning off the engine, he drew in a deep breath and let it out. Time to bite the bullet and pretend he was enjoying himself, even if he really wasn't.

The four men entered the dim interior of the large building. It had been decorated in a fall theme with bales of hay, ears of Indian corn tied together hanging from the posts and leaves scattered across the floor. This was the first community dance Wade was attending in close to five years. He still had a clear memory of the women who had bombarded him with offers and innuendos. Every time he turned around, there was another woman coming at him. Chad had laughed, but Wade had no idea of how to handle them. Instead, he avoided going to community functions as much as possible. He hoped his age and time away from the social scene would prevent a repetition of that nightmarish evening. Those women had done an excellent job of scaring him off without realizing what they were doing.

Chad and the ranch hand took off together. Jamie headed to where the old-timers where holding court. Wade scanned the room before his noted Jerry, his best friend talking to a few men from town. Striding across the expansive room, his boots creating a tattoo, he stopped behind Jerry, smiling.

When Wade topped his friend on the shoulder, Jerry rotated his head to see who was behind him. A big smile creased his face as he turned to Wade. "Well, well, well. Looky what the cat done dragged in!" he said as they greeted each other.

Wade chuckled. "Yeah. Chad threatened to get the others to drag me here, so I figured I'd better come a long nicely."

Jerry chortled, clapping Wade on the shoulder. "It's about time you quit hiding out there at the ranch. There's a whole big world away from there, you know."

"I know that, but you're an old married man. You don't have to put up with the women chasing you like you're a prized stallion at auction."

Jerry and the others laughed at his accurate description of how the town women viewed eligible bachelors. He draped an arm across Wade's shoulders. "Yeah, it much be tough fighting them off," he teased. "I can't believe you and Chad are brothers. You attract them, and he plays with them." Jerry took away his arm before saying, "How's your boy doing?"

"He's getting there. He got an acceptance as one of the better veterinarian schools next year. It's going to cost me on an arm and a leg, but hopefully, it'll be worth it in the end."

"Jake's a good kid. He'll do well," Jerry raised his brows. "Want to trade him for a girl?"

Wade chuckled, shaking his head while holding up a hand palm out toward Jerry. "Not in this lifetime. It's bad enough with a boy. You can keep your girls."

Jerry gave an exaggerated sigh and rolled his eyes. "I can't eve give them away. They're driving me to drink with all the boys hanging around, including your brother's two."

Wade picked up on what Jerry was hinting at. "Let Chad know if they disrespect your girls. They're aware of what will happen if they do."

Jerry nodded. "You meet the new lady yet?"

"No, but I guess I saw her at the store yesterday."

"Come on. I'll introduce you. She's over there talking to Maddie."

Jerry took off. Wade followed him toward his wife who was engaged in conversation with several other women. The lady he'd seen in the store was there, listening to what Maddie was saying. Tonight, she was dressed in a while blouse with the top buttons open, loosely tucked into the waistband a full denim skirt with a wide ruffle at the bottom. She wore plain black boots with low heels. Her hair was loosely pulled back with a clasp at the nape of her neck, a few stray tendrils curling around her face and ears. The necklace she wore drew his eyes downward to the rounded breasts.

Pulling his gaze from where it shouldn't be, Wade waited as Jerry kissed, Maddie, his wife before turning to the person he now knew was the A. Brown they were expecting. Considering how Chad and he hadn't recognized her in the store, the real person looked a lot different from the studio photos they had been given. She was much prettier and a lot more vibrant in person. Then there was that voice.

"Abilene, let me introduce you to Wade Chapman, one of the ranchers in the area. His brother Chad is right over there," Jerry said, pointing out Chad. "Wade, this is Abilene Brown. She's staying out at the Haskell place for the next six months."

"Pleased to meet you, ma'am," Wade said with a smile. He shook the offered hand, remembering her green eyes looking up at him in the store.

"Same here. I take it you're from the infamous Triple C Ranch."

"Yes, ma'am. Seem like we always have three Chapmans to run it. We hope you'll enjoy your stay here."

Her smile widened. "I believe I will. The people here are so nice and friendly."

Wade noticed the women listening and watching them. Abilene must have noticed the attention they were getting. She moved away from the group of women, motioning for him to come with her with a motion of her head and a smile. As they ambled across the floor, she said, "I'm so glad you decided to come tonight. Jerry said you most likely wouldn't show up."

Wade turned to her, brows drawn together. "You say that like you knew who I was."

She chuckled. "Well, Mrs. Collins happily informed me about you and your brother. Her description was quite accurate." Quiet for a few steps, she stopped and rotated to face him, her face serious. "Your being here saves me a trip to your place. I understand your ranch borders on the Haskell place on all sides. I'd like to request permission to explore on your land. I'm doing some geological research. There are a couple of areas I'd like to study, but they're over the border, so to speak."

Wade almost missed what she was saying, mesmerized by her low whiskey voice as it wrapped around him. This didn't bode well for him is she had him daydreaming by talking to him. He mentally shook himself before responding.

"And what sort of research are you doing?" He knew what she was doing, but he needed her to tell him. They didn't want her to know they had enticed her here to help her. At least not yet. She would eventually learn about them and what they were doing. For now, she had to believe she had found this place on her own and they were helping her because they liked her.

She met his gaze as he tried to keep his mind from going places where it had no reason to go. One thing he did know: Chad wasn't going to get a chance with her. Her voice pulled him from his thoughts.

"Mostly looking at the age of the area, content of the soil and various rocks and formations, water content. That type of thing.

All surface thing. No digging other than a few inches. I'm not looking for gold, silver, gas or oil. I'm studying the geological makeup of the area. If you want o see what I'm doing, feel free to stop by and I'll show you the research I've done in other areas."

Wade sifted through what she said, "I believe that might be best as it would give me a better idea of what to expect. We've had other who wanted to do 'research' but they were after the gold, silver, oil and gas."

A hopeful look crossed her face. "Then when may I expect you?"

Wade shrugged. "Tomorrow after church if that's all right with you."

"Great. May I plan on you for lunch then?"

Wade's eyes narrowed, but all he noticed was an innocent invitation in her direct gaze. "Sounds good. Sort of tired of eating my own cooking. Our housekeeper's on vacation and Chad and I aren't the best of cooks."

A grin spread across her face. "Then I guess I'd better dust off my cooking skill. I'll show you what I'm doing and explain it over lunch."

To verify what she said earlier, Wade said, "So, you came here to do research?" There was no reason to let her know he already knew the answer.

"Mostly. I—um—needed to find a place off the beaten track to keep a low profile for a while."

He noticed the change in her when she lowered her head. Her bottom lip caught in her teeth as she scuffed the toe of her boot on the floor. He wanted to enfold her in his arms, protecting her while telling her it would be alright. He knew better but she had given them the opened he needed.

"Want to talk about it?" he probed, his voice soft, concerned. He needed to hear her version of what he already knew.

She darted a glance at him before making a half turn away from him, gazing at the wall. "Not now. Tomorrow."

He could live with that, not that she was going to tell him something he didn't already know. Now that the business portion was done, it was time to get to the personal things he wanted to know. Just because he was part of a case his family was working didn't mean he couldn't get to know her better and enjoy her company.

"Okay, so any fellas waiting on you back home?" Wade asked with a smile.

Her eyes crinkled as she shook head, grinning. "No. No attachments." She rotated and faced him, her eyes merry, she stopped the rest of his questions. "Before you ask, one child, a girl, grown and on her own. I'm a widow and have been for over twenty years. I haven't found a good enough reason to remarry. I have a doctorate in geology and teach part-time while doing research the rest of the time. I've taken some contract jobs at times but refuse to work for companies which destroy the land. I've been all over the states and love what I do. Your turn."

Wade couldn't help by laugh. She had nicely circumvented all his questions.

"Alright. I've lived here all my life but have done some traveling in the states. Been divorced for close to twenty years and haven't found a good enough reason to remarry. I breed, raise and train horses for a living. My one child is a boy who's away at school studying to be a vet. I share the ranch with my father and Chad, my brother, and his two teenage sons. I have a master's degree in animal husbandry and also enjoy what I do."

Abilene's right brow rose. I've a feeling my stay here is going to be quite interesting. Being my normal self, I'll admit to finding you fascinating. Gentlemen are few and far between and I like your style."

Wade assessed her, considering what she said. Time to be honest. "I'll admit you got my attention, and that's no easy task for most women. I don't meet many who are ladies and as direct as you. I find it quite refreshing. I dislike the games most of the women play when I meet them."

She chuckled. "And here I expected you to start running for the hills form what I was told."

It was his turn to lift and eyebrow, his face serious with a hint of a smile at the corners of her mouth. "I still might."

Her laugher, like her voice, drew him to her. It was natural and full. Quickly scanning the room, he noted many of both sexes watching them, not that it mattered. His plan, not that he had actually met her, was to monopolize her time while she was here. When she placed a hand on his arm, his attention was redirected to her mesmerizing green eyes.

"I'll trust you to introduce me to the non-lechers in town. Like you, I prefer solitude to being chased everywhere I go."

At a loss for words, Wade's eyes rounded as he stared at her. It took a minute for him to pull himself together. "And just how did you figure that out?"

She grinned. "Easy. Mrs. Collins said you seldom came to town, but each time you did, there was always a line of women waiting to bump into you because you were one of the more eligible bachelors in the area, along with your brother. If you put it all together, you avoid coming to town because of the lecherous women who want to get a hold on you."

The analysis was right on target. She went up another notch in his book. Apparently, she understood how he felt. He studied her for a few seconds. "I can imagine you have much the same problem."

Abilene glanced over the room. "I do but I ignore most of the men. There are times when it gets to be a hassle to do anything with all the attention I get by being the new woman in town. I came this evening to discover what I was up against."

With a chuckle, Wade said, "Well, you've made enemies of most of the single women in the room with me talking to you for so long. The men will back off if they believe I'm interested in you since most of them know me from my younger days and how I react to someone cutting in on someone I'm interested in at the time. I can only see good from banding together while you're here. I get to enjoy things, and you get left alone."

"Enjoy what types of things?" Abilene asked sharply, taking a step back from him, her eyes narrowed.

It was his turn to grin. "Nothing bad. Things like going out to eat occasionally, dancing, having someone other than my brother to go riding with—that type of thing."

Abilene visibly relaxed. "Okay. I can handle that since I don't get out much either."

With a conspiratorial wink, he said, "Than I'll let them know I'm going to be hanging out with you. That'll make most of the leave you alone."

"And how many women will I have to fight?" Abilene asked, staring at him.

Wake let out a bark of laughter. "None. They'll shun you instead unless they want information about you going out with me."

She studies him with serious eyes, then shrugged. "Sounds good to me. I don't need the women hanging around gossiping or the lechers accosting me.

Wade put his hand at her waist. "In that case, let me introduce you to those who'll be nice to you while treating you as a friend."

He guided her around the room, introducing her to his close friends. What she didn't know was how he was giving her a ring of protection. She had made it easy for him by accepting his proposal to band together, but she didn't know there was a secondary reason for the proposal. He was attracted to the new lady in a way he hadn't expected.

When they got to Chad, Wade expected him to make an off-the-wall comment. To his surprise, Chad greeted Abilene with a smile and a simple handshake. Wade could see he was holding back his laugher.

Abilene studied him for a few seconds before saying, "Alright. Out with it. You can't believe your brother has attached himself to the new woman so quickly."

Chad's laugh rang out before he glanced at Wade then back to her. "No, I can't, but then again, my brother isn't really all that normal as you seem to have already discovered." He leaned close to her and lowered his voice to a stage whisper. "I only request at least one dance. Have to at least make a showing as if I'm compete against him for the beautiful newcomer. I need to keep my standing around here, you know."

Abilene, her eyes showing merriment, whispered back. "Okay, I'll save you one, but I don't promise not to step on your toes."

Straightening up, Chad said, "Let me worry about my toes. Would you like something to drink?"

"An ale if they have one. If not, a glass of white wine."

"Coming right up. I'll bring you back one, too," Chad said to Wade before heading to the bar.

Wade watched as his brother charmed the barmaid. Glancing down at Abilene, ne noticed she was also watching his brother.

"You're a decent judge of character to guess what Chad was thinking."

"He's easy to read on the surface. He gave himself away when he was watching you introduce me to your friends."

The tone of her voice drew his attention. "You see something else in him, don't you?"

She sighed. "Yes. A deep pain that's never left. He's developed this cavalier playboy façade to cover that pain to keep from getting hurt again. As much as he plays, he's actually lonely." She pivoted to Wad with raised eyebrows. "Meanwhile, back at the ranch, you hide from them, not wanting to be bothered with those you see as grasping and greedy. It's an easy out and works."

Tilting her head away from him, she admitted, "I know how well it works. I've used it for most of my adult life. Like me, you aren't lonely, preferring the solitude to the games."

Wade leaned a hip against the counter for drinks behind him, folding his arms before him. "There wouldn't be a bit of gypsy in you, would there?" She'd been correct in the analysis of both him and Chad.

"No gypsy. I'm a habitual people watcher, honing my skill over the years. That's how I know you're trustworthy and will hold to your word."

Chad rejoined them, handing Abilene a mug of dark ale and Wade a beer. They chatted about the town and their jobs until the band started to play. Setting his beer on the counter, Wade took the mug of ale from Abilene before leading her to the dance floor. He hoped he could remember the steps of the line dance they were doing.

The next dance was a country waltz. Abilene openly flirted with him as they danced opposite each other. Her green eyes were merry, ignoring the dirty looks she was getting. For the first time in many years, he was having a fun time at a dance and the woman across from him was the reason. She couldn't be called ordinary in any sense of the word.

When the band segued into a slow dance, Wade finally got to hold the woman who created a big stir among the locals.

She gleefully, "I guess this should get them talking. Nothing like being the center of a gossip storm in a small town."

"Yeah. Well, I was beginning to wonder if I would have to pull you out of a pile of women during that waltz."

With a shake of her head, she chuckled, "Not yet. Let's see what happens when I dance with your brother. It should really set them on their ears."

"Living a bit dangerously, don't you think?"

"Not really. I'm setting the stage for them to leave me alone," she responded with a smile.

Wade didn't understand, but she seemed to know what she was doing. He would play along, hoping things didn't get ugly before they left. He planned to enjoy the sparkling green eyes inviting him to do more than dance.

When the slow dance ended, Chad came to claim his dance as they were leaving the dancefloor. Reluctantly, Wade let Chad take her from him. He moved to where he could see them dancing. Chad winked at him as he whirled Abilene to the music. Wade felt a spike of jealousy go through him as he watched.

Chapter 3

Chad glanced back at Wade, then grinned at her. "I'm not sure what magic you've worked on him, but you've gotten his total attention without even trying."

"No magic. He'll forget about me in a couple of weeks."

"I don't believe so, just wait and see."

With and smile, she ignored Chad's words, fully believing if things went as they normally did, Wade would be back on the ranch, not bothering with her by the end of the week, two at the most.

Chad made a turn and she was facing where a corner where the wallflowers sat. It was the spot where she would have ended up if Wade had walked away and left her alone. Among those there, was a pretty younger woman with dark red hair talking to one of the older ladies. Abilene brought her attention back to Chad.

"What's with the nice-looking redhead sitting over there with no one going near her other than the old ladies?"

Chad rotated them until he could see the person she mentions.

"I don't so. Maybe she prefers to watch."

"Hm. I bet she would love to dance if someone asked her," Abilene commented, watching the woman before turning back to Chad, who gave the woman another glance.

"You might be right. We sort of ignore the women over there because it's where the old ladies go to sit and gossip."

Abilene met his gaze. "If it wasn't for Wade hanging out with me, I would be sitting there with her. I guess that means I'd have become invisible and ignored too."

His eyes snapped back to hers. A smile appeared on his face, showing he understood what she was saying. It gave her a reason to believe one nice-looking redhead was about to have some fun for one evening.

Chad escorted her back to Wade at the end of the song, bowed, and thanked her for the dance. He pivoted and strolled to no-man's-land and the girl she pointed out to him. Wade observed Chad's progress around the edge of the dance floor. His voice came to Abilene.

"I've a feeling you've done something tricky here," he said. Abilene smiled, watching Chad talking to the woman.

"Nothing tricky. If you hadn't shown up or had left after meeting me, I would have been right there beside her, unseen by all the men here."

Wade's eyes widened, disbelief showing on his face. "I can't imagine you being unseen, even with the old ladies."

With a slight frown, she shook her head. "You're quite wrong. That's the corner of the unseen. Most men won't even look over there. It's the place for the elderly, the outcasts, the exceedingly shy, and a few who are hoping for only one dance for the evening. I know from experience because that's where I normally end up. I'm not comfortable around strangers."

Wade stared at her, blurting out, "I find that hard to believe."

Turning away from Chad, she took a sip of her ale, her back to the dance floor. "Jerry threw me out there, and if you hadn't shown up, I would have joined them in that corner, not willing to participate in the meat-market scene. Even Chad would have looked right past me once I was there. We wallflowers have a tendency to blend into the woodwork one we choose our spots."

"So, you pointed her out to Chad, having been there with lone like her," he said before turning and leaning on the counter beside her, his gaze boring into her."

"Yes. It'll make her night to be noticed by someone like Chad, not counting having a dance with him."

Abilene met Wade's assessing stare. She still wanted to go and hide but couldn't now. After acting out of character and would now have to pay the price. Hopefully, she would be able to blend in with the woodwork after tonight.

Wade took her arm and guided her out to the dancefloor where Chad was dancing with the woman no one noticed until now. She was striking with her dark red shoulder-length hair, slightly freckled pale skin, and soft brown eyes. It was evident she was shy but smiled as Chad held her loosely in his arms.

Wade and Chad grinned at each other as Abilene winked at the woman who was finally being noticed. She hoped Chad, or someone else, would see beneath the shyness. Abilene had a feeling this woman who was more than she seemed on the surface. Wen the dance ended, Chad escorted the woman to the spot they claimed as theirs.

"Wade, Abilene, let me introduce you to Eveline, or Eve."

With a friendly smile, Abilene shook Eve's hand. "You can call me Abby. Pleasure to meet you."

Eve's grip was firm while her smile remained shy.

"Same here," Wade stated.

"What would you like to drink, Eve?" Chad inquired.

"A cola, if you don't mind," she replied.

When Chad headed to the bar area to get Eve a soda, Abilene politely inquired, "Are you fairly new here?"

Eve shook her head. "No. I've been where for a couple of years. I was transferred to the band here when the one I worked at was merged with this one." Her honeyed Southern drawl signaled she wasn't from New Mexico.

Wade studied the woman. His face showed when he recognized her. "You're the business account manager at the bank. I didn't recognize you with the different hairstyle. It looks good down."

His compliment made Eve blush. "Thank you," she said, nervously moving her fingers, her eyelids shuttering her eyes.

Abilene moved closer to Eve, examining the necklace Eve was wearing. "That necklace and earrings are quite striking. Where did you get them?"

Eve's fingers touched the necklace. She smiled at Chad, who handed her a soda. "I made it. It's a hobby of mine. I found the stones up near a canyon not far from where you're staying. Mr. Chapman gave me permission to hunt for rocks there. The only restriction is to not go into the canyon since it's sacred ground."

"It's an old Indian burial ground and is protected," Wade said. "There's guard dogs roaming the canyon, so I wouldn't advise anyone to try and enter it without one of us with them."

Abilene returned her gaze to Eve. "So you find the stones, cut and polish them before making them in to wearable art."

Eve nodded. "Yes. My mother taught me how. She did some wonderful pieces. I have one of her pieces which has a large wild horses in the center. She gave it to me on my sixteenth birthday."

Abilene was familiar with the type of jasper used in the necklace Eve mentions. When they jasper was cut, it would have what appeared to be mountains under bluish sky. There would be rolling greenish brown plains with what appeared to be dark horses running on the grass. The stones weren't common, and it was rare to find a large one.

"I'm a geologist and I'd love to see it. You mother taught you well since the necklace you're wearing is quite beautiful. The setting complements the stones without over powering them."

Eve beamed. "Let me know when you'd like to see it. I have others I'm working on which may be of interest to you. All the stones I'm using were found in this area.

Rummaging in her purse, Abilene pulled out a card, handing it to Eve. "Call me when you have the time. I'm free most of the time. I'd love to see your work and where you found those particular stones."

Eve slipped the card into her purse. Abilene hoped Eve would call her. This was someone she would like to befriend. They had a lot in common to talk about.

Wade kept Abilene with him for the evening, enjoying dancing with her. The longer he spent in her company, the more he liked her. This was one time he didn't mind staying late.

It was close to midnight when Abilene glanced up at Wade. "Well, I hate to break up the party, but I need to get home before I turn into a pumpkin."

Wade chuckled before he went into gentleman mode. "Let me walk you out."

"I also need to get home. I need to be up early in the morning," Eve stated.

Chad nodded, putting a hand at her waist as the four or them wended their way to the door through the still-crowded room. Chad followed Eve when she turned to the right, and Wade followed Abilene to the jeep beside his truck.

She turned and peered up at him. "Thank you for the wonderful evening."

"My pleasure. I'll see you tomorrow after church. You be careful going home."

She turned, unlocked the door to the jeep, and said, "You be careful, too. See you tomorrow."

Wade watched as he backed out of the parking space. He now had something to look forward to tomorrow after church. The books could wait. It should be an interesting six months with Abilene here. He hoped they could solve her problem quickly because he wanted to spend some time with her other than part of his job.

Chapter 4

Abilene couldn't believe Wade has spent the entire evening with her. She hadn't been lying when she told him she normally hid in the corner of the 'unseen' when going to dances while at home. There had been an older man who danced with all the women in the corner once during the evening. A person would think if you were out there on the dance floor, dancing with an older man, at least one male would notice and ask you for a dance, or at least seek you out to talk. Only it didn't work that way. Once the dance was over, she was overlooked as soon as she returned to her seat.

Six months was the term of her lease. Six months of peace and quiet while blending in with the countryside, or so she hoped. There wasn't mush hope of Wade continuing to notice her. In another couple of week, he would forget she existed just as Chad would most likely forget Eve. The most she could hope for was a friendship with the shy redhead who loved rocks. It would be great to have at least one friend in the area to talk to, and hang out with occasionally, who had at least a passing interest in geology.

Hopefully it would be at least a couple of months before she needed to make plans. There were the three job offers for later in the year, but until then, keeping a low profile was a priority. Staying hidden from the past would be great, but over the past few years it always seemed to catch up to her. If all went according to plan, she would be gone before Ron found her again. Maybe this time he wouldn't find her at all. Abilene knew it was wishful thinking even though she blocked her phone from giving her location, doing the same with her laptop while deleting everything Ron sent to her without opening it.

With a sigh, she began preparing the lunch for her and Wade. If only Ron wouldn't show up this time. She liked it here and the man who had offered her friendship. If Ron blew into town, no one would believe she wasn't working for him, including Wade. Ron would make sure of it in no time flat as he had done over the past five years in almost every place she had gone.

No matter what she did, there didn't seem to be any way to get rid of the man other than to quit working on her research and take a full-time teaching position. It wasn't what she wanted to do, but with what had happened over the past five years, it appeared to be the only option. It would pay the bills and keep Ron from bothering her.

The problem with taking a full-time position was how she could be easily found. There would be no place to hide after she left here. How long would it take before they came for her once she stopped moving around? That was the million-dollar question and wasn't something she could share.

Abilene straightened her shoulders, going to work fixing the simple meal. It remained to be seen if she would be safe here for a few weeks, or if, like the last place, Ron would show up within the first three days.

Everything was ready for Wade. She finished setting the table before checking the pie in the oven. The sound of a truck in the driveway prompted her to go to the porch, have expecting to see Ron instead of Wade.

She leaned against the post watching the good-looking man get out of the highly polished blue double-cab pickup. He was dressed in a dark blue three-piece suit, a light blue dress shirt and a matching tie with discrete strips. He wore dress shoes instead of the expected fancy boots. There wasn't a Stetson in sight to cover the neatly trimmed full head of glossy black hair with silver at the temples glinting in the sunlight. Her heart skipped a beat. This man appeared to be a powerful businessman in the suit. He broke into a smile when he noticed her waiting on the porch.

She chose to wear a simple loose, light green top with a rounded neckline to match the green in her colorful, flowing midi skirt. On her feet were a pair of basic sandals. The only concession to cooking was to fasten her hair back with a clasp to keep it out of her face. Abilene returned his smile, waiting for him to come to her.

"You look as nice in dresses as you do in jeans," Wade said. He didn't bother to hide his obvious assessment of her.

"Thank you," she replied, her face heating. I had to be a nice red color at his compliment. She waited for him to climb the three steps to where she was standing. "Well, the suit takes you from the ranch to the boardroom in one fell swoop."

Wade glanced down at his outfit. "So I've been told. You should join us on Sundays at church. The fashion parade can be quite fun."

"I'll think about it," She replied with a shake of her head at the broad smile on his face. "Come on in and make yourself at home." She turned and led the way into the house.

Wade followed her into the dim interior. This was the first time to be here since the last renters left. The place was simply furnished with basic rugged furniture covered in a durable chestnut brown material. He did notice the few touches she added to the room, making homier. Abilene had also added colorful pillows with matching throws in the sofa and chairs along with what he assumed were family pictures placed about the room. There were cut flowers in a vase on the table beside the big overstuffed chair.

He loosened the tie and took off the jacket, draping it over the back of the wingchair, taking her up on her offer to make himself at home. The tie quickly followed. He opened the top two button on the shirt before removing the cufflinks and rolling up the cuffs. It was similar what he would have done if he had gone home.

The house smelled good. A mixture of cooked food and what he could only describe as a clean scent. He strolled into the kitchen. It was spotless and the woman in it eye-catching. He noted the small table covered in a white tablecloth, simply set with plain plates and silverware.

He watched Abilene moving about the kitchen, imagining more than one meal with her. It was a strange feeling to want to see a woman in the kitchen, let alone wanting her to be there for him. A sharp longing shot thought him as he followed her movements. It had been a long, long time since he'd wanted to be with a woman for more than a few hours.

Abilene felt his eyes on her, but she ignored him as she dished up the food and set it on the table. The food was simple: baked chicken, green beans and baked potatoes with a salad she removed from the refrigerator. She was keeping the apple pie warm in the oven for dessert. Not sure of what he liked, she figured simplicity was best.

Wade ambled to the table when she glanced at him with a smile, inviting him to join her. She hoped he would like what she had made. "If you don't mind, I'll leave it to you to give the blessing," Abilene said after they took their seats. She felt as if it was something he did with each meal.

Wade recited a short grace. When finished, Abilene said, "Help yourself."

He did so while she filled her plate. They ate in companionable silence, neither of them feeling the need to talk. When Wade sat back, having eaten his fill, Abilene cleared the table. She placed two small plates and dessert forks on the table before pulling the apple pie from the over, setting it in the center of the table. She refilled their coffee cups before sitting again.

She didn't miss the way his eyes lit as he helped himself to a generous piece of the pie. After taking a small slice, Abilene decided to open the discussion about what she wanted to do in the area.

"Last night, I understood your reluctance to let me explore on your property. Apparently there have been a few not so forthright explorers trying to get at the resourced in the area."

"True. There have been a few over the past several years."

His reserve made her believe there had been more than a few. The stones Eve used in her necklace gave Abilene reason to believe this would be an area rich in information if she could only get to what she wanted to see before Ron showed up. She picked up the folder which she placed on the table. "Here's what I'm working on now." The folder contained a sheaf of loose paper which she printed off this morning.

Wade took the folder from her and scanned the printed pages while eating the homemade pie. He noted how she was using the minor fault lines throughout the country. In each area she analyzed the geological formations and surface makeup for that particular spot. The conclusions as to how the areas were formed, the relationship to eons past and the specific events which caused the surface makeup were clear and concise.

There were multiple drawings labeled with precise time lines detailing when each layer had formed. There were notations on weather, flora and fauna attached. It was thorough and professionally written. Her references to the earth plates and fault lines were shown in more hand drawn graphics. He was impressed with the detailed information and how it was written so anyone, with some basic knowledge of geology, could understand it.

When he finished, Wade met her gaze. "I notice you're concentrating on the various fault lines."

"Yes, I am. I believe it will give us a good idea of what has happened in the past and may give us some clues about what to expect in the future along those lines. The weathering of the formations also gives us a clue as to the weather cycles and rate of erosion based on when the formation was created and the number of years it's been exposed."

Wade tilted his head, asking one simple, yet complicated question: "Why?"

Abilene understood what he was asking. "I'm doing this for myself to gain a better understanding of how this planet cooled, shaping the land masses. I'm specifically interested in this continent. It hasn't been done with a focus on the various faults other than the major ones which most people know about. My plan is to write a geology text based on what I'm finding on the surface. I could care less what's beneath it. That's for others who are after money and not the history of the earth. There are so few unspoiled areas along the minor fault lines, so I go to places that are off the beaten path, so to speak."

Abilene knew it was a partial truth. She went to the out-of-the-way areas to avoid her past. Namely one particular person, as well as those behind him, who used her research for nefarious dealings. In a way it helped her find unspoiled areas over several of the smaller fault lines.

"I don't see how you would create a problem, but I'll need to clear it with my father first. He still has the final say in who explores on our land. If he gives you the okay, please don't take anyone other than Eve with you. Pop gave her permission to hunt for stones because he likes her work."

"I don't have a problem with that. I made a mistake a few years ago, and believe me, it won't happen again as I'm still attempting to distance myself from him."

It was the truth. She had been running from Ron for five years. No matter what she did, he managed to find her. What she wouldn't give to have him disappear from her life.

"I take it this person keep finding where you are."

Her head popped up, her face frozen in fear.

He shrugged and calmly said, "Hey, it was a good guess. If this person shows up here, let me know. We'll see what we can do to make him leave you alone. Now tell me about him what happened."

Abilene fidgeted with her fork, gazing at the plate in front of her. How do you tell a man you just met about being stupid enough to give a weasel like Ron what she surmised was under the ground? She peered up at Wade. Maybe, just maybe, he might be her knight in shining armor. If only he could make Ron leave her alone. The worst which could happen would be his running for the hills and leaving her to waste the six months she was to be here doing nothing.

"Okay. You deserve to have the full truth. I was in Tennessee working on this elderly man's land. I found this great area with all sorts of unusual properties. I knew form the formation I was studying there would be oil or gas under it. Because it wasn't what I was interested in, I didn't even think to tell the owner what might be under his land.

"I attended this party one of my former college classmates was giving. There was this man named Ronald McGuire who attended the party. He was a smooth talker and seemed to be interested in what I was doing. The conversation turned into what the various formations held under them. I made the mistake of telling Ron about the one where I was working. I stupidly explained how it probably had oil, gas or water under it based on the way it had been formed and the likelihood of pockets being formed at the time the plates shifted in that area.

"Within days, he began to buy up the mineral rights all around the area, then the land. The land was sold for next to nothing because it wasn't good for farming and most of it wasn't being used for anything productive. Before I knew what was happening, they began drilling and ruined the area with the rigs and shantytowns.

"The elderly man, who property I had been using, ended up with nothing left of the fifty thousand dollars they paid him for the property. Ron and company scammed him out of it by selling the land back to him when they were done. He ended up owing the government for the cleanup from the drilling. His share of the profits didn't even come close to covering the bill her received. In the end, he lost his land, his house and then died soon afterward.

"It wasn't until several months later that Ron found me. I refused to talk to him, but he discovered where I was working and did the same thing again. It got so I was associated with them and couldn't do my work.

"I've attempted to hide. I've run. I've even put everything on hold, but to no avail. He always seems to find me and does the same thing all over again because I made the mistake of telling him about the oil in the one formation. They've found oil or gas in almost every place I've gone based on my conclusions regarding what's beneath the surface of each area I study. What upsets me is, in each place they've been, it's the people living there who have been hurt, along with the environment. I can't let it happen here."

Wade now had confirmation as to why she was here. She was hiding from the syndicate tracking her. What she didn't have ws how his family owned the mineral rights to almost all the land in, not one, but several counties. Her research couldn't be used here.

"I don't believe you have anything to worry about here," Wade said with a smile.

She leaned back in the chair and let out a sigh. He noted she didn't believe his assessment.

"I hope you're right. Ron will show up here sooner or later. I've no idea of how he finds me, but he always does."

As if it was cued, there was a knock at the door. Wade watched as she closed her eyes, resignation and defeat on her face. More than anything, he wanted to tell her everything would work out, but knew he couldn't. There were some secrets which need to be kept until the time was right. His father and Jamie were correct. She needed their help.

Chapter 5

"Well, he's here. It took him less than three days to find me this time." Abilene pushed herself from the chair, plodding toward the front door with Wade following her.

Her next six months would be spent doing nothing of any real value. She blinked back the tears as anger rose to the surface. How does someone take their life back from a stalker like McGuire who is using their research without permission for profit while destroying the land and people? She didn't have any more ideas of how to circumvent what he was doing other than giving up her research.

Abilene opened the inside door to a man who looked like a used care salesman. The man was around six-foot-tall with poorly dyed, slicked back hair. The red cheeks and nose were ruddy. He was dressed in an ill-fitting black suit with the jacket open exposing the white shirt pulled tight across his protruding abdomen cut by the thin bright tie. The pants below his belly were held in place by a belt with a large, fancy silver buckle. The rounded face was creased in a big grin showing teeth which resembled those of a horse. She wanted to slap the grin from his face but knew it would only make matters worse.

"Go away, Ron. I'm not exploring this area. I'm here for a vacation." She kept he door closed, not wanting him near her.

The man sneered. "Yeah, and I'm a monkey's uncle. Come on, doll. Let me in."

From his reply, he hadn't seen Wade. It didn't matter. She had no intention of letting him into the house. The man made her skin crawl. How could she have been so stupid to have talked to him in the first place?

"I'm not letting you in. Now go away and leave me alone!"

"Sweetheart, I'm not going anywhere, so you might as well let me in and show me where you're working."

"No." There was no way she was giving him any information now or in the future.

"Now, baby doll, you need to be nicer to me. I'm the one who's keeping you in a job."

"I'm not your 'baby doll', and you have nothing at all to do with my job. Now go away and leave me alone."

"Never sweetheart. You might as well tell me what I want to know now. I'll find out anyway, so why not save me some time?"

"There's no way I'm going to help you. I'm not doing any more research, so might as well leave."

Ron leaned a hand on the door frame and chuckled. "Right." He sobered, glaring at her. "Don't lie to me. I know why you're here, and it ain't no vacation."

Wade moved to where Ron could see him. He stood up straight, eyes narrowing and his face turning hard, the smile upending into a frown.

"Oh, I see the way it is. You pick up some dude the minute my back's turned."

"There has never been a relationship between us and you know it. Now go away."

Ron's mouth formed an evil grin which made Abilene shiver. She was familiar with what he was capable of doing. The last man who attempted to protect her ended up in the hospital after severe beating. The last thing she wanted was for something to happen to Wade and his family.

"Now, Abby, you know that isn't true. We have a five-year history here."

Anger boiled to the surface. Her instinct was to scream at him and the assertion of having a relationship with her. Her teeth gritted as she glared at him. It wasn't true. None of it.

"We have no 'history' together. Your chasing me all over the country isn't a history and you know it. I'm *not* your girl. Never was and never will be. Now Leave. Me. Alone," Abilene demanded with force, her voice shaking with barely controlled anger.

"Hey, working together is a history…"

"I've never worked with you. I haven't received one penny from you or your company and would have returned it if I had. I want nothing to do with you or your scams."

Ron grinned and shook his head. "I don't run scams, doll. Everything's all above board. Not my fault they didn't ask for more money for the land. All you have to do is ask and you could be a rich lady."

Abilene blinked to hold back the tears welling in her eyes. "Ron, please leave me alone. I'm not going to allow you to use me again."

Wade moved forward, placing a protective arm around her shoulders. She leaned into his embrace, praying he could handle the persistent con artist.

Staring at the oily man, Wade stated in a calm voice, "I believe they lady has asked you nicely to leave."

Ron laughed. "Dude, you know nothing about this so-called lady. I'd advise you to do a bit of research."

Wade moved Abilene behind him, opening the screen door. Ron backed up two steps on the porch. "I did my research. I know who she is, and I also know what she does for a living and it isn't working for you. My best advice, McGuire, is for you to leave—no just here, but the area—or you may find you have bitten off more than you can chew this time."

Ron took another step backwards. Wade let the screen door slam shut before crossing his arms, daring Ron to take a swing at him. Instead, Ron backed up, putting a foot on the top step, peering around Wade. "Abby, I'll be back when your guard here is gone."

Wade kept his eyes on Ron. His demeanor showed he didn't trust the man not to do something stupid. "I wouldn't advise it. This place is off limits to you. In case you haven't noticed, the fence says no trespassers and you are trespassing. I wouldn't advise your returning her any time in the future."

Ron's lips turned up in an evil grin. He pivoted and descended the steps, proceeding to the Cadillac he was driving. After opening the door, he faced Wade, who remained on the porch, arms crossed, and feet spread, staring at him.

"You may have bitten off more than you can chew, mister. That little lady will get you hurt."

"I don't think so. If anything happens to me, it will lead right to you, and you and take that to the bank."

Ron's eyes rounded when he noticed the cellphone in Wade's hand. Wade didn't look away from Ron as he entered the big car and sped away. Meanwhile, Abilene returned to the living room, listening as Ron started his car and left. She sat on the overstuffed wing chair where Wade had hung his jacket. Her arms were wrapped around herself as if she was in pain, tears streaming over her cheeks. She couldn't face Wade when he reentered the house.

"Forget I asked about exploring on your land. I can't now." Her shoulders slumped in defeat. "I guess I'm out six months' rent. I can't stay here. He'll create havoc if I do. If I leave, he'll follow me and leave this area alone." She lowered her head, burying her face in her hands.

Wade squatted before her and cupped her face with a gentle calloused hand. He wiped away tears with his thumb. "Abby, you can't keep running. He'll destroy you and your work. I didn't like when I said I researched you and your work. You're a respected geologist with a lot of highly lauded work out there. It's well documented that you're not associated with McGuire or his organization.

Turning stricken eyes to him, Abilene knew she couldn't stay even though she wanted to in the worst way. "I can't let him destroy you, your family, the ranch or this area. If I leave, he will too, because he won't have anything to latch onto to create a problem. He's waiting for me to go into the field. If I do, he'll repeat what he's done everywhere else. I can't let it happen again."

"Abby, listen to me. You can't keep running."

"I can't stay here," she cried, her hand resting on his arm. "It puts you and Chad at risk of getting her. Severely hurt. He's done it before." She was terrified for him and Chad, both of whom she liked.

It was the same no matter what she did or where she went. It was also the main reason she hadn't gotten involved with anyone. They would hurt him to keep her from settling in one place.

Wade's calm voice had her staring at him. "He knows if anything happens to me, he'll go to jail. I have his threat on a nice little card here, and it'll show who to question first. Abby, let us help you get rid of him once and for all."

She threw back her head, eyes closed, noisily blowing out a breath of air. She faced him. "Wade, you don't know what they're capable of doing. I am." She studied his face, tears streaming over hers.

Turning away from him, Abilene knew better than involving anyone else in her problems. There was no way she could justify a death or near death because of her. This finalized her plan to take one of the teaching positions she had been offered. There was no other choice. Not now. Lowering her head to her hands, she began to sob. Her life's work wouldn't be completed while she did a job she didn't want to do.

Wade ran a hand over her head before pleading with her. "Abby, please stay here. Don't let him control you and your life."

Her voice was muffled by her hands. "I can't let you take that risk." She sniffed, raising her head from her hand, but not facing him. "I can teach. Once I'm not longer doing the research, he'll leave me alone."

Wade held her hands, turning her head with a curled finger under her chin so she was looking at him. "If you do that, he'll have taken away something you've put a lot of time, money and energy into which is important to you. It takes you in a direction you rejected many years ago, and you know that too. Let me help you. He can't do what he's done elsewhere. If he tries, he'll go to jail. Until you get him out of your life permanently, you won't have one."

Reaching out, she lightly touched his arm, giving him a weak smile. "I do appreciate the offer, but I can't let you spend the money and time to fight him and his cronies. Like I said, I know what they'll do, and I can't let it happen again here. I was hoping for a couple of weeks and got two days."

Rising from the chair, she plodded to the kitchen, wiping tears from her face with her hands. Wade followed her. She stood at the sink, her hands resting on the narrow strip out counter, staring out the window at what had started as a beautiful sunny day.

Wade put his hands on her shoulders, turning her to face him before enfolding her in his arms. Her arms slipped around his waist before she began to cry again, unable to stop the sadness and fear Ron's visit caused. Wade rubbed her back as her tears wet his shirt.

"Abby, promise me you won't leave," Wade pleaded.

"I can't stay here," she repeated, her voice tired and defeated, not moving from his arms.

"Yes you can. Let us handle Ron while you do what you came here to do."

"You've no idea of what you're saying. He'll destroy you and your family."

Wade chuckled. "I don't think so. He may try, but he hasn't had the pleasure of dealing with my father and his lawyers. Trust me when I say, it'll be over on one court date. In federal court no less."

She leaned back to study his face. "How can you be so sure of that?"

"Trust me. He hasn't done his research, and I don't believe he will. If he had, he wouldn't have even come here. Like I said, let me and my family take care of this."

"Why are you so willing to do this for me?"

"I have my reasons, with one being how I don't like the Rons of this world who cheat, lie and steal."

Moving from his embrace, she turned her back to him, needing to decide what to do. She leaned her hip on the edge of the sink, again staring out the window. If she left, Ron would follow her. If she stayed, she would be putting everyone who helped her at risk of getting hurt or being forced into financial ruin. If she ran, it meant continuing to try to hide from them. They would eventually find her no matter where she hid. How, she didn't know, but they always managed to track her down and she would be on the run again.

It was a pattern she wanted to break more than anything in the world. For twenty long years she'd been running from them. Wade was offering to help her have a life. The question was: could they really get rid of Ron? Wade seemed to think they could. Maybe it was worth a try. If things began going down the tubes, she could always leave.

She turned to face Wade, meeting the eyes which were watching her. There was something there she couldn't read but it was time to trust someone. With a deep inhale, she made up her mind.

"I promise I won't leave for at least a month." Abilene hoped he wouldn't regret her decision.

His lips turned up in a smile, his fingers brushing a strand of hair behind her ear. "Good. I need to get home, but I'll be back with a couple of guard dogs who'll keep Ron away from the place. I'll also have one of the hands come and stay in the bunk house. He'll do the repairs the place needs. Also, he'll be an extra set of eyes and act as backup if McGuire returns.

She could only imagine what he would be paying someone to stay and guard her. The dogs should be enough. "You don't need to have one of your men stay. I'm sure you can put them to better use."

"Wrong. Considering I own this place, I don't want anyone bothering my tenant."

Abilene stared at him for a few seconds before beginning to laugh. He grinned at her. She shook her head and scolded, "It figures. You don't want to lose a tenant."

"Sort of. Jamie's a good handyman and I was planning on fixing the place up anyway. This way I get started on it earlier than planned."

Abilene put her hands on his shoulders, stood on her tiptoes and kissed his cheek. "Thank you. If this works, I'll be in your debt for giving me back my life."

"It'll work. You'll see. I'll be back in a couple of hours."

Abilene walked with him to the door, handing him his coat and tie. He rotated and gave her a hug. He removed his phone from his pocket as the stepped off the porch on his way to his truck. He continued the conversation as he backed the truck around, following the driveway to the dirt road.

She leaned against the doorframe, letting sigh escape as the truck moved from view. This may have been an unwise decision, but then again, if he was right about taking care of Ron and making him leave her alone, she could have a life. She would love to stay here and find out if what she had seen in Wade's eyes was her imagination of if it was real.

Chapter 6

It was closer to four hours before Wade returned. There were two trucks and three men. Wade and a wizened old man exited from the first truck. Chad emerged from the second one, which was pulling a horse trailer with two horses in it. There were two large dogs in the back of Wade's truck. They jumped to the ground and headed for the porch. Abilene froze when the dogs began to growl when she took a step toward the edge of the porch.

"Waldo. Arf. Down," Wade commanded. The two dogs dropped to a sitting position where they were. He strode to her, took her hand and led her to the yard toward the dogs. "Let me introduce you to your two guards. They'll obey Jamie like they do me." He turned to the dogs. "Waldo, here," he said, pointing to a spot at his feet.

The big dog with short red hair and floppy ears trotted over and sat at his feet, staring at him, waiting for the next command.

"Friend," Wade said, putting his arm around her, moving her so her hip was next to his. With a motion of his hand, the dog came over, sniffed her hand then licked it. Abilene bent over and scratched his jaw. The dog's tail wagged. She squatted so she was on eye level with the dog, hugging the now gentle animal. He licked her face as she giggled.

Arf, an obvious mixed breed with short hair and markings like a collie, whined at Waldo for getting all the attention. Wade motioned for Arf to join Abilene, again saying "Friend." She included Arf in the meet-and-greet. When she stood, the two dogs ran to the older man, whom she assumed was Jamie.

Wade guided her to the elderly man who was assigned to be her guard. He wasn't much taller than she was with a lean face of skin which appeared to be creased leather. It was the deep-set, dark brown eyes which captured her attention. Something about them made her feel as if she had met him before, yet she didn't remember ever having seen, let alone met, him prior to today. He didn't speak while assessing her as she did him. What she saw, she liked.

"Jamie, this is Abby. She has a problem in the form of one Ronald McGuire."

Jamie spat into the dirt, raising a small puff of dust. "Heard of him. Sidewinder if you ask me."

Abilene cocked her head, a crease between her brows. His voice added to the impression she had met him at some time in the past. The terse statement made her wonder what he knew about McGuire.

"You know him?" she asked.

"Yep. Been through up yonder. Didn't get nothin'. Sure tried though. Ain't too bright."

Chad's eyes showed merriment which gave her the distinct impression they knew more about her nemesis than they were sharing.

"Alright. Out with it. What do you two know that I don't?" She crossed her arms, her gaze snapping between the men.

Chad winked. "Our secret. Let's let him dig a big hole and watch as he buries himself in it."

Jamie apparently had nothing more to say since he had gone to work unloading the horses they had brought with them. She watched as a white horse backed down the lowered ramp with nothing more than a command from Jamie. He then backed a pinto off the trailer then led him to the barn, ignoring the white horse which began to graze on the long grass in the large yard.

Chad unloaded the tack from the trailer. They hadn't brought hay or straw for the horses as there was plenty in the barn. Abilene had gone through all the buildings when she was exploring the place after unpacking. The only extra they brought was oats.

Wade put an arm around her and walked to where the white horse was standing. The horse nuzzled him. He patted the horse before pulling a lump of sugar from his pocket. The horse gently took the sugar from his hand. Abilene reached out and ran a hand down the horse's jaw. Wade slipped her a sugar cube. The horse took it from her hand before nudging her as he had Wade. With a smile, she ran her hand over the big horse's neck. He was so beautiful with the shimmering white coat, long flowing mane and tail and light brown eyes. She knew he was a true white with his skin being a pink in color.

"This guy is a lady's mount. He's gentle and well trained. Don't use a bit on him as he hates them. As the result of that, he's rien and pressure trained. Jamie will right with you until you get used of controlling him. All I ask if for you to take good care of him for me."

"I haven't had a horse around in a few years. It'll be fun to ride again." She ran her hand over the side of the beautiful horse's head. "What's his name?"

"Ghost."

She couldn't imagine why they would name him something so different. "There's got to be a story behind that name."

Chad, who had been listening, joined them, laying an arm across her shoulders. "Sure is. We attempted to catch him as a colt, but he would vanish into thin air every time we would get close to him. Ended up he walked into the pen one day, leading a good-sized herd of yearlings with a few older horses. He laughed as he jumped over the fence and disappeared again. This went on for close to five years. I won't forget the day he led this herd of beautiful horses into the corral. You could tell they were his. He didn't leave that time, standing there are proud as could be while the rest milled around him. Been the best damn stallion we've ever had. He frequently takes off like a ghost, but he always comes back."

Staring at the horse, Abilene guessed he needed his fun occasionally. It was easy to imagine him running across the landscape for the pleasure of running. He was that type of horse. The question was: why were they giving him to her to use? Wade answered the question as if he had read her thoughts.

"He's another layer of protection. The paint and him are like big guard dogs, but ones you don't expect. Let him run loose in the fenced area. He and Jamie's horse don't like strangers, especially men they don't know."

Abilene turned her head to face Chad. "Why are you doing this?"

With a grin, Chad said, "We believe ladies in distress, especially interesting ones, are deserving of knights in shining armor to protect them. We're those knights, just minus the armor."

Turning back to the horse, in a soft voice, laced with sadness, she said, "Right now, I'll take a knight or two, sans armor."

Chad kissed her cheek before grinning at Wade as he ambled off to take the rest of the tack to the barn. Abilene noted the glare Wade aimed at his brother's back.

"Ignore him. He's teasing you." She rotated to him, tilting her head to the side. "Have you all eaten yet?"

"No. We'll eat when we get back."

"I have some soup on and fresh bread if you want to eat before you leave."

Wade studied her, then shrugged. "Sounds good. It'll save me from whatever Chad planned to cook later."

Her arm went around his waist. "It'll be my way of saying thank you for what you've already done."

With his arm around her waist, he walked with her to the house, not commenting other than to say, "Not having to eat hotdogs is worth everything we've done." She now knew he didn't care much for hotdogs.

The brothers stayed for he meal, then left, saying they needed to return home. She didn't mind, liking Jamie as he was pleasant in a gruff manner. He helped her with the dishes and in cleaning up the kitchen. When the work was finished, he turned to her.

"Want to stay in the house. Need to be closer to you. Bunkhouse's to far away."

Abilene considered what he was saying. There was no reason for him to stay in the bunkhouse. The house held four bedrooms, so there was no lack of room. It gave her a good excuse to move to the second floor where she could see more of the magnificent landscape in the morning sun from the window.

"Sounds good. Let me move upstairs and you take the bedroom on the first floor." She noticed him about to object. "I didn't see any reason to use the top floor when I moved in, but I would prefer it. I considered making my room upstairs on the east side of the house, and now I have a good excuse to move to there."

With a nod, he didn't object; instead he helped her to move her things. When done, he brought in the few items he had brought with him and put them in the vacated room. When done, he brought out a book and sat in the large overstuffed chair as if he belonged there. As he read, she worked without interruption until bedtime, enjoying his quiet companionship. Having Jaimie in the house wasn't going to be a problem. In fact, it would be nice to have someone to share the big house with, even if he didn't speak much.

Chapter 7

The week was uneventful. On Saturday night, Chad headed for town as planned, leaving Wade to keep an eye on his boys. Chad was looking forward to meeting the man who was bothering Abby, his brother's woman. It was how he thought of the lovely lady he came to care for and respect in the few times he had been around her.

Something about Abby drew him to her in a way no other woman had in the past. Letting Wade have a go at her first knocked him out of ever having a chance to date her or get to know her better. Never would he act on those emotions out of respect for Wade, but he couldn't stop how he felt. She was everything a man could want in a woman, plus.

In a way, he regretted offering Wade the first chance with her; then again, if he hadn't misread his brother, Wade already had strong feelings for Abby. From what he had noticed, she was drawn to him, too.

It would all work out. He had Eve, who was the perfect Southern belle. He cared a lot for her, but Abby had him under her spell. She was that unattainable woman most men admire from a distance, like a movie star. At least this time, his big brother had found a decent woman who wasn't chasing him. She didn't seem to care about what he had or would inherit. That was a definite plus.

Wade had wanted to do this part of the plan, but Chad talked him out of it. This was one of the few things he could do for her.

On top of that, if they could get Ron out of the picture, Abby would stay. Even if he couldn't have her, he didn't want her to leave, wanting that sister-in-law he would tease, protect and love.

In the second bar he entered, the man he was searching for was bellied up to the bar with a mixed drink in his hand. He was talking to a man a few stools away to his right. The smell of horses mixed with stale beer hit him as he entered the rundown bar where he was well known.

Chad took a seat next to Ron on the stool which had seen better days. He ordered a beer. Ron's choice of a dilapidated saloon in the poorest section of town had him questioning how much money the man made for what he was doing. Then again, maybe he was only comfortable with the less well-to-do of society. Chad waited until the men stopped talking before speaking.

"New in town?" Chad asked before taking a sip of the beer in the mug before him.

"Yes." Ron gave him a friendly grin.

"The name's Chad."

"Ron."

"Planning on staying long?" Chad took another sip of his beer, holding it between his hands, waiting for the man he instinctively disliked to answer him.

"Depends on one pretty lady."

"Her name wouldn't happen to be Abby, would it?"

"You know her?" Ron asked with interest, rotating on his stool to face him. Chad's gaze bored into the unsuspecting man's eyes.

"Sort of. I got to dance with her at the town dance," Chad broke eye contact before taking another swallow of his beer.

"You wouldn't happen to know the man who's moving in on her, would you?"

"I take it she's your girl?" Chad sipped his beer again, hiding the disgust at the thought of this man ever touching her. He kept his face blank, gazing straight ahead at the mirror on the wall, watching Ron's expression.

"Sort of. We have, um, worked together in the past."

Chad glanced at the rotund man who had a big grin on his face. A brow rose when he commented, "Really. She didn't mention any partner."

"I'm a silent partner, so to speak."

"I see." Chad swallowed his anger at Ron's assertion of Abby working with him. There was no way she would work with a slime ball like him.

"Yeah. She just don't know we're partner." Ron gave a short chuckle before sucking down half of the drink he had in before him.

Chad took another swig of his beer to hide the spike of anger Ron's statement had sent through him. Pivoting on the stool, he faced the man the thought of as a fat weasel in clothes. "Leave her alone." His voice was soft, holding a noticeable threat laced into the three words.

With narrowed eyes, Ron glared at Chad, who had indicated he was on Abby's side.

"Make me," Ron challenged with a sneer, his fetid breath washing over Chad.

"I believe that's a challenge I'll take, sir." Chad carefully placed his mug at the back of the bar, tensing for whatever the slime next to him was planning.

Ron laughed, heaving his heavy frame from the barstool as if he was going to walk away. Pivoting, Ron swung a beefy fist at Chad, only to find empty air where he had been sitting. A fist slammed into Ron's blubbery abdomen, knocking the air from his lung. He bent over, gasping, his hands holding where Chad had hit him.

With a shake of his head, Ron lumbered toward the smiling man who had hit him, attempting to take him off his feet. With a sidestep, Chad avoided the charge, before bringing a elbow down onto Ron's back at the base of his neck. The big man fell heavily to the floor, stunned and panting for breath.

When Ron rolled over, Chad held out a hand in an offer to help him up. Ron took it, giving a quick jerk only to fine a foot on his throat and the arm stretched tight, the shoulder screaming in pain.

Staring down at the big man, his eyes filled with hatred, Chad's voice was icy. "This is the only warning you'll get. Leave her alone."

"Fuck you," Ron croaked through the pressure on his neck.

Chad leaned on the foot on Ron's neck as the big man's hand pushed against his foot. "Not in my lifetime, mister."

He released the pressure, moving back, allowing the big man to pull himself up from the floor. Once he regained his feet, Ron pulled out a dirty handkerchief and wiped his hands and face. He stuffed the filthy rag back into his pocket.

With a sneer and a voice full of threat, Ron said, "You'll regret this, pretty boy. Trust me on that. You'll regret this."

Chad stuffed his anger down. He'd done what he was supposed to do. "Threats will get you in big trouble around here, especially with, let's see, seven witnesses."

The bartender snapped, "You owe twelve dollars. Pay up and get out."

Ron tossed a twenty on the bar before striding to the door. He looked back over his shoulder and with a sneer, not caring who heard him, "You'll not like what's coming to you, pretty boy."

The bartender had called the police as soon as Ron had swung at Chad. They arrived before Chad had finished his one beer. The officers took statements from all the customers, along with Chad and the bartender. The all described what had transpired prior to McGuire leaving. The threats were duly recorded. The second step in Wade's plan was completed. They were letting him dig his hole.

When the police left, Chad grinned at the men who knew him quite well. "Thanks guys. That pretty new lady appreciates your help, and so do I. A round for the house."

Chad left a fifty on the bar, well aware the bartender would use it to pay their bills after giving them a round on the house as Chad requested. He smiled on his way back to the ranch. The plan was coming together nicely.

Chapter 8

The week had passed quickly. Wade had gone and checked on Abilene and Jamie twice. Each time he had gone, he hadn't wanted to leave. She was this wonderful woman with a good sense of humor. She liked him, but…

He didn't want her to leave. Ron hadn't returned, but it was only a matter of time before the man began trouble again. For now, it was a waiting game for them.

On Saturday evening, Wade was working on the books when he heard a vehicle pull into the drive at the front of the house. He went to the door, expecting to see Chad, only to find his father climbing the steps to the porch. It was good to have him home. He had missed him and his subtle guidance when things weren't quite making sense.

Wade also hoped he'd look as good as his father when he hit his late sixties and early seventies. At six one, lean, with gray hair and piercing blue eyes, Nolan still attracted the attention of women and men alike. The Stetson hat and western suit reinforced the wealth and power of the man who wore it.

Even though he was 'retired' from ranching, he still enjoyed doing a full day's work on the ranch, working beside him and Chad, and the hands. Most of those cowboys had been with them for years. Yes, he had slowed down, but he was there when needed. It was good to have him here to help with handling Ron and whatever he was going to do the next.

With a big smile, Wade waited for his father to join him. They greeted each other with a clap on the shoulder before heading into the large living room. His father's deep voice filled the room.

"Boy, it's good to be here. Nothing like a trip away to make you appreciate being at home." He placed his valise on the chair and removed his hat. "Anything exciting happen while I've been languishing away in the capital?"

Wade didn't know where to start. A lot had happened, most of it concerning Abby, but none of it exciting. He ran a hang through his hair, mentally cataloging the things his father would need to know.

"Why don't you go and get comfortable? I'll pour you a Scotch and meet you in the den. There are some issues we need to discuss concerning the new renter." There was no question in Wade's mind that his father wanted to get out of the suit he was wearing. It would give him time to decide where to start with Abby and her problems.

"Sounds like you have a lot to tell me," Nolan drawled.

"I do." Wade noticed his father assessing him. He had kept his face blank, but Nolan seemed to have a sixth sense where he was concerned.

With a nod, Nolan ascended the stairs while Wade strode to the den to pour him the drink he had offered. He knew his father would return in his usual jeans and plaid shirt. It was the uniform for most of them on the ranch.

Nolan joined him in the den, taking a seat in his favorite chair before Wade handed him the Scotch on the rocks. "Well son, what's going on?"

Wade took the chair opposite his father, staring at the amber liquid in his glass of whiskey, attempting to decide where to begin. This Ron character hadn't met his father yet. If trouble was brewing, he wanted him nearby. It wasn't that he wasn't capable for handling things, but Nolan's wisdom and experience regarding what they were doing was invaluable. As far as he knew, Ron had been doing nothing more than talking to the other ranchers. They had a good idea of what the man was telling them, but for now, it didn't matter. He decided to begin with Abby. Everything that was happening circled around her.

"The renter for the Haskell place arrived right on time. A. Brown happens to be an attractive woman who's a geologist, as I'm sure you already know."

Nolan took a sip of his drink, then studied it as he said, "Abilene Brown. Does good work but been having a major problem with a fella named McGuire."

"So we discovered last Sunday."

Nolan watched Wade. Yes, there was something going on with Wade, and he suspected it had a lot to do with one Abilene Brown. "Describe her for me."

A smile formed on Wade's lips. It told Nolan more than Wade's words ever would. "Well, she's about five eight and curved in all the right places. She's got this gorgeous long mane of mahogany brown hair with a few strands of silver. It hangs in these waves and curls down past her shoulders. When she speaks, her whiskey voice warps around you, making you think of a stormy spring day with the rain falling. Her green eyes are like cat's in the way she watches you.

"Throughout all of what's been happening to her, she's maintained this great sense of humor. Abby's this lovely woman who seems to pull you to her with her strength and gentleness." He raised his eyes from the partially filled glass he had been staring at while talking to meet his father's unwavering gaze. "She's been having a real hard time with McGuire, and it's taking a big toll on her."

Nolan figured one Abilene Brown had Wade's full attention from the description and tone of voice. He hoped Jaimie wasn't going to give Wade a problem where Abilene was concerned sine Wade had more than a passing interest in her.

"What does McGuire have to do with her?" He needed to know what Chad and Wade had discovered beyond the information given to them. He wouldn't be around forever to help them out.

"He follows her around, sees where she's working. Then he buys up the mineral rights, then the land for a song. He sells leases to the wildcatters who are controlled by the syndicate, which controls him. These drillers don't follow the rules and end up with a lot of contamination with each well. They also don't pull all the permits needed to drill.

"She told me how she mentioned oil could be found on this place in Tennessee at a party and he's been dogging her after a big field was discovered right where she said it would be. The places where she works are along fault lines, and you know what that means: oil and gas are usually close by. He's been using her work and scamming those around the areas to get the mineral rights or the land. Both if he can, and, as she put it, totally destroying the areas with their drilling."

"So he tracks her down and uses her work for nefarious purposes," Nolan paraphrased. He sat with his lips pursed and eyes narrowed. "When did he show up?"

"Abby arrived Thursday night and he showed up Sunday afternoon at the house. He made some threats when I ran him off the property. Abby was ready to run again, but I got her to agree to stay for a month."

Chad ambled into the den, a beer in his hand. He perched on the arm of Wade's chair after a glance in Nolan's direction.

"Thanks for watching the boys. You were right when you said Ron would fall in with our plan. I couldn't believe how he went for it hook, line and sinker. It's all on record with the police. I wanted to laugh at how he looked lying there on the floor, looking up at me. It was the last place he expected to be when he came after me and attempted to deck me.

"He's a real piece of work. I do know he needn't come sniffing around here. I, for one, will make sure he pays the price if he does."

Nolan's gaze bounced between the two boy's faces, wondering what they had done. "Care of explain what happened?" he requested, his voice soft, before taking a sip of his drink. The boys knew it was a command, not a request.

"Just letting him dig a hole in which to bury himself when he goofs up." Chad had a happy smile on his face.

"He already has," Wade said with a grin. "He threatened me when I told him to leave Abby alone. The Chief has it in his hands on a SIM card."

Chad added, "And he made some nasty threats against me tonight after taking a swing at me when I told him to leave her alone. There were seven witnesses who all gave pretty much the same story with how I didn't threaten him before he swung at me."

"And the lady in question? How is she being protected?"

"Waldo, Arf, Ghost and Spot with Jamie thrown in for good measure," Chad recited.

Nolan grinned. "I hope the man attempts to get to her. He won't know what hit him. You did warn him not to trespass, I hope."

Wade nodded, almost offended at his lack of trusting him to do the right thing. "Very clearly. Again, all on the video card form my phone. It's times and dated from the phone. I had the Chief removed it."

"Alright. Let's see what he tries nest before we do anything else."

"Well, he was researching the mineral rights to the area on Wednesday at the land recorder's office. He was frustrated when he couldn't find out who owned them, so I'm guessing he'll attempt a legal maneuver to get them," Wade stated.

Chad added, "He's also talking up the other ranchers. We may get some flak from them depending on what he's telling them."

"Won't do him any good, but he can try. Is she getting any work done?"

"Not really. She's afraid to do anything due to McGuire hanging around the area. I also told her I needed to clear it with you," Wade said before lowering his eyes to his drink.

Nolan was aware Wade wouldn't allow anyone out on the ranch without his approval. Wade ran the ranch, but he didn't own it. That meant he would defer to him when decisions came to people being on the ranch.

"Hm. Looks like I need to go show her around some. You did leave the tack for Ghost, I hope."

"Sure did," Chad told him with a smile. "Ghost likes her, and Jamie said she didn't have a problem riding him."

Nolan kept his face neural when he questioned, "How did you convince Jamie to stay with her."

Chad chuckled. "It was the darnedest thing. We didn't have to convince him. He'd seen her at the dance and said any lady that pretty needed to be guarded from the riffraff."

Nolan studied his glass, lips pursed. It appeared Abilene had all the men falling at her feet; only he knew why Jamie wanted to guard her. Soon he would have to fill the boys in on the shy, but for now he wanted to see how things panned out. "You two aren't going to start fighting over her, I hope."

Chad punched Wade on the upper arm, grinning. "Nah. She's Wade's. Besides, I've got a girl. A downright pretty redhead who also had curves in all the right places and a honeyed Southern accent you can cut with a knife."

Nolan stared at Chad, frowning. "You wouldn't be talking about Eveline from the bank, would you?"

Chad licked his lips, the grin leaving his face. "Yes, I am." He glanced to Wade as if asking for support. "We're planning on going for a ride tomorrow afternoon. Why don't you and Abilene join us?"

Wade shot a glance to Nolan, who had wiped all emotion from his face. "I'll ask Abby when I pick her up for church and let you know." Wade swirled his drink, eyes on the glass.

Chad chugged the last of his beer before standing. "Great. I'm off to bed. See ya in the morning. Glad to have you home, Dad."

"Good to be here. Good night, Chad."

Nolan watched as Chad as he left, then returned to Wade, who faced him, his face a mask.

"I take it you like this Abilene, or Abby, as you call her." He waited not sure if Wade was going to answer him. When his lid lowered, hiding his eyes, Nolan had his answer, but he wanted to hear Wade say it.

"Dad, I can't explain it, but it's like she reached out and told hold of me with her first words and smile. Those green eyes set me spinning. When I'm with her—" he sifted uncomfortably in his seat," well, I don't want to leave when I'm with her. She's never far from my thoughts and…I don't know. She isn't like any other woman I've ever met." He finally raised his head and faced Nolan, the misery and uncertainty showing in his eyes and one his face.

Nolan sipped his drink as he assessed Wade. Abilene had done in a few days what other women had been wanting to do over many years. She had captured Wade's heart, only he didn't know it yet.

"Son, my best advice is to hand on for the ride or your life. A woman like her most men only meet once in a lifetime. Twice if you're blessed. She'll ties you up in knots until you find out she's right there with you. I believe you've met the woman you have wanted to find but didn't realize it. Just don't let her slip away or you'll regret it for the rest of your life."

Wade downed the rest of his drink. "Dad, if she were to leave, I would be like McGuire and follow her no matter where she went."

The hint of a smile lifted Nolan's lips. He could hardly wait to meet this woman who had his oldest son turning in the wind, not sure which way to turn. She had to be something special to have captured Wade in such a brief time.

"Well, I'm heading for bed unless there were problems with the ranch you need to tell me about." Nolan finished his drink, waiting for Wade to answer.

"Everything went smoothly. Got the back stallion to saddle and Chad has the filly almost ready for sale."

Standing and stretching, Nolan said, "In that case, I'll see you in the morning."

"Night, Dad, Wade responded. He remained sitting lost in his thoughts.

Nolan smiled as he climbed the stairs to the second story. It was going to be interesting to see how Wade would handle a relationship with Abilene. From everything he had learned about her, she was one extraordinarily strong woman who would give Wade a run for his money. They had one month to get things moving to keep her here with them.

Chapter 9

Monday morning, Nolan saddled his horse and rode to the Haskell spread, which had been a good addition to the ranch. The buildings were solid, and, like now, it brought in some extra income. His hope was one of the boys would get married and move into the big house. It wasn't that he minded them at the house, but he wanted them to be happy and in their own places. It was a given Wade would be living in the main house sooner or later when he inherited the ranch, but he needed some time away from the family. He was the boy who had never left home, preferring to stay at the house and work the large ranch. Wade would benefit by marrying and moving out to be on his won for a few years.

Nolan's thought returned to the lovey lady he'd spent the last two weeks wooing. The widow was a cultured lady he met at one of the parties he attended the trip before to the capital. In that one meeting, he fell for her, like Wade with Abilene.

Truthfully, he hadn't wanted to leave her this time, but he would see her again in a month or so and they would remain in contact via phone calls and video calls. Maybe by then, he wouldn't have to worry about what the boys would think. If they were busy with their own women, they wouldn't care what he did. This was one woman he wasn't going to let get away.

Nolan noticed Waldo sitting at the gate, waiting for him. He dismounted to open the gate, walking the horse through before closing and latching it. With a whistle he called the Arf as he walked up the driveway. The dog bounded around the corner of the house with a happy bark. He played with the dogs for a few minutes before turning to the house and seeing a woman on the porch leaning against the post, her feet bare. She was dressed in snug jeans and a big white shirt with her hair tumbling around her face. From Wade's description, he knew this was Abilene.

The two of them assessed each other. She returned his smile. "You must be Mr. Chapman," she said.

Her husky voice wrapped around him as he nodded, fully understanding what Wade had been saying the night before. "I am. Name's Nolan. Figured I'd stop by and see what all the ruckus was about."

Abilene chuckled. "Well, come on in. Jamie's out back. I'm sure he knows you are here by now."

Nolan dropped the reins to his horse before mounting the steps to join the woman who had bewitched his son. She held the screen, welcoming him into the house.

"I just made some fresh coffee if you'd like some."

"Wouldn't mind a cup," Nolan said, noticing the homey feel to the house. He hung his hat on the coat rack by the door before following her into the kitchen. She was a good housekeeper. The other rooms were neat, and the old kitchen gleamed in the morning sun. She poured the coffee and set the mugs on the table, placing sugar and cream within his reach.

It's a pleasure to finally meet you, Mrs. Brown," Nolan said.

"Please, call me Abby, or Abilene. Mrs. Brown makes me feel like an old dowager."

He nodded, understanding her aversion to titles, feeling much the same when addressed as Mr. Chapman. "Alright, Abilene it is." He tilted his head, studying her face. "I've followed your work for quite some time now. I was wondering how long it's take you to get here."

With wide eyes and parted lips, she stared at him. It was a statement she hadn't expected. "You know my work?" she queried with surprise lacing her voice. The perfect brows pulled together in a frown.

"Of course I do. I loved geology and archaeology. They sort of go hand in hand. I got interested in the fault lines and found your research while looking for more information on this area. I loved how you wrote it so I could understand all the details. I guessed you'd show up in these parts sooner of later since we're right on top of one the lines."

Abilene played with her cup. "You do know I'm having trouble with a man who follows me and ends up destroying almost every place I've stayed for more than a day or two.?"

She was guessing Wade would have talked to him. "Don't worry about McGuire," Nolan said in a matter-of-fact tone. What he wanted to do was to take her in his arms and protect her. If he was twenty years younger, he would give Wade competition like he wouldn't believe. This was a woman worth fighting for, which made him wonder about Chad. Than again, the boy said he had Eveline to take up his time.

"I have to worry about McGuire. He's going to make trouble here. I've no doubt about it and I'll be the cause of it."

"You aren't causing a thing, my dear. He's doing it without your participation. Let us handle him."

After running her hands over her face, Abilene gave a frustrated sigh. "You all keep saying that, but you don't know him like I do. Ron has been stalking me for the last five-plus years. Trust me, he'll disrupt this town, and you won't be able to do a thing about it."

"Again, let us deal with him. You have work to do." Nolan kept his voice calm, hoping to refocus her on her work instead of the man who was stalking her.

"I can't go anywhere. He'll follow and tear everything up. I promised Wade I'd stay for the month, but I'm only going to fine-tun what I've done while I'm here. I can't let him destroy another place."

"What? And give up your work?" Nolan glared at her.

Abilene bowed her head, playing with her mug as tears welled in her eyes. "I don't have much of a choice." She let out a breath, her shoulders slumping. "I've been offered a teaching job and I'll probably take it. There are a lot of other things I can do which won't be of any interest to Ron and others like him."

Nolan could hear the defeat in her voice and in the slumped posture. She had resigned herself to doing a job she didn't like. The green eyes held hurt and sadness, along with the brimming tears.

His attention went to the kitchen door. Jamie entered from the mudroom without knocking, leading Nolan to believe he had somehow convinced Abilene to let him stay in the house.

"Nolan," he said with a nod in greeting. "The boys fill you in?"

"Yes, they did. Thanks for staying with Abilene."

"Place needs work. Keeps me busy. Want me to saddle Ghost?"

"Yes. Abilene needs to see part of the country around here and there's not better way then by taking a ride." He refocused on Abilene. Her face showed she was about to refuse. "Don't even think of saying no. I insist. Take some of the tools of your trade as you'll want them," Nolan commanded in a gentle voice.

With a huff, Abilene said, "You're only asking for more trouble than you can imagine."

"Again, let me worry about it. You worry about your work."

Without further argument, she stalked out of the kitchen. Nolan leaned back in the old wooden kitchen chair. He liked this woman who worried about the effect of her stalker on those around her. Not many would care about the consequences of what McGuire was doing to the land.

"I'd advise some boots there, missy. Jamie will have Ghost ready in a few minutes. Where I want to take you is a good piece from here."

Nolan didn't miss the controlled anger, aware of what caused it: McGuire and her fear for him and his family. After meeting her, he was looking forward to the confrontation with McGuire. The woman deserved a decent life.

Boots on and hat in hand, Abilene returned with a bag and a smile in place as he finished his coffee. She sent a sidelong glance at him before saying, "Alright, you win. Ron is your problem, not mine. Just don't say later that I didn't warn you."

Nolan didn't react. He was aware of what he was getting into with helping her. She was worth every penny it would cost if it benefited everyone concerned about her.

Jamie had Ghost saddled when they left through the mudroom. Abilene fed the semi-tame stallion a lump of sugar, running her hand along his jaw. The horse pushed at her, eliciting a giggle from her. Abilene easily mounted the big horse, settling herself in the saddle with an ease which showed experience. She took the reins Jamie handed her.

"Missy, you have fun now," Jamie said to her.

"Thanks Jamie. Watch for snakes slithering around," she said with a smile and nod.

Jamie's face creased into a seldom seen grin. "No worries. Don't care much for 'em when they ain't where the belong."

He stepped back as Nolan winked at him. The old man didn't care much for most women. This was the most he'd heard him say to any female in years. But then again, he knew why Jamie was partial to her. It was time for that talk with Wade. He needed to understand what he was getting into by wooing Abilene.

Nolan led the way at a slow walk until past the gate. Waldo and Arf sat forlornly behind the gate as they rode away, leaving them to guard the house with Jamie and Spot. Picking up the pace, Nolan headed in the direction of a large outcropping they could see in the distance. He glanced at the woman on the white horse. She was comfortable in the saddle.

"Ready for a run?" he asked with an impish grin. She returned the grin, nodding she was ready.

The gave the horses a gentle nudge, encouraging them to run on the reasonably smooth path. Ghost took the lead as Abilene leaned over, letting him choose his way, the reins slack. Nolan followed, appreciated the view of the woman and horse enjoying the exercise. It was easy to understand why Jamie didn't complain about saddle Ghost. She was a good rider, understanding the horse she was riding.

Ghost slowed as the trail became rougher, snorting and shaking his head. Abilene rubbed his neck in appreciation. Nolan caught up to them. His horse was blowing from the long run.

"Good riding, girl. He likes to run. You should ride him in the races next month. Not only would he enjoy it, I believe you would too."

With a smile she shook her head no. "I don't think so. Let one of the boys ride him."

"Uh-uh. He won't run for them like he does for you. He likes you."

Abilene laughed, shaking her head again. "He also likes Wade. Don't pull that on me. Let Wade ride him. I've no experience in racing and don't care to learn."

Nolan let it drop. He would get Wade to work on her. The girl had no idea of how good she was with the half-wild stallion. He took the lead around an outcropping of rocks to find a man taking pictures. Abilene stopped Ghost, her face changing from happiness to fear. The man had to be the infamous Ronald McGuire.

With a nudge, his horse moved forward between Abilene and the man. "I'd like to know what you are doing here?" Nolan asked, his voice soft and calm.

Ron rotated at the calm words to face Nolan, whose face had settled into a mask, alert eyes assessing the stranger.

"Doing some preliminary work," Ron said, grinning at her. "Good to see you, Abby. I believe I've found the right place without you."

Nolan's gaze shifted to Abilene. She scanned the area, but from her face, he knew Ron was mistaken. This wasn't the area she was here to find.

Keeping his voice controlled, Nolan informed Ron, "You're trespassing. This area is off limits to everyone. I'd advise you to leave."

Ron sneered at the older man who leaned on the pommel of his saddle, watching him. "You can't make me leave open range and you know it, old man." There was a challenge in his voice.

Nolan reached to his side causing Ron to stiffen momentarily. There was a phone in his hand which he dialed calmly and waited. Ron went back to grinning. "Bill, I have a problem her near the burial grounds."

Nolan listened then lowered the phone. "McGuire, I'd advise you to leave as I previously requested."

Ron laughed, rotating back to the edge of the ridge, resuming taking pictures.

Nolan spoke into the phone. "Nope. Taking pictures. Yep."

He returned the phone to the holder before saying, "Sir, you're on private land, not public. You're trespassing, and I'm again advising you to leave."

Ron ignored him. When he finished with taking the pictures he wanted, he moved toward Abilene. Ghose shook his head, pawing the ground in warning. Abilene slipped from the horse's back, moving to beside Nolan while Ghost blocked Ron from getting to her.

Unable to see her, Ron stopped, chuckling. "You needn't hide, Abby. I can see you, and you'll show me where to go sooner or later. Oh, by the way, those two men won't be enough to stop me, so you needn't get them all riled up."

Nolan didn't change his position. Ghost moved, blocking Ron when he moved in order to get a better view of her.

"Those two men are my sons. You need to heed their warnings," Nolan said. His voice was soft but this a threads of steel coming through. The face remained neutral, but his eyes bored into the man, watching his every move.

Ron either didn't hear the soft threat, or didn't care, dismissing the old man. "Abby, you know better than involving others in this. I'm sure you remember what happens to them," Ron said, an evil grin on his face.

She turned to Nolan, eyes pleading as tears tracked over her cheeks. Nolan winked at her as the sound of a helicopter came to them. Ron's demeanor changed when he noticed the helicopter speeding toward them with the insignia of the sheriff's department on its sides. He didn't move as the pilot hovered then set the chopper down in a flat area.

Four police officers exited the open door, moving toward them. Nolan hadn't changed his position. His eyes had turned icy as he stared at Ron. "As I said before, you're trespassing. You were asked to leave more than once. This is private land. This particular area is off limits to everyone but the tribes." Nolan raised his voice so the officers could hear him. "My best advice to you, Mr. McGuire, is to leave this town. Let me also warn you that if anything happens to Abilene or my family, you'll be the one charged due to the multiple threats against us and her."

One of the officers handed Nolan a folder containing papers and a pen. He signed the papers, then handed it back. "Let Judge Wainwright know I'm pressing charges and will be there for the hearing."

The change in Ron's expression was worth the confrontation with him. "Who are you?" he asked.

"Nolan Chapman. I own this land. You're persona non grata around here."

With narrowed eyes and a frown, Ron stared at Nolan as an officer handcuffed him. He then pulled him toward the helicopter. When Ron stumbled, the officer wasn't exactly gentle in pulling him back to his feet. Nolan hadn't moved other than to follow the progress of the officers and their prisoner with his eyes.

They watched until the helicopter took off. Nolan peered down at Abilene. "Like I said, let me worry about him," he said, dismounting from his horse.

She stared at him, obvious confusion on her face. Nolan smiled, surveying the area before him. "I knew he was going to be here. The hands let me know when he went through the fence. This may be a big spread, but we do know who is here and why. This particular area is totally off limits and is well guarded."

"This is where the Indian burial grounds are located." It was a statement, not a question.

"Yes. They're down yonder in the canyon. It's sacred ground. No one is going in there without the tribe's permission. Not eve my family. I bought this parcel to protect that canyon when their leader came to me when it came up for sale. It borders the reservation and I'm working on having the reservation expanded to include this area. That was why I was in the capital when you arrived instead of being here to greet you."

Nolan walked her to the edge of the canyon as he talked. Below them was a natural arch, decorated with feathers. On each side of the opening was a totem carved of sandstone with faded colors. They were weathered, showing they had been there for several hundred years.

"Ron will have his cronies try and destroy that area if he noticed it," Abilene stated with sadness.

With arms crossed and feet spread, Nolan glanced at her before saying, "I wouldn't advise them to try it. What you don't see are the posted guards. From the minute he showed up, the tribe has had guards posted all around this area. That's how I knew Ron was here. Those pictures he took will hang him on the trespassing charges. I'll push for the maximum sentence based on his past habit of ignoring trespassing signs.

"You already knew about him before I got here."

There were a few seconds of silence. She had picked up on what he had left unsaid. "Yes. I check out tenants. I was aware of who you were and how he was stalking you. Until now, he has skirted the law and managed to get away with a few things. Not here. I don't care for scum like them and neither does our judge. This time he won't get away with him scheme of threats and bullying since we don't like bullies."

"I have the distinct feeling you have an ulterior motive for taking on Ron and his buddies."

Nolan smiled, aware her feelings where correct. She was almost too smart for her own good. Yes, he had a reason for taking on McGuire. An exceptionally good one with the state and federal law enforcement behind him. Ron wasn't aware of how hard they had worked to get her here, hoping he would follow. What they weren't expecting was the woman who had a magnetic attraction for the three of them.

Abilene removed a small camera from her bag before surveying the area. She moved to an natural formation of rocks, squatting to take a picture. With a squeal of surprise, she lost her balance, ending up sitting in the dirt when a man, who had blended in with the rock, stood. Nolan and the man laughed.

"Sorry, ma'am, but I didn't think you'd want me in your picture," the man who could have been anywhere from thirty to fifty offered her his hand.

She took the proffered hand, letting him pull her to her feet. She brushed the dust off her jeans. "I didn't even see you. I was concentrating on the colors about where you were."

"Figured as much," the man, who looked to be one of the tribe, said before turning to Nolan. "You were right. We have his conversation on record. There are planning on raiding the canyon tomorrow night in the belief there are artifacts they can sell in the graves."

"I'll let the Feds know since it's a federal offence to desecrate tribal burial ground. Excellent work, Leland. They'll find a reception they weren't expecting when they get here."

Nolan watched a Abilene ignored them, examining the striations on the rocks where Leland had been sitting. She stooped, picking up a good-sized stone, then smiled. It was deposited into a baggie along with several others before she took a sample of soil form a few inches below the surface. Her eyes narrowed, staring at a rock at the base of a pile of larger rocks. She examined the rock, turning it over.

The two men watched as she carefully put the rock back into position, unwilling to take any of the similar stones with her. Nolan pointed to where she had noticed another rock with a metallic yellow going through it. Leland nodded.

When Nolan touched her shoulder, Abilene jumped before meeting his eyes. "If he sees this, you're doomed," she pronounced.

"This is sacred land. Even here. No mining. No drilling. No trespassers. We're aware of that small vein and others throughout the area. It's one of the reasons the area is off limits."

He understood her fear which was valid as far as she was concerned. For him, it was the sacred ground which mattered, not the small amount of gold to be found.

She stood, studying him with troubled eyes. "Then you're also aware of the silver over there in those rocks, the copper along the ridge over on the other side of the canyon, and the semiprecious stones scattered around the area. The rock over here has turquoise in it and the one over there has what appears to be sapphire. If he gets even a hint of what's around here, you'll be overrun with trespassers."

Leland chuckled. "Lady, you're the first one to notice the gold, let alone all the other stuff. Even Eve hasn't seen what you do. McGuire is here for oil and gas, or even coal if he sees it on the surface. As to the rest of the stuff, he's totally clueless since he has no training in geology and is using what you do to point them in the right direction." Leland winked at Nolan when Abilene rolled her eyes, gritting her teeth. "Lady, unless someone finds out from you about this, I don't believe there'll be any problems." He was confident in what he was saying.

Glaring at Leland, Abilene snapped, "They won't find out from me. I can't use this area other than for comparison to the other place I'd like to record. It will be done in broad generalities without being identified as to the exact location. Nor will I give and exact chemical makeup because that would tell anyone with a rudimentary knowledge of geology what could be found here."

Satisfied she wouldn't jeopardize the area, Nolan drawled, "We need to be getting back. Leland, the Feds will contact you later today."

Nolan held Ghost as Abilene mounted. The big horse hadn't moved from where she had left him. Everyone had agreed she needed to know what they were protecting. He trusted her to do as she said she would. In all the research on her, she had been up front and truthful. Plus, her story hadn't changed from day one.

Chapter 10

Leland followed Nolan and Abilene as they rode away from him. He chuckled, recalling Abby's face when he stood from where he had been hiding. There were advantages to being a half-breed. He was able to have the best of both worlds. His mother's father encouraged him to embrace what was called 'the old ways.' The end result was becoming an expert in tracking, using a bow and arrow while blending into the countryside. He had also learned to live off the land, able to travel miles on foot with minimal food and water.

Meanwhile, his father encouraged him to choose a profession where he could use his mind along with his skills. Leland had a degree in criminal justice, but had decided to work for Nolan, liking what he and the Chapmans were doing for the innocent people sent to them.

Like Abby, McGuire hadn't see him sitting at the base of the rock. Ron walked past him several times, not seeing him in the shadows. Nolan had noticed him when he moved his head as they rode past him. It was like playing hide-and-seek a s kid. You hid and the one who was 'it' had to find you; only in this game, it could get deadly if someone found you in the wrong place.

Leland's two oldest sons had joined him in learning the old-time skills of the tribe. They also joined him in working for Nolan. The work was dangerous at times, but it was mostly a lot of fun for them. The Chapmans paid well for their help, and they got to use the unexpected skills only a few knew today.

Returning to where he had been sitting, Leland again blended into the colors of the rock as he watched over the area. Close to an hour later, his cell phone vibrated. A quick glance around didn't turn up any strangers in the area. He pulled the phone from his pocket.

"Hello, Trent," he answered, keeping his voice low.

"Hi, bro. I hear you need some backup at the canyon."

"We do. McGuire was just here. He's under arrest, but there are plans afoot to raid the burial grounds."

"Not to worry. I'm sending a contingent of the National Guard to assist. They should be there this afternoon. It's up to you how you position them."

"Thanks. I'll make good use of them. There's a little nook in the canyon where they can camp without being seen. Hopefully they're bringing enough supplies for a couple of weeks.

Trent chuckled. "I told them to plan on a month. Not sure how long this operation will last. Did you get to see Abilene?"

"Yes. She sure is something else. Not only is she beautiful, she's smart. The lady knows her stuff."

"Really?"

"Yep, she identified all the gems, turquoise, gold, and I'm sure she saw a more than she mentioned." Leland chuckled. "But she didn't see me. How could she see all that other stuff and not see me sitting right in front of her out in the open?"

Trent laughed. "Leland, you have hiding in the open perfected to the point where your own people can't see you." He sobered. "You be careful. These guys play for keeps."

"I've no intention of getting hurt. But I'm curious how Wade is handling Abilene. From what Chad said, he's so smitten he doesn't know which way to turn next."

There was silence. Trent finally uttered, "It's about time. I hope he remembers the job he's supposed to do where she is concerned."

"Well, if what Chad said is true, Wade may convince her to stay here. She was ready to run when McGuire showed up while he was with her.

"He better not let her disappear. If she does, we'll never get them. We need her to get what we don't have on the rest of the group."

"From what Nolan said, she's going to stay for a month for sure. You need to get things pulled together, buddy. She's sacred. Real scared of what they'll do to us here."

"What makes you believe she's that frightened?"

A vision of Abby's face when she saw McGuire flashed through his mind. Terrified would be a better word to describe her reaction to him. "You should have seen her face when she saw McGuire. I'm guessing there's more going on than meets the eye."

"Maybe," was Trent's short reply.

"Got to go. I'll wait around until the troops get here and are settled. Thanks again."

Leland cut the connection as he again scanned the area. No new trespassers were noted. Trent's brief replay confirmed there was more to this than what he had given them. Trent indicated Abilene was a key, but why? What Leland did know was how they better not let anything happen to her or there would be hell to pay for all of them.

A birdcall got his attention. He moved closer to the rock beside him, moving nothing but his eyes while following the dust trail of a motorized vehicle in the distance. Whoever it was, wasn't afraid of being seen. Who was it and why were this person on the reservation?

It was close to a half hour before he recognized the vehicle. Whipping out his phone and hit autodial. When the person answered, Leland snapped, "Why in the hell didn't you call me?"

"Hello, Leland. It's no nice to hear your voice," the person on the other end replied cheerfully.

"Look, you can't go for joy rides around the area without checking in with me."

"Having a problem?" the man asked without concern.

Biting off what he was going to say, Leland didn't need to make things worse than they already were. "Yes, there's a problem. You need to stay away from the burial grounds unless you like getting shot first and questioned later."

The silence on the other end indicated the man got the message. "Okay. I'm going in to relieve Fred. I'll warn the others to let you know before coming out.,"

"Tell them to use horses. That ATV could be seen for miles."

"Gotcha."

"Eddy?"

"Yeah."

"Don't pull that stunt again our you're off the team. Understand?"

"I get it. I'll let the others know the call first. Thought this was a training exercise."

Leland gritted his teeth. "Never assume it's a practice session. You know that Eddy. You could blow the whole operation with antics. One more stupid act and you're out."

He didn't give Eddy a chance to respond. Furious at the young man's excuse, he settled against the rock again. A few seconds later, he made another call.

"What's up?" Trent answered on the first ring.

"I need you to check on someone for me."

"Who?"

"Eddy Alvarez. He's from the Albuquerque area."

"Why?"

"I have my suspicions where he's concerned. When a person keeps jeopardizing operations, I want to know why."

"Got it. I'll get back to you in the next couple of days. Keep an eye on him. When did he join your team?"

"About a year ago, right after our last run-in with McGuire's bosses."

"Uh-huh. Getting on it now. Don't let him know you suspect anything. He might come in handy down the road."

"I won't be trusting him with any sensitive information. So far, I've used him for guard duty, but he just let anyone within ten miles know there are guards at the canyon."

"Get him out of there. He doesn't need to know about the extra troops. Pair him up and have him do reservation rounds," Trent advised.

After doing a quick survey of who was working where and how he could get Eddy off duty at the canyon. "Will do. I'll let you know if there are any other hiccups on this end."

Leland broke the connection before calling one of his friends, telling him to go home sick and to continue to play sick for a week. He would get paid. There was no argument from his friend. Now to get the problem man back to the town.

"Eddy, I have a problem. I need you to fill in for Billy. He went home sick. Take his shift for today. I'll let you know about tomorrow."

"Sure thing, boss."

Leland hung up, watching as Eddy turned and headed back to the reservation. He had a week reprieve. Hopefully Trent would get back with him in a day or two. The last thing needed was someone on the inside passing information to the criminals.

Two hours later, his relief showed up. Instead of going home, he headed to the ranch, needing to talk to Nolan. If Eddy was a mole, they had to plan on how to use him to their advantage and there was no one better than Nolan and Jamie in setting up a good plan.

He was in luck when he got to the ranch. Nolan, Jamie, Wade and Chad were all there. He explained his problem with Eddy and his suspicions. Jamie came up with a plan on how to feed the man false information to pass onto McGuire's setup. It would all work out.

Before he could leave, Nolan stopped him. "I believe we need to have a discussion about Abilene."

Leland sat back done, waiting to see what Nolan wanted to say.

Nolan turned to Jamie. "You want to tell them or me?"

All eyes were on Nolan when he began to talk. When he finished, that all had more the think about. Leland had been right. Abilene was important, but he hadn't realized how important. A lot of the extra pieces fell into place with the information Nolan gave them.

Chapter 11

Ron didn't mind going to jail. He'd been there more times than he wanted to admit. Relaxing on what passed for a bed, he smiled at the thought of how easily Abilene had fallen into their plans. She had no clue as to how easy she was to track after she opened the first e-mail he sent her. She was clueless in more ways than one.

Ron reviewed the plan. The lawyer said the mineral rights would soon belong to them. Nolan Chapman wouldn't know what hit him when the orders started coming down. Chad and Wade would discover how much fun it was to be on the receiving end of a beating. This was going to be a lot of fun. A whole lot of fun. Abilene had only made the mistake of getting involved with a man once before now. After their roughing him up like they had, he couldn't believe she was making the same mistake again. This time roughing up those helping here was personal, not a job.

Ron sat up when the door to his cell was unlocked.

"Time for court, McGuire," the officer said, indicating he needed to turn and face the wall to be cuffed.

The lawyer had fallen down on the job but not getting him out on bail before the hearing. Two days in jail wasn't the best use of his time. Then again, some of these small towns were a big hassle in this business. Once the handcuffs clicked into place, Ron let the officer lead him to the courtroom, smiling at the thought of leaving the dreary cell. He was placed at the table beside the lawyer. The smile disappeared when the lawyer who had always won, frowned.

"What's the problem?" Ron whispered.

"Not sure. The judge wouldn't set bail. Also, I know the lawyer over there. He's no pushover." The lawyer had nodded in the direction of the table where two men sat.

A sliver of fear sliced through him. This hick town was different. The old man who he now recognized that *the* Mr. Chapman was sitting at the other table, ignoring him and his lawyer. Today he was dressed in a suit, looking ever inch the powerful businessman. The two boys were behind him, also dressed in suits, clones of their father. Ron rotated back to the lawyer who avoided making eye contact with him while they waited for the hearing to start.

The judge entered the court and called it to order. The charges were read and duly noted. Ron's lawyer entered a plea of not guilty.

The judge said, "Mr. Wellington, you may start."

The Chapman lawyer simply stated, "You Honor, Mr. McGuire willfully broke the law by trespassing on the Triple C Ranch after being warned by Wade Chapman to stay off their land. Also, he was found in a restricted area which is sacred to the local tribe. It contains an ancient burial ground. These pictures from his camera are proof he was there along with the arrest report." The lawyer handed the bailiff the documents then sat.

The judge said, "Mr. Matthews, you may state your case."

The wily lawyer laid out their case based on proof he had dug up after Ron had called him. It showed the land didn't belong to the Chapmans and, in fact, belonged to the government and was open range. He produced maps, deeds, and government records to prove the case. It had taken him two days to meticulously trace the deeds and ownership of the land in question. Ron didn't see how the Chapman could win.

When Matthews sat down, Wellington rose. "Your honor, I'm sure Mr. Matthews believes what he has shown, but if you look at this map, you'll see a notation showing it's from a long, long time ago."

Wellington tacked up an new map over the one Matthews had used. "This current map of the area, with the county and state lines, clearly defines the land owned by Mr. Chapman. The progression of the deeds from the original land grant, have been recorded in the state capital. They are contained in this document from the State Department of Records which supports Mr. Chapman's ownership."

He handed a file to the bailiff before continuing.

"As you can see, the area is posted with no trespassing sign which are clearly visible at the required intervals. Mr. McGuire was asked to leave three times. The proof is here in the transcript of the conversation recorded on a SIM card from Mr. Chapman's cellphone. He was also warned not to trespass prior to his doing so as is shown in this transcript of a conversation in which he also threatened the owners with bodily harm."

Again, the bailiff was handed the paperwork containing the evidence he had recited.

"Your Honor, I also have records here showing this is a pattern for Mr. McGuire. In light of his willful breaking of trespassing laws in multiple places, the prosecution is requesting a maximum sentence be given in light of the past offenses and the threats against the Chapmans and one Abilene Brown. We would also like to request a restraining order preventing him from contacting or being within five hundred feet of any of the Chapman family and Ms. Brown."

The paperwork was handed to the judge along with a file containing a dossier on Ron and his history. He didn't have a good feeling about this at all. These people had gone above and beyond any of the other places they had been.

Matthews rose. "I object, Your Honor. This hearing is based on the present, and my client's past doesn't have any bearing or connection to this offense."

"Objection overruled. IF there's a pattern to you client's actions, it must be considered. There will be a recess of thirty minutes as I look over all the evidence presented."

The gavel came down, and the judge left the courtroom, taking all the paperwork with him. Matthews turned to Ron. "Be prepared for a big fine, jail time or both."

Ron gritted his teeth, tightening the muscles at his jaw. It was time for Zeke to shop up. The upside to this was how his sitting in jail would keep him from being blamed for what was about to happen. These yahoos would learn what an organized takeover was within the next month.

In exactly thirty minutes, the judge returned and called the court to order. "I have reviewed the evidence on both sides. Mr. McGuire and Mr. Matthews, you need to us updated maps and do a better research as to who owns what in this territory. You were clearly trespassing and, from the records I've been given, ignored all requests to leave. All of this after being warned to stay off the Chapman ranch. If this was a one-time offense, I'd have been willing to give you a minimum penalty, but from what I was given and have verified, this is a regular pattern for you.

"Therefore, I'm sentencing you to a year and a day in the county jail with a no early release stipulation along with a fine of twenty-five thousand dollars. Also, from the records given to me, the restraining order is approved. I caution you to not contact any of the Chapman family or Ms. Brown in any way."

The gavel came down and the judge stated, "Court is adjourned."

Ron turned to Matthews. "Do something! I can't sit in jail for a year."

Matthews glared at him. "It will take close to a year to get an appeal. Suck it up. It's only a year and a day." Snapping his brief case closed, he left Ron to his fate.

Anger radiating off him, Ron turned to where the Chapmans had been sitting. His eyes widened. They were gone. Maybe it was time to get another lawyer.

Two weeks later, Ron walked out of the county jail. His appeal had changed the sentence to a fifty thousand dollar fine and time served. The restraining order remained in effect.

Wellington hadn't objected. If anything, he appeared happy with Ron getting out of jail. It made Ron uneasy when the lawyer nodded at him with a smile as he left the hearing. Something was up, but what?

Zeke was waiting on him when he returned to the house he had rented. The short, thin man with a shaved head, goatee and tattoos was dressed in his usual printed T-shirt and jeans with worn boots. His grin, showing crooked, nicotine-stained teeth, set Ron on edge.

Straightening his jacket, Ron asked, "What do you have to report?"

Zeke continued cleaning his nails with a pocket knife, while slouched in a chair, the television turned to a news channel with the sound muted. "Well, it looks like these folks are putting blame on the Chapman clan and Abby. They are seeing dollar signs but have discovered Chapman owns the mineral rights to the whole area and isn't willing to allow any drilling."

Ron paced as he talked. "Good. We need to get them fired up about his underhanded way of getting the mineral right, then have them fight to get them back. A class action suit should make him sit up and take notice."

Zeke didn't say anything. He had his orders. Time to rile the locals into action.

The Saturday after Ron went to jail, Wade and Abilene had gone on a ride with Chad and Eve so Abilene could see more of the ranch. It had been a pleasant day spent in her company. As they played around, Wade had held her. He hadn't wanted to let her go after giving her a playful peck of a kiss the situation had demanded.

Her eyes dared him to do more, but he backed away, afraid if he took the dare, things would spiral out of control. She was only here for six months. As much as he could imagine her staying, the likelihood was slim.

During the wait for what Ron was going to do next, Wade visited Abilene and Jaimie several times during the week once he was finished with work. Each time he found it harder and harder to walk out the door and return home. Even though things were calm, he was so afraid she was going to leave before the end of the month she promised to stay.

What he wouldn't give to have all the right words like Chad to tell her how he felt. Their conversations had been pleasant, but he couldn't seem to get past the friend stage. Something about her made it difficult for him to talk to her. The good things was how she didn't seem to mind him hanging around and accepted his timid advances. He smiled as he planned his next move. A real kiss. One she would remember.

Chapter 12

It didn't take long for many of the smaller ranchers to call for town meeting. Three weeks from the time Ron had been released to be exact. The ranchers were angry at what they saw as the Chapmans controlling them with their money and power. Most of them wanted their mineral rights back to make money with the oil Ron's minions said was under their land. They were assured they could continue to run their ranches while getting passive from wells drilling on their land,

They had been told there was a lot of oil in the area and they wanted their share of the profits. Before they would agree to a class action suit, the ranchers requested a town hall meeting to confront Nolan.

Abilene know the routine. It was a similar scenario to those which played out in the other communities. She decided to attend the meeting after packing all her things, hoping against hope Nolan wouldn't be tarred and feathered before it was over. Only a miracle would make it so she didn't have to leave, but that wasn't likely to happen.

The Chapmans had tried. It wasn't their fault they had failed. This was a lot bigger than they could ever imagine. She didn't want to leave. Wade was a big part of that reluctance to run again, along with not having many places left where she could hide.

It was a matter of time before they came for her, but it wouldn't be Ron. He was the one charged with keeping track of her through her research. No, he wasn't the one she was worried about. The secret she had lived with for twenty-some years was the problem. Soon she would need a miracle or suffer the same fate as her husband.

Choosing a seat close to the door of the large town hall for a quick getaway if needed, Abilene listened to the ranchers making their case. Nolan listened calmly, his face not showing what he was thinking. Most of the ranchers expressed their anger at not controlling the mineral rights on their own land. While most had been respectful to Nolan, several weren't above calling him names while being accusatory in their remarks. He listened, leaning back in the chair, an elbow resting on the table beside him, waiting his turn to speak.

Once all the ranchers had stated their cases, Nolan stood, moving to the podium where he took the microphone from the mayor. He was calm, scanning those gathered in the room, noting those who were glaring at him. It took several minutes for the room to quiet until all you could hear was the rustling of the people shifting in the seats.

His sonorous voice was clear and carried to the back of the large hall, drawing the attention of all those in the room. Abby could see how he had gotten to where he was today. With his voice and sense of timing, he would make a great statesman if he ever decided to enter the political arena.

"I've sat here and listened to you all state your views. I've heard the anger many of you expressed over being denied the ability to get rich quick. On the surface, many of your arguments make sense, but overall, it's obvious you haven't delved into all the pros and cons of what Mr. McGuire is proposing.

"First of all, yes, I own the mineral rights. You all sold them to me fifty some years ago. Not a one of you objects at the time, even though you were aware of the possibility of there being gas and oil in the area. Every last one of you agreed you were ranchers, not prospectors. We also agreed at the time how we didn't want our ranches on the land destroyed by wildcatters and others who have no respect for this area."

He paced by the podium, holding the microphone, scanning those who had come to the meeting. He stopped at the podium, leaning on it, facing the ranchers, his face showing concern.

"I'd like to know what changed. Are you all so greedy you can't see what's happening here?" He again scanned the room, giving them time to answer his question. "Let me show you what's happened to other places where Mr. McGuire and the group behind him have prospered, and what the other communities' greed brought them."

A picture came on the screen behind him. Abilene recognized it as one she had taken over five years ago. It was the first time Ron pulled his scam using her work.

"This photo is from Tennessee. Notice how peaceful and beautify it is." He gave them time to study the picture. The next picture came up. "This is what it looks like today."

There was low murmur from the ranchers as they stared at the picture. It showed the massive damage the drillers had created and left. Nolan made his way through every site where Ron had used her work to drill, giving those in the room plenty of time to study the picture. Unlike them, he had done his homework. The comments he made were short and to the point as he scrolled through the before and after pictures.

When a picture of the land outside of town came onto the screen, Nolan turned and faced the now quiet men and women. His countenance showed concern as he faced them. Again, he leaned on the podium, allowing them to look at the picture behind him.

"Is that what you want? If so, come to me and I'll sell you back your mineral rights. But, before you make that decisions, take a good look at this picture for it will be the last time you'll see it like this."

He took a deep breath and released it slowly, beginning to pace again. He wasn't finished.

"You've now seen the results of Mr. McGuire's use of your land. He rapes it, destroys it, then moves on for you to deal with the mess. If you take him up on his offer of steady big money, be prepared for the federal mandates for you, not the drillers, to clean up the mess they leave behind. What you receive from the oil or gas won't even come close to paying for the cleanup."

He brought up a letter with the name blacked out. It was from the EPA. Abilene heard the collective gasp from the room as the read the letter. Nolan stopped pacing before saying, "Here's the cost from the last site they used."

A listing of the federal and state government charges and requirements for cleaning up the drilling site and making it meet the standards for the area were showing on the screen. With the fines and costs, the total was over a million dollars. The room held total silence. Nolan had made his case. The landowners would end up owing the government more than they could ever hope to earn from the oil. There would be ongoing fines if they missed deadlines from mandated corrections and environmental adjustments.

"Like I've told you before, know all the ins, outs and costs before you believe you'll strike it rich. Mr. McGuire has been doing this for the past five years what we're aware of, leaving the landowners in massive debt the can never pay back. If that's your goal, then have at it. As for me, he's not going to set foot on my land to destroy it like he did those other places.

Nolan handed the microphone back to the mayor. When he took his seat, a tall thin woman, whose hair was done up in a bun at the back of her head, marched to the front, taking the microphone from the mayor. Her face was pinched as if she had eaten something sour. The dark eyes found Abilene. The angry words cut into Abilene like a knife, each word slicing deeper, destroying what hope she had for staying.

"I know who to blame for this scammer coming here. It's Abilene Brown, She's a geologist, and Mr. McGuire uses her research to find the oil. It's on her head for what's happened in every other place. And to think we accepted her into our community."

Abilene rose and left as the woman spoke, noticing how many were looking around the room for her. It was enough for her to know what was going to happen now. Ron's sneer was all she needed to see to know he had engineered this meeting to ensure they would blame her, not him, even though she had nothing to do with his business. He would get off scot free while she took the brunt of the anger from his underhanded dealings.

Wiping the tears from her face, she pulled out of the parking space and drove to the small ranch. There was no longer any reason to stay. She efficiently packed the boxes into her jeep, aware she still owed four months rent on the house, having stayed over the month she promised Wade. It would take the rest of her savings. But she would honor her lease. The teaching job was her only option now to make ends meet. The years of research were wasted since she couldn't complete it. So much time and money spent, only to see it washed away by something she couldn't stop or control.

When the last box was in the jeep, she gave the place one last scan, missing it already. They had tried. At least Ron didn't get his way here. All he had done was to destroy her reputation for this area. It was also time to forget her dreams. They would never come true because Wade was lost to her. There was no way he would have anything to do with her now.

She slid behind the wheel, wiped the tears from her face and pulled away from the house, heading for the highway. There was no choice now. Teaching it would be, Maybe in another ten or fifteen years she could go back to her research as a hobby.

She wiped away the tears which didn't want to stop before merging onto the interstate, heading northwest. All she needed to do now was to notify the university by the deadline she would take the job. It meant she had four months to waste. There was only one place left to go to enjoy the last of her freedom from a normal job. It was her home. Hopefully Ron wouldn't find her there. If he did, there was nowhere else to hide.

Chapter 13

Wade stayed until the end of the meeting. He had seen Abby leave, but wanted to see if their plan would work. It went much better than expected. This meant she would be safe for the time being. He couldn't stop grinning, elated with the way everything had gone. Now if the rest would go as smoothly.

When he arrived at the house, Jamie met him on the porch. His smile faded when the saw the frown on Jamie's face. Dread coursed through him. He hoped he was wrong; then Jamie's words destroyed that hope.

"She left 'bout an hour ago." Jamie leaned against the porch post, watching him, his face unreadable and the voice held no emotion.

"Didn't you try and stop her?" How could Jamie let her leave without attempting to convince her to stay.

"Nope. Not my place."

Wade ran a hand through his hair, gnawing on him bottom lip, turning to stare at Ghost. "Did she give any indication of where she was going?"

"Nope. Didn't talk to her."

Wade took a seat on the steps, running a hand over his face. He knew where she would be in the fall, but he wanted to find her before then. His shoulders slumped, leaning forward to rest his elbows on his knees, hand clasped to keep them from shaking.

"Any ideas on where she would hole up for a few months?" Wade questioned, staring at his folded hands, praying she had told Jamie where she might go from here.

"Yep."

Twisting to stare at the old man, Wade noticed he was watching him closely. Anger mixed with concern boiled to the surface. He was wasting time, and Jamie wasn't helping by not answering his questions.

"Well, are you going to tell me or not?" Wade asked, his tone sharp with anger.

"Depends."

Wade glared at him, unable to get want he needed from the old man who had continued to stare at him. "On what, Jamie?"

"You."

Wade's brow furrowed, confusion, irritation and impatience warring inside of him. "What are you talking about?"

"Why do you want to find her?"

Wade stared at Jamie, his mouth grim, attempting to figure out what Jamie wanted from him. Rotating away from the man who had arched an eyebrow, waiting for his answer, he knew he would have to tell him why he wanted to find Abilene. But what exactly did he want to know?

The minutes ticked by as he went through everything the old man might mean until her remembered the story of a woman from a long time ago. Jamie had loved her and planned on marrying her. She suddenly disappeared. Jamie left the ranch in search of where the woman had gone. He had found her. According to the story Jamie told them when he returned, she had been sick and hadn't wanted him to suffer along with her. He convinced her to marry him and stayed with her until she died before coming back to the ranch.

Jamie's words to his father when he returned came back to Wade. "If you love someone, you go after them and stay with them through thick and thin. Don't let the one you love slip away."

Why did he want to find Abilene? Jamie wouldn't' accept anything but the raw truth. Because of his job wouldn't be acceptable. No, he wanted Wade's personal reason for wanting to know where she went. It meant he would have to admit how he felt about her. If he didn't, she would be lost to him. That was something he wasn't sure he could handle. In the short time she had been here, he had gone from being attracted to her to not wanting to be away from her. It was time to be honest with himself. He loved her.

Hanging his head, Wade divulged the truth about his attachment to Abilene. "Jamie, I love her. I can't let what Phyllis said drive her away from me. It's like a big hole has been torn out of me with her laving. I have to find her." He tamped down the fear which entered him as he begged, "Please, Jamie. Help me find her."

Wade turned pleading eyes to the man who was like a second father to him. It all rested with Jamie since he had no idea of where to begin. With a sigh, he turned back around, studying his hands again, not sure if he was right in what Jamie wanted to know.

"Might want to find her hidey-hole in Colorado then," the matter-of-fact voice stated from behind him.

Relief washed over him. It was a start and a lot more than what he had before. He glanced at the man who had given him what he needed. "Thanks," he said before heading to his truck, planning how he could find her place in Colorado.

"You better marry that girl, or you'll have to deal with me," Jamie warned as Wade opened the door to his truck.

With a crooked grin, Wade said, "Planning on it. Just have to convince her to say yes."

Jamie gave a curt nod before going back into the house. Wade now had a general area of where to look. He would overturn every rock in in the state to find her if necessary. He would worry about convincing her to come back with him once he discovered where she was hiding.

Back at the ranch, Wade turned on the computer and began his search. During the time-consuming, county by county hunt, frustration continued to build. Finally, her name popped up on the screen during the search in San Juan county.

"Bingo!" he exclaimed, smiling at the screen. After coping all the information on her property and the county seat, he shut off the computer. Pivoting without looking, Wade sidestepped his father, avoiding running into him by a quick step, rushing to his room. Nolan followed him, standing in the doorway watching him pack.

"Dad, I not sure how long I'll be gone, but I'm going after Abilene. It shouldn't be more than a few days, two weeks at the most."

"You sure you want to go chasing after her, son?" Nolan asked, eyes filled with concern.

"I have to. If she doesn't want me, I won't be gone long, but I have to try."

"I take it you care a lot about her."

Wade paused then resumed his packing. "I've not met another like her. I can't let her slip away."

Nolan put a hand on his shoulder, holding him in place for a few seconds. "I know what you men. If I was you age, I'd be giving you some competition for her. As it is, I have my own lady who's just as compelling. I hope she'll agree to marry me soon."

Wade chuckled before giving his father a hug. "You neve cease to surprise me. Glad you understand."

"Understand, I do. Totally. Go and find her. You'd better bring her back."

Wade let out the breath he'd been holding. "I will if at all possible." He wasn't' sure what would happen when he found Abby.

Now wasn't the time to tell him he wanted to marry Abby. He hoped to convincer her to return if for no other reason than how she couldn't continue to run away. The bad thing was, he didn't know what he would do if she refused to come back with him.

After she left the town hall, Chad, the most unlikely speaker rose and challenged her to prove Abby was working with Ron. Phyllis received what she had been told.

When Eveline stood to say her piece, the room had gotten quiet. Eveline held as much respect as the Chapmans did in the town. They listened to her cultured Southern voice question Phyllis's version of Abby working for McGuire.

"Why, if Abilene was working for Ron, wasn't she getting paid for it?" She held up a sheaf of papers. "I have her tax returns going back ten years. There's not one shred of evidence of any money being given to one Abilene Brown by any oil company. She gave these to me because she knew what was going to be said about her. I'm sure she'll be gone before this meeting ends. She cares enough about us to attempt to stop what happened elsewhere from happening here.

"We had several long talks about Mr. McGuire over the past few weeks. He had used her and has destroyed any hope she had of competing her research. I believe we, as a town, owe her an apology for believing the accusation Mr. McGuire has spread which are totally unfounded."

It was then the ranchers and townspeople turned on Ron and his minions. Wade grinned as he remembered their hasty retreat. The senior reporter was planning on doing an exposé on McGuire and those behind him. The plan was to get it published nationwide and essentially shutting them down. Now all he needed to do was to find Abilene, who had left like Eveline said, and get her back to safety.

Chapter 14

After driving for over twelve hours, Wade pulled into Silverton, the county seat where Abilene's place was located. It was the early hours of the morning, so he leaned his head back against the headrest and slept. The slamming of a care door awakened him. It was daylight, but was still before nine, the time the office opened.

There was an open café across the street. Coffee and food sounded good since he'd had minimal to eat since lunch yesterday. By the time he finished breakfast, the door to the county courthouse was open. It was great timing for him as he should be able to find Abby's place and get there prior to noon.

He was the first customer of the day. When called to the counter, he asked if someone would show him where the property was located and how to get there. The older lady pulled out a map and marked the location then drew a line from the town to the property before handing it to him. As he was leaving, clerk said. "Say hi to Abilene for me. I wish you the best of luck. She's a special lady."

Wade nodded with a tired grin. "Will do. I appreciate that. You're right. She's one extra special lady."

It took over an hour to get to the turn-off to the hidden house. When he finally found it, he understood why she had come home. Outwardly, it appeared to be an old log cabin set on a large natural shelf on the side of the mountain, surrounded by pine and aspen trees. There was a brook bubbling merrily as it tumbled down to the road on the far side of the building. He turned to the view of the mountains through the trees to his right. The view alone was worth the trip to come here. It was a perfect retreat from a world which had been anything but kind to her.

The old jeep was in the drive, pulled close to the house. Wade pulled in behind it, parking the truck so she couldn't get around him. Stepping down from the driver's seat, he stood, breathing in the mountain air, feeling the peacefulness of the rustic setting. He climbed the steps to the wide porch and knocked on the door. When there was no answer, he sat on the porch steps to wait for her, using the time to figure out what to say to convince her to return with him.

As the time dragged on, Wade began to wonder if he had done the right thing in coming after her. What if she didn't feel the same about him as he did her? Should he use McGuire as an excuse to get her to come back, or should he tell her the truth about how he loved her? The longer he thought about it, the less sure he was about why had had come after her. He was on the verge of getting up to leave when Abilene's low voice startled him out of his thoughts.

"How did you find me?"

With deliberate slowness, he turned to the woman whose face showed she had been crying. "Jamie," he blurted out, his mind seeming to quit functioning at seeing her so upset.

With a sigh, she sat beside him on the step. "Figures. How did you pry it out of him?"

"By telling him the truth."

Abilene stared at him, her head was tilted, and brows drawn together in a frown. "Truth about what?"

Wade hesitated, realizing too late he should have said something different. He might as well tell her the rest, hoping it wouldn't cause her to run from him. "How I feel about you."

Another sigh escaped her as she watched a squirrel in the tree before her. Even though she didn't look at him, he could see the resignation on her face and in the slumped shoulders.

He leaned forward, resting his elbows on his knees as he studied his hands, aware he needed to tell her the whole truth. The most she could do would be to negate it. Screw up his courage, he said, "Abilene, in what little time we've been together, I've fallen in love with you. I couldn't let you run away and not let you know."

He rotated his head to view her face. Tears were running over her cheeks. The sad look in her eyes had him fearing the worst before her lowered her head. He waited, unsure of what to do now.

"Wade, I can't go back there. They believe I was the cause of Ron showing up. If I didn't misunderstand what was being said, they also believe I was working for him. Those are things I can't change."

He turned to face her, a hand tenderly pushing the tendrils of hair from her face before letting it rest on her shoulder.

"They know you weren't working for him. In case you weren't aware of it, you have a lot of friends in town. Eveline came to your defense as did Chad, Jerry and a few others. If you stayed, you could have seen McGuire and his cronies essentially run out of town."

"You know it doesn't change a thing. He'll do it again the next place I go."

"I don't think so. Once the national exposé is out there, he'll have no place to hide. His days are numbered in the oil industry. Never underestimate the power of a few good people who aren't afraid to do the right thing." Wade reached over to gently turn her head until she was facing him. Abilene, I love you. There's nothing I wouldn't do for you, but you have to help me here. You need to come back and help us expose him and the companies who were paying him. Part of that is being honest about how he used you. Until you do, it will keep happening over and over again. Don't' let them win and destroy what could be."

The fear took the place of the sadness. "You don't know what he and his friends are capable of doing. I do. The last person who attempted to help me ended up disfigured and permanently disabled. They broke both arms, both legs, then beat him until he was close to dying. He sent me away, afraid they would come back. I can't let that happen to you or your family. They will come after me and you."

The ringing of her cellphone cause Abby to jump as if she had received a shock. Taking the phone from the holder, she frowned at the screen. It was on speaker when she asked, "What do you want, Ron?"

"You to get back to work. I'm coming for you and you'd better be ready to go to the next place by the time I get there."

"I'm dropping the research, so go find another patsy to use."

"Not happening, dearie. I'll be there in an hour." Ron's voice was harsh with an audible threat lacing the words.

The phone went dead, not allowing her to respond. She rotated her head to him, ready to cry again. "Now do you believe me?"

He surveyed the area, planning what he was going to do. Going to his truck, he took a rifle with a scope from the holder on the back window before pulling out a magazine of ammunition from behind the seat. The last thing the two-faced weasel expected was a high-powered rifle and a man who knew how to use it.

Wade checked several spot before taking up a position which allowed him a clear view of the road. He prepared for the man who was threatening the woman he loved. With a click, the magazine seated in the rifle before he put a round in the chamber. It was now a matter of having the best view he would get of the road and waiting for Ron to show up.

"Go and pack your things in the jeep. As soon as Ron is taken care of, we need to go back to the ranch. It's a safe place for all of us. We can deal with the threats from there."

Abilene didn't argue, pivoting to the cabin to do as requested. There was no choice now. Ron knew where her house was, which meant the others would know its location also. Wade and his family were her only hope of surviving to see her next birthday. There was no place else to hide.

Within the half hour, she had the jeep repacked and ready to go since she hadn't begun to unpack yet. Instead, she had needed the time to grieve the losses which were piling up. There were a couple of extra boxes she included, afraid to leave the contents here now that her home had been located.

Wade was on the phone when she had finished with the jeep. She listened to his end of the conversation.

"Yes, sir. He's made threats against her and me. I'm going to attempt to stop him before he can get to her." Wade listened, then said, "I'll do everything I can to keep him in one piece for you." There was another pause which brought a smile to his face. "Thank you, sir. You should be close behind him. He said he would be here in and hour and there's only about thirty minutes of that hour left."

Wade hung up before giving her a reassuring smile. "It appears there's a warrant for Ron's arrest here on Colorado. Something to do with environmental destruction and illegal and shady deals. There are also warrants for all the oil conglomerate's head honchos. They feel I'm doing them a service by tying to stop him from getting to you. I'm not sure he knows it or not. But he's not allowed within a mile of this place without violating a restraining order someone filed for you in this county."

"I wonder who would do that?" Abilene muttered to herself, her forehead crinkling in a confused frown.

"My guess would be my father, but I've been wrong before."

"Why would he get a restraining order for me?"

"He likes you. Believes in you, and if I didn't misinterpret what he said before I left, he cares a lot about you."

"I still don't understand."

"Trust me. You'll understand when we get back?"

He let it drop, not willing to discuss the family dynamics with her at this time. The minutes crept by until the sound of a car moving slowly on the road reached them. Wade sighted the rifle in on the spot he had chosen and waited. Ron's Cadillac came into view. One shot was quickly followed by a second. The car veered to the left side of road in a slow skid. The sound of a crash told them the car had either gone off the road or run into the bank.

Before either one of them moved, two cars with flashing lights came into view. One stopped where they could see it. Two officers exited the cars, walking fast in the direction the Cadillac had gone. Wade and Abilene made their way down the steep driveway to the road. When they could see what had happened, the noticed Ron sitting on a rock at the side of the road. His hands were cuffed behind him with blood running down his face as an officer talked to him. Another officer put a dressing on his head wound before they pulled him to his feet and placed him in the back of the first car.

The flat front tire on the driver's side had pulled him into the mountain when he had hit his brakes. The windshield showed where his head had hit it. Apparently he didn't' believe in using a seat belt.

Abilene nastily said, "Too bad he didn't go through the windshield and sever his head from the rest of him. It would have saved everyone a lot of time and money."

Wade put an arm around her, pulling her close to him. He didn't comment on her remark. It was one of the few times she had let the anger show.

The officer who had been talking to Ron strolled over to them. He was smiling. "I'd like to thank you for keeping him all in one piece. There are a lot of angry people out to get him. We plan on making an example of him.

"Ms. Brown, you take care. I'm looking forward to seeing that completed research. My kid's been keeping up with it online. He's real interested in what your final conclusions will be." He didn't wait for her to respond before returning to his car, backing in around to face back in the direction they came in from before yelling back at them, "We'll get rid of the Caddy in a couple of hours." He followed the other car down the road to book the man who had been bothering her for five long years.

She turned to Wade before saying, "Do we need to leave right away?"

The answer was on his face. "I hate to say it as I'd like the stay here for a few days also, but yet. Once they discover you're not at the ranch, they'll come after you. The quicker we get back, the safer you'll be. We can protect you there where we can't here."

She turned to take what she felt would be the last look at her home. The tears began again. "I hope it's still here when I get back," she said before going and locking the doors. It was with reluctance eh got into the jeep, waiting until Wade backed out of the driveway and waited for her to fall in behind him.

When they reached the highway, she went around him so he could see her. There was no guarantee they would get back to the ranch before being found. Ron wasn't the only one who wanted her and the others were more dangerous than him. Maybe they would back off with McGuire being out of action. Then again, they hadn't backed off in the years before Ron showed up, so why would they leave her alone now?

Chapter 15

It took them until late the following day to get back. Abilene kept the pace steady at a speed which wouldn't task the fully loaded old jeep. Wade paid for her gas. She didn't object. Her funds were limited at bets. Besides, it was his choice for her to return to the ranch, not hers. She didn't care if it was rationalization or anger, but she didn't believe she should have to put out the extra expenses.

When they stopped for the night, he made sure they had rooms next to each other. After they ate, he walked her to her room. Before letting her enter, he checked the room. She rotated into his arms, not realizing he was directly behind her. His head lowered to plant a short, tender kiss on her lips.

It wasn't much as far as kisses went, but she continued to feel the touch of his lips on hers as she drifted off to sleep. It was enough to show her how he felt. The dreams were on him and the simple kiss which lead to what she wanted: a life with the man she was afraid to love for fear it would get him killed.

It was late afternoon before they arrived at the Haskell spread. When she pulled into the yard, Jamie ambled toward them from the barn. He came over to her and gave her a hug before saying, "Now that you're back, don't believe I'll let you leave again, missy."

She gave the old man a smile before kissing his cheek. "I won't be leaving anytime soon, so I guess you'll have to put up with my cooking for a while longer."

Jamie gave her a curt nod before opening the back of the jeep and unloading the boxes. She knew he loved her cooking and their short conversations. Meanwhile, she loved the old man's close friendship. He had told her if she left Wade would come after her before leaving for the town hall meeting. Other than the comment, he hadn't stopped her while she packed when she explained what was happening. He had been right. Wade did come after her, but not for the reason she expected.

Ghost had moved to behind her without making a sound. When he nipped her shoulder, she moved away before rotating to the big stallion. Her arms went around his neck. He was one of the many things she would miss if she ever had to leave here.

If Wade told her the truth, maybe she could stay. Then again, he could always decide she wasn't what he wanted. If that was the case, she would go back to the loneliness which accompanied her ever since Kristen, her daughter, had moved out to live on her own.

"I'm sorry, big guy. I didn't forget about you." Abby reached into the jeep then held out an apple for the horse. He took it from her hand and ate it before moving closer to put his head over her shoulder, holding her in place.

Wade and Jamie had all the boxes and bags in the house within a few minute. She gave Ghost a pat before going inside to unpack again. Wade stopped her at the door with a hand on her arm.

"Abilene, I meant what I said at your place."

She swallowed, the nodded. "I know you did." Rotating her head to face him, she couldn't rid herself of the fear of losing him. "Wade, my being here makes you and your family targets. If anything happens to you or any one of them, I don't know if I can live with the guilt of being the cause."

He wrapped his arms around her. "We're doing this of our own free will. You have nothing to feel guilty about."

Her arms encircled his waist, as she leaned into him, gathering strength from him. She loved him, but when he found out the rest of the story, he might end up hating her instead. For now, she needed to keep her secrets. If the person who was controlling everything had one iota of suspicion that she shared what she knew, they would do everything the could to kill her and those she had met during her time here.

Leaning back in his arms, she imprinted what she saw on his face into her memory. When his lips met hers, her breathing stopped. This time it was a kiss not to be forgotten. She was breathless when he raised his head, a crooked smile forming on the lips which had turned her into mush. "Go unpack. I'll be back in the morning."

Going up the steps to the porch, she rotated, holding onto the post to watch him leave. Her mind screamed for him to come back, afraid of what could happen while he was away from her.

Jamie sifted to study her from where he sat on the steps. "That man's plumb crazy about you. Don't you go an' hurt him. Don't think he could stand it. Took him twenty years of waitin' to find you." He got up and headed to the barn, having said what he wanted.

She stared at the old man's back, now understanding why he had told Wade where to find her. He loved Wade as if he was his. It confirmed what Wade had said at the cabin. He had told Jamie he loved her to find out where she went. No matter what she did, these men were going to protect her if for no other reason than Wade's love for her.

It didn't take Abilene long to unpack. She looked up to find Jamie smiling at the picture she had put back in place on the end table.

"Looks like home again. Good to have you back."

She stood straight, meeting his gaze. "I'm terrified. These men won't give up, and they'll come after everyone here in revenge for what was done to them."

"Been there. Done that. Not to worry."

"I can't help it."

"You love him?" Jamie asked, putting a hand on her shoulder.

There was no way she could lie to him. "Yes."

"Then trust him."

"I do. It's the reason I came back. But I'm still afraid."

Jamie patted her cheek. "Fear's good. Keeps you alive. Let us do our job. You and Wade'll be fine." His arm came across her shoulder, guiding her to the kitchen. "I'm here by choice. Remember that. We choose our friends and who to protect."

She stopped, studying his face for hidden meanings. "Okay. I get the point." She kissed his cheek before going to the kitchen to fix supper.

Abilene was setting the meal on the table when Chad came to the back door. "Come on in," she said with a smile.

"Hm. Something smells good," he said, entering the kitchen. He moved next to her to kiss her cheek.

"Have you eaten," she asked moving away from him.

"No. Haven't had a chance. Didn't know you were back until I saw the jeep out front. I was looking for Jamie."

She turned to the doorway to the living room. Jamie was standing there watching them. Chad's mouth opened and closed like a fish out of water, speechless for a change. The last thing he had expected was Jamie socializing with her, a woman.

Jamie quirked and eyebrow. "Need Somethin', Chad?" he asked.

"Yeah. I need to run some stuff by you."

"Jaw at me over supper."

Abilene chuckled at the expression of disbelief on Chad's face. "I like to cook, and Jamie likes to eat. There's no reason for him to forage a meal of for me to eat alone," she explained.

Jamie watched Chad for a few seconds as if waiting on a comment from him. Chad kept his mouth shut, but she knew he was wondering about the relationship between her and Jamie. Walking over to the table, Jamie pulled out a chair and sat, waiting from them to join him. Abby set the rest of the food on the table before taking her normal seat in the corner. She waited for Jamie to say the blessing before passing the food.

One they were all eating, Jaimie, said, "Tell me what you found."

Chad glanced at her.

"It's about her. She needs to hear it."

With that, Chad related what they had discovered. "Well, McGuire is only a front guy, as we all knew. Behind him are several powerful people who have a lot of money. There's a group who keeps changing the company's name to keep out of the limelight, but the same men are behind all the different shell companies."

He paused to eat a couple of bites of the meatloaf and mashed potatoes, his eyes flicking to her, then back the Jamie.

The last names of the men are Garvin and Ringwood. There's a man by the name of Zeke Hatfield who stirs up problems then keeps them boiling. Every place which had been hit, all of these men have been involved. Matthews is only one of a cordon of lawyers they have on retainer. There've been payoffs, forged papers, missing documents and so forth. I have it all put together and in the Feds' hands. No matter what they do, they're going down."

Abilene kept her eyes on her plate when she said, "They have Ron on a federal warrant in Colorado, along with going against a restraining order."

"On down. Three more to go. It's Zeke I'm worried about. He's the one who controls the goons," Chad said before spearing some broccoli.

"What do you think they'll do?" Jamie asked, eating another bit of meatloaf.

"My guess is they'll try to get to the burial grounds. They want to get the tribes riled up against Dad for no protecting them."

"Yep. Won't make it," Jamie said concentrating on eating.

"How can you be so sure?" Chad asked.

"Feds and tribe already there. Been for weeks."

Chad glanced at her. She nodded. "They're there. Ron made a big mistake by going there first, so they're waiting on them to show up. It's the only place I've visited since being here."

"That may be, but they're going after the herd of horses. If they find them, we'll have to start all over again."

"Won't find them."

Chad frowned. "Why not?"

"Sent Ghost for them."

Chad shook his head, a crooked grin on his mouth. "Well, looks like you're all prepared. I'd best get on home then."

"Nope. Need you here tonight."

Abilene glared at Jamie. "What do you mean? Why do you need him here tonight?"

"'Specting visitors. Waldo and Arf aren't here. Nolan took them to the canyon."

Chad nodded. Without a word, he left the table and went out the back door. His truck started then came around the house, headed for the barn. He returned with two rifles, ammunition and night-vision goggles.

"You notify the sheriff?" Chad asked, loading the rifle he was holding.

"Yep. Can't do nothin' yet. They be close. Some Feds too."

I saw Leland over by the tree. Did he bring friends?"

"Yep. Five."

The two men sat at the table drinking coffee and talking as she began cleaning up from their meal. She was washing the dishes when a bird trilled. Jamie and Chad melted into the shadows while she continued with the dishes, aware she was the bait. As she was wiping the counter, Zeke slipped in the door from the mudroom into the kitchen.

"Well, looky here. You do need to get better guards, sweetie," he said, a triumphant grin on his face.

Abilene dropped the dishrag into the sink before turning to rest her hip against the counter, facing the nasty little man. "What makes you think I have none?"

Zeke sneered, taking two more steps into the kitchen. "If you did, they wouldn't have let me get this close to you."

"What do you want, Zeke?"

"You. Seems the bosses think you're pretty valuable. Because Ron's in jail, it doesn't mean we still can't use you and that brain of yours. Now you can come quietly, or you can come bound and gagged. Makes no difference to me."

She glanced behind him but didn't see anyone. "And how to they propose to make me give them information I don't have?"

"Oh, you have it. All you need to do is show us how to find the oil."

Abilene stared at her hands resting on the counter. "I'm no longer working on the research. You'll have to find someone else."

He let out a bark of laughter. "Garvin doesn't believe that for one minute. You remember him, don't you? He took you to the prom, dated you while in collage before you married Mr. Brown." Her head popped up at the last words. The smirk on his face made her believe he knew more than what he had said. The next words sent dread and fear coursing through her. "Too bad he died so young."

Not showing her thoughts on her face, she asked. "What are you hinting at, Zeke?"

The evil grin had her holding her breath, fear slapping around inside of her.

"Well, Mr. Garvin didn't take kindly to your leaving him for another man. Even though twenty-five years have passed, doesn't mean he's forgotten you. He feels it's time for you to come home to him."

She stared at him, lips slightly parted before breaking out in to laughter while Zeke stared at her. The expression on his face was priceless. When she got control of her mirth, she shook her head, unable to believe Garvin was such an idiot.

"You can go back an tell Garvin he's nuts. Yes, I went to the prom with him because every other boy was afraid to ask me. As for college, I talked to him and went out with him twice. I let him know I wasn't attracted to him. He's a total idiot if he thinks I want anything to do with him, especially now."

Zeke grinned. "That may be, but he wants you and what he wants, he gets."

"Not this time," Jamie said from the doorway, a rifle aimed at Zeke. "On the floor and spread 'em," he commanded, his eyes as steady as the rifle he held.

Zeke gave a whistle which was cut short by the ring of cast iron skillet hitting his head. Abilene hoped she hadn't killed him. At least not yet. Zeke know who killed Steven, and after all this time, she wanted the ones how had ordered his murder, along with the ones who had committed it, to pay.

She dropped to the floor as Zeke fell, aware he had brought some of his men with him. Bullets shattered the window over the sink where she had been standing a split second later. Jamie turned off the lights and pulled the goggles down over his eyes from the top of his head. He raised his rifle and fired a shot. The report echoed throughout the kitchen. Abilene covered her ears as the men exchanged shots. She began to cry, wanting it to be over.

The silence, when the shooting stopped, was a deafening as the gunfire. Jamie came to where she lay in the glass on the floor, unable to move. The truth finally sank in from what Zeke had said. Garvin had ordered her husband killed which meant he wasn't above killing her to keep someone else from having her. Several more pieces of the puzzle slipped into place.

"It's alright, Abby. Come one."

Jamie brushed the glass away from her before he lifted her up so she was sitting. Her wide eyes met his, the pupils dilated as she shivered, unable to make her muscles work. He hugged her go him, holding her as he leaned into him, sobbing.

A man entered the kitchen. He checked on Zeke who was still breathing. "I'll have the medic come and get him."

Another man entered and squatted beside Jamie.

"She alright?" he asked in a voice filled with concern.

"Will be," Jamie said, glancing down at her clinging to him. His eyes went to Chad.

"Get your brother," he commanded, not moving.

Chad pulled out his cellphone. When Wade answered, he only said, "Abilene needs you," before disconnecting the call.

Chapter 16

Wade was at the house in ten minutes, having ridden bareback from the ranch. Fear of what he would find had him pushing the horse over the dark landscape. Upon entering the kitchen, he stopped, staring at Jamie holding a sobbing Abilene amid shattered glass. He took a tentative step forward. "Abilene?"

She turned to him, a shaking hand reaching in his direction, her eyes pleading with him. In two strides Wade stood beside them. He took her from Jamie's arms, lifting her to her feet before sweeping her off her feet to carry her from the bullet riddled kitchen to the living room sofa. She clung to him, the harsh sobs not slowing.

He sat with her on his lap, cradling her like a small child as the harsh sobs continued, not easing.

"What happened, Chad?" There was no way he was bout to play question and answers with Jamie.

Only, it was Jamie who answered the question, sitting on the arm of the sofa, his hand on Abilene's head. He didn't turn away from Wade's glare, a frown on his face.

"Zeke showed up. Found out a boy she dated killed her husband and been dogging her for the past twenty-five years. A man by the name of Garvin. He wants her real bad."

Wade laid a cheek against her head. His voice was barely audible to those around them. "Abby, sweetheart, you didn't do anything wrong. You can't control other people."

She raised her head, the fear showing on her face. "He's after you now. He'll kill you if he can."

Wade tightened his arms. "Not likely. You took care of Zeke, Ron's in jail and they picked up Ringwood earlier this evening. They're searching for Garvin as we speak. They should have him in custody soon."

She sniffed, resting her head against his shoulder again. "It won't stop him. He wants me. He said he'd see me dead before allowing anyone else to have me."

Wade, glanced at Jamie, before concentrating on the woman I his arms, processing what she had revealed. "When did he tell you that?" he asked, needing to know when she had last talked to the man.

"At my husband's funeral. He means it."

She didn't need to say she was afraid. Wade could see it.

Jamie stood. "Need to take her to the ranch. Chad, get the truck."

Chad paused before asking, "Does your jeep have four-wheel drive?"

"Yes. Why?" She sniffed, watching Chad from the safety of Wade's arms.

"Come on. We can go the back way using the jeep and no lights. It'll take the terrain better than the truck and it'll be quicker and safer off the roads."

Jamie pulled her from Wade's lap, refusing the let go of her as he and Wade guided her to the waiting jeep. Chad had picked up three rifles for them. Wade handed goggles to Jamie. They checked the area before leaving the house to get into the Jeep.

"Leland, please tell the other thanks. We're taking her to the ranch." Wade said to the man who was standing by the jeep, dressed in dark clothes which enabled him to blend into the shadows of foliage around the house.

"My men will stay here and guard this place. They may come back. You all be careful." Leland moved to a horse standing in the shadows. He rode through the gate, heading to the burial grounds.

Wade joined Abilene in the backseat of the Jeep. Chad was driving with Jamie riding shotgun. Wade was praying the arrived safely.

Somewhere around fifteen minutes later, they arrived at the main compound. Armed men standing in groups, preparing for an assault on the ranch house. There was gunfire in the distance indicating the canyon was under attack.

The men got out of the jeep first, checking the area before helping Abilene to stand. She surveyed the area as they guided her to the house. She froze, almost in midstride, eyes locked on a group of men by the corral. Her hand gripped Wade's arm, drawing his attention to a tall, blonde-haired man who was grinning, aiming a rifle in their direction.

The man's voice was pleasant as he said, "I told you, and you didn't believe me. If I can't have you, no one will," He sighted in on her as she stood, petrified, unable to look away from the man who had killed her husband and was now going to kill her.

A hard shove to her right shoulder threw her off balance. Unable to regain her feet, she headed to the ground. All movement, including her fall, changed into slow motion.

The sound of a gun firing echoed in the night. A red flash of the gun powder streamed into the darkness from the muzzle as the bullet left the rifle. Her scream took forever to be heard as she twisted of follow the direction of the bullet. Jamie pivoted away to the right, his hand going to his left shoulder before his legs crumpled and he began to fall into Wade, blood spraying as the bullet hit him.

Wade reached out, catching Jamie before he hit the ground. Several rifle reports from around her, deafened her. As she hit the ground her head swiveled in time to watch Garvin collapse backward like a rag doll thrown onto the ground, the rifle falling from his hands.

The air in her lungs left from the impact with the ground. She lay still for several seconds, watching as several men surrounded Garvin, the rest running to where Jamie lay on the ground with Wade talking to him.

When she could breathe again, she crawled to Jamie. The breath she had sucked in released when his dark eyes turned to her. He grimaced before saying, "Nothing major. Only my shoulder. I'll be fine."

"You better be," she said, a tear dropping onto the dusty ground. "I need someone who likes my cooking to eat with me."

"Hope you're as good a nurse as you are a cook."

It was high praise from him. She stripped off her cotton blouse, turning it inside out to hold against the wound, hoping to stop the flow of blood pooling on the ground. He sucked in a breath when she put it under the shoulder, wrapping it over top to hold pressure on the wound. She found his hand and held it, afraid for the man who had become her best friend.

While concentrating on Jamie, she didn't seem to notice her state of undress. Sirens wailed in the distance when she felt a warm material across her back and shoulder. She gave Chad a quick glance. He had placed his shirt over her. With a nod and a smile, he turned to crowd control, keeping those who had gathered around them back to allow Wade and her to care for the injured man.

Flashing lights lit up the yard as multiple vehicles pulled to a stop. Two paramedics ran to where they were while two more went to check on Garvin who was still surrounded by a group of men. Nolan materialized and squatted close to Wade, eyes on Jamie.

"You going to be alright?" he asked, a hand on Jamie's uninjured shoulder.

"Yep. Shoulder wound. Hurts like hell though." Jamie's jaw clenched, his face creasing in pain.

Nolan turned to Wade. "You okay, son?"

"Yeah." He glanced at his shirt. "I didn't get hit."

Nolan squeezed his shoulder before heading to where Garvin was laying.

A medic nudged Abilene away. She released the pressure on the wound before giving Jamie's hand a squeeze. "I'll see you later. Do as they say. Understand?" She moved away to allow the emergency personnel to do their job.

"Yes, ma'am," Jamie agreed before his face scrunched up in pain at the tech probing his wound.

Chad lifted her from the ground, her eyes gravitating to Wade, who had also moved to allow the medical personnel to do their job. He was bloody, but it wasn't his blood. She slipped her arms into Chad's shirt, pulling it closed over her exposed chest.

Gavin could no longer threaten her, but it wasn't over yet. Inside, she began to fall apart. The night consisted of one jolt after another. She forced her legs to hold her as Wade joined her, guiding her to the house. As relief that no one other than Jamie was hurt, washed through her, her legs began to buckle, a violent shivering incapacitating her. Wade caught her as her before she could fall, lifting her into his arms to carry her the rest of the way to the house.

A paramedic followed them, having seen her collapse. He began to question her as she stared at him blankly, unable to process his words. The scene of Jamie getting shot played in her head, fulfilling her fear of someone getting hurt.

Wade answered the paramedics questions as time slowed again, unable to process what was happening. Something cold was put on her arm, then a sharp prick as she continued to shiver as she saw the blood splattering as Jamie fell. She clung to Wade's hand as a river of tears flowed from her eyes, unable to stop the loop from playing. It was all her fault.

Words came to her. "She'll be fine in a few hours. The medication will put her to sleep but I'd advise you to not leave her alone for the night." The snap of his bag closing registered before he disappeared. The words flitted past her, incomprehensible.

Nolan's face appeared over the back of the sofa where Wade had placed her. He put a hand on her shoulder, encouraging her to look at him. "You're safe. Wade's going to put you to bed and stay with you."

Her eyes went back to Wade, unable to figure out what Nolan had said. Wade stood and lifted her from the couch. He shouldn't be carrying her. She was too heavy to be carted around like a child.

Nolan had pulled back the covers on a bed where Wade placed her. Nolan removed her shoes before Wade pulled the coverlet over her. He leaned over and kissed her forehead. "I'll be right back. Dad will be here until I return."

Nolan took a seat on the edge of the bed. A hand brushed the strands of hair back from her face. She could see the concern but couldn't grasp why. A few seconds later, she remembered the events of the evening. Her eyes found his.

"What about the canyon?" she asked, eyes wide with dilated pupils.

"They didn't get past the mouth of the canyon." He smiled at her, his hand rhythmically running over her cheek and had. "It's real hard to find a person who's shooting arrows, not guns."

She digested his words. "Jamie will be fine, won't he?"

"Yes, he will. Might help to make a case for him to retire."

She fought to keep her eyes open. "Is Garvin dead?"

"Yes. He's dead. He can't hurt you any longer."

She stared at the wall, not seeing it before moving her unfocused gaze to Nolan. "Good. Then I can love Wade." Her eyelids were drooping as the medication took effect.

"Yes, you can," he said. "As much as you want."

Nolan continued to rub her head, holding her hand as the medication took effect. He gave her a fatherly smile, understanding more than she had said. Wade came up behind him. Nolan stood, pulling his eyes from the now sleeping woman.

"She should be more relaxed now that Garvin is dead. He was the one who was threatening her the most since her husband died." Nolan studied Wade, wondering if her cared for Abilene as much as she did him.

Wade's gaze went to the woman who was in a drugged sleep before facing his father. "What is it about her which makes a man not want to let her go?"

Nolan chuckled. "Son, if I had the answer to that, I could make millions. She loves you, that much I do know. You'd better do right by her. It took her as long to find you as it did for you to find her."

Wade, grinned. "Working on it."

Nolan left, closing the door. He trusted Wade to not take advantage of Abilene. Things were coming together, slowly but surely. Damn, he wished Jamie was here to celebrate.

Chapter 17

Leland had gone over all the plans to protect the burial grounds with Trent, Jamie, and Nolan. Everything was in place. Then Jamie called for him and a few of his men to come and protect Abby. It had pulled him from where he had planned to be that evening, but he needed to do as Jamie requested. Something was up or Jamie wouldn't have called.

Earlier he had fed Eddy the information they wanted him to have. There was a contingent of ten with bows and arrows covering the opening to the burial grounds. The troops Trent sent were hidden in the rocks where they could see the top of the ridge and the approaches to the entrance. They were are ready as they were going to be for whatever McGuire's minions and bosses had planned.

Nothing had happened in the canyon while Leland was guarding Abby. Jamie was right. He had been needed there to keep Abby safe. Wade was taking her to the big house when he left. He left his horse in a grouping of trees, taking his place in the shadows of the rocks where he could see the entrance the path the raiders were most likely to take to the canyon. He settled in to wait.

The sound of motorized vehicles moving down the canyon reached the defenders as the lay in wait. The invaders weren't hiding their arrival, believing the troops had been pulled and the burial ground was unguarded. Eddy had done as expected, giving them the false information. Laughter reached Leland as they closed the distance to the waiting men.

Leland was proud of his group as they waited until the men turned off the engines and moved away from the multiple ATVs with trailers they were using as transportation. The moon was low in the sky, throwing a silvery light over the landscape while leaving dark shadows where it couldn't reach. One of the shadows made a slight movement, unnoticed by the approaching men.

An owl hooted. Immediately afterward several arrows found their marks before the men could react. Within seconds, they were firing blindly into the shadows as more arrows flew into their ranks. The men on top of the walls fired, dropping three of the men. It only took seconds for the men to realize they were outnumbered and had no where to hide. Five men were on the ground when they dropped their guns and raised their hands. One man who hadn't done so was quickly dispatched with an arrow when he aimed at the officer who was approaching the group.

In the silence, Leland heard distant gunfire. A spike of fear shot through him. The sounds had come from the direction of the ranch. Before he could speak, there was silence. Whatever had gone on was over, be it good or bad.

The troops waiting at the side of the canyon rounded up the men and arranged to take them to the local jail. Leland ensured there was coverage for the rest of the night before heading to the ranch by horse. He needed to reassure himself everything was okay there.

A half hour later, he slipped past the guards into an open area where there were flashing lights from police and emergency vehicles. A body covered with a plastic sheet was on the ground, guarded by several police officers. Scanning the rest of the grounds, he noted the congealed blood behind two policemen. The question was who had been shot?

He entered through the side door into the kitchen. Nolan and Chad were at the table. Nolan's head turned to him, his face haggard, worry in his eyes.

"Take a seat," Nolan said, his voice gruff.

Leland sat beside Chad, opposite Nolan. Nancy, the housekeeper who had returned from her vacation, set a cup of coffee before him. He smiled his thanks to her, before she returned to her cleaning. When he looked back a Nolan, he couldn't shake the idea of something being wrong.

"I guess you noticed the body out there," Nolan said.

"Yes. Who is it?" Leland was sure he wanted the answer.

"A man named Garvin. He came after Abilene. Jamie pushed her out of the line of fire. Four of our men got him, but Jamie was shot." Nolan was watching him.

Jamie. Figured. Leland took a deep breath, forcing himself to relax. "How bad?"

"A shoulder wound. He'll live. They took him to surgery to remove the bullet and repair the damage."

"Abilene okay?"

"She was shaken up pretty bad. The medic gave her a sedative. She should sleep for the rest of the night."

"Where's Wade?" It was odd for Wade not to be here with his family.

"With Abilene. Only Garvin and Jamie got hurt."

Leland's muscles relaxed. Jamie being out of action for a few weeks was better than what he was imagining when he saw the blood and the body.

"Eddy passed the information along as expected. We got them before they reached the entrance to the burial grounds. I left a contingent of guards there. It's be nice if the rest of the night was quiet." He paused then asked, "Mind if I stay the night?"

"Nolan smiled. "Not at all. You know where your room is. We might need you in the morning. Abilene will want to go see him, I'm sure."

"I get to play guard if she does as I want to go see him, too."

"Figured you would."

Nolan's cellphone rang. "Hello, Nolan Chapman speaking."

He listened then smiled. "Thank you for calling, Dr. Moore. I appreciate it." He disconnected the call. "Jamie's doing fine. They're going to keep him tomorrow for sure. The bullet went through, missing all the bones. They had to repair a few muscles and ligaments."

Leland chuckled. "Not a good thing for them. I can hear him grumping and growling already."

The three men laughed, aware he was correct. Nolan rotated to Nancy who was crying. "He's fine. Go to bed. We'll clean up here."

She hurried out of the kitchen, wiping tears from her face. Nolan shook his head but didn't comment.

"I don't know about the rest of you, but I'm going to bed also. It's been a long day." Nolan stood and left, leaving Chad and Leland at the table. Chad took their coffee cups, putting them in the sink before opening the fridge and pulling out two beers. He handed one to Leland. They popped the tops, taking big swigs before setting the cans on the table. Leland turned his with his long fingers, still worried about Jamie.

"You know Chad, the last thing I would have expected was Jamie getting hurt."

"Me too. It happened so fast. He saved Abby's life. If hadn't shoved her out of the way, Garvin would have killed her."

Leland studied the can. "Yeah, figures. He's saved me from getting trampled to death in a cattle stampede. You'd think he didn't care a hoot about you, then he'd show it in a dramatic fashion. I'm not sure what I'd do if anything happened to him."

Chad sighed. "I get it. Seems like he's always there to rescue us when we did something stupid."

The two grinned at each other, both having stories of the times Jamie saved them from disaster. They finished their beers, washed out the coffee cups then headed for bed. Tomorrow would be another busy day.

Leland hoped things would settle now that Garvin was dead, and Ron was out of the way. Abby needed some time to relax and recuperate from all the stress she had been under for the past five years. More than anything, he wanted her to stay for a few months. He wanted to get to know her better and didn't want to do it when she was looking over her shoulder for the next person to come after her.

Chapter 18

Abilene gradually awakened the drugged sleep which had kept her from dreaming for the night. She was still groggy, needed to get up but not want to leave the comfort of the soft bed. She burrowed into the warmth which surrounded her, closing her eyes, relaxing as he avoided analyzing the pleasant sensations. Her eyes popped open when a kiss was planted on her head. The warmth had moved against her back. There was an arm across her, firmly holding her next to the warmth.

Abilene rolled over, her eyes meeting the worried face of Wade, staring t her.

"You alright, Abby?" His voice added sound to what she was seeing.

"I think so." She took a quick inventory. Other than being somewhat stressed, she was wasn't hurt. "How's Jamie?" popped out, afraid for the man who had saved her life.

"According to dad, grumping and growling. We'll go visit him later. Maybe you can settle him down." His lips turned up and his arms tugged her closer to him.

She relaxed against him, not sure how she got here or why Wade was with her. "I don't remember much after the police and ambulance got here."

"Nothing to remember," he said.

There was on question she needed verified. Lowering her eyes to his check, she asked, "Gave is dead, isn't he?"

"Yes."

She reached up to lightly touch his face, blinking to hold back the tears which were forming. He kissed her hand.

"Wade?"

"Hm?"

"Please don't leave me." She knew it sounded insecure, but she needed him and the love he was willing to share with her.

In stead of answering her, he kissed her, putting his emotions in to the kiss. To clarify, he said, "I've no intention of leaving you—ever."

"I love you," she mumbled, her head tucked into his shoulder.

"Good, I don't have to worry about it being one-sided now."

"True," she said, with a giggle moving so she could see his face. "Does your father know you're in bed with me in his house?"

Wade laughed. "I hope so, considering he was the one who told me to stay with you."

"He did?"

"He did. Speaking of Dad, we'd better get up before he comes to make sure I'm behaving."

An impish grin formed on her lips. "What if I don't want to you to behave?"

Wade grinned, kissed her forehead then rolled away from her, getting out of the bed. "That's as much misbehaving as you'll get from me for how. Up and at 'em."

She sighed. "If I have to." She would have preferred him stay and hold her. His arms made her believe she was safe.

"You have to. It's time to eat breakfast. Chad brought you some clothes. They're over there on the chair in the bag. I'll see you in a few."

He left, closing the door behind him. She must have been totally out to not remember Nolan telling Wade to stay with her or Chad being in the room. She sat up before noticing the open shirt. Her face heated. It was bad enough she couldn't remember much, but then to have him in bed with her partially undressed!

She pushed to her feet, having lean on the bed until her head stopped spinning. Her memory was still fuzzy from the drug. She went through what Chad had brought before heading to the bathroom. It didn't matter if breakfast was ready, she needed show if for no other reason than to feel clean from all the events of the night before.

Dressed, she made the bed before following the sound of men's voices. It led her to the kitchen. The family was gathered around the table talking. Her eyes gravitated to the woman who was cooking. Unable to look away, she stared at the familiar figure. Abilene took a step into the room, not believing what she was seeing.

"Nancy?" she tentatively questioned, not sure if she was right.

The woman turned at Abilene's voice. A big smile lit the face of the woman who had helped to raise her.

"Abilene!" Nancy left the stove, coming to her to enfold her in a warm hug. "Child, it's so good to see you again. I wasn't sure if it was really you when they told me who was here. Come. Sit down. I'll have your breakfast ready in a jiffy."

Abilene returned the hug before taking the empty chair at the table next to Wade. "I can't believe it. Never in a million years would I have expected you to be the housekeeper and cook here. How long have you been here?"

"About twenty years. I came right after you grandmother died and the house was sold. I've been following you through your website. Child, I'm amazed at how good you've done. You're quite famous with that research of yours."

Nancy set her favorite breakfast before her. It was pancakes with an over easy egg on top with two slices of bacon. The syrup was already on the table. Abilene poured the syrup over the egg and pancakes.

"I swear, you have the strangest taste in food," Chad commented with a chuckle, staring at her plate.

She grinned at the two men who were examining her plate. "Don't knock it until you've tried it. I love it like this." She broke the yolk to the egg with a bite of pancakes before putting it in her mouth. She grinned at Chad who shook his head, glancing at Wade.

A knock on the kitchen door grabbed their attention, preventing him for making a comment. A police officer was standing there. Nancy let him into the kitchen. Abilene tensed, staring at his somber demeanor.

"Morning, Nolan. Boys. I've got some bad news. McGuire is out of jail. He managed to get some forged release papers. We have reason to believe he's on his way here for Ms. Brown."

Abilene put her fork on the plate, catching her bottom lip with her teeth. Unable to speak, she stood and left the room, tears running over her face. It wasn't over. It didn't appear as if it would ever end. She stood, her hands on the back of the sofa, staring out the big front window of the house.

Wade ran his hands up and down her upper arms. "You're safe here with us. We know what he looks like, so he can't sneak in like Garvin."

Just when she thought things would become normal, something else would go wrong. It was a never-ending back dream from which she couldn't seem to awaken. Now the Chapman's were involved, their lives on the line like hers.

"You all can't keep this up. You have a business to run and my problems are disrupting it big time. You shouldn't have to be involved in my ongoing issues with them."

Wade turned her to face him. "Our business will survive with a few weeks of downtime. We know what we're doing. For now, you're our focus. Your problems became ours because of how we feel about you."

She moved into his arms. He had no idea of what he was saying. None of them had a clue as to what they had stepping into with keeping her here.

"Wade, my being here is putting all of you in grave danger. They won't stop, even with Garvin dead and Ringwald in jail."

"As I've said before, it's our choice to do this. We're willingly helping you. I'm not going to allow you to run again. If you love me like you said, then let me and my family do what we can to extradite you from this."

Her hand went to his cheek as she searched his face. He was sincere in the offer to help. More than anything, she wanted to believe they could help end her nightmare.

"I do love you. It's so hard with what happened with Steven to put you in that type of danger. I can't handle the thought of something happening to you."

Wade enfolded her in his arms. "I'm aware of the dangers. This isn't the first time we've done something like this."

Abilene hoped he was right. She didn't want to lose him now that she had found him.

"Come and finish your breakfast so we can go and see Jamie."

For now, she had no real options. It was stay here and accept their offer of help or continue running. As Jamie said, she needed to trust him.

They returned to the kitchen and took their seats. She attempted to finish the breakfast she loved. Worry about McGuire being free, and Jamie had her withdrawing while mechanically eating, no longer enjoying the meal.

Nolan's calm voice brought her back to the here and now. "Don't you worry yourself about McGuire. We'll take care of him. You stay here and don't go anywhere without one of us with you until he's found."

She played with a piece of pancake in the syrup. "I'm disrupting your life." She couldn't hide the defeat lacing through her voice.

Nolan patted her shoulder. "Not in the least. You need to understand this is life for us. Besides, this is something we need to do. If we don't, they'll make live miserable for a lot more people than you. We work with the authorities on a lot of things and this is only one of them."

Her eyes examined his face. She wanted to believe him. With a slight shrug, Abilene lowered her eyes to her plate. "You win. I'll stay put and you can take the heat for me being here."

Chad threw a balled-up napkin at her. She glared at him. He was grinning. "We don't mind taking the heat for you, so chill."

If they were all saying the same thing, then she needed to chill like Chad said. It was if they were building a wall of protection around her. Hopefully it wouldn't get them hurt.

She finished the last of her meal as the men planned their day. Once done, Wade said, "I'm taking Abby to see Jamie. He's creating havoc on the floor. He seems to listen to her, so we need to see if she can get him to calm down."

Nolan laughed. "It figures. Take Leland with you to ride shotgun to be safe. I don't believe our escapee will show up here until late tonight or tomorrow at the earliest."

Chapter 19

A few minutes later, they were on the road to the hospital and Jamie. Leland and Wade chatted as she sat quietly in the back worried about what type of havoc Jamie was causing. Why they though a visit from her would calm him down was beyond her, but then again, it might. At least it would decrease her worry about him being alright. As with Wade, she wasn't' sure what she would do if she lost him. He had become the voice of reason in the chaos which surrounded her.

It took a half hour to get to the hospital. Wade and Leland kept her between them on the way from the car to the entrance. She didn't miss how they continuously scanned the area for any threats.

The heard Jamie's voice as soon as the elevator opened on the second floor. He was complaining they were trying to poison him with the food. Abilene attempted to hide her smile. Nancy had prepared food for the irascible old man, away he wasn't fond of most mass prepared food. Shaking her head with ha grin, she followed his voice of the man who had become like a father to her.

When Abilene entered the room, bag of food in hand, the harried nurse made a hasty exit. After kissing Jamie's cheek, she sat on the bed, attempting to glare at him. Using his good arm, he pulled her over to kiss her cheek, all smiles now that she was there.

"Girl, you sure are a sight for sore eyes."

"Nancy sent some food for you," she said, scanning him to make sure he really was alright.

"They been trying to poison me with the swill here," he grumped, eyes on the bag she had placed on the table over his bed.

With a chuckle, she opened the bag, took out the top container and opened it for him. Jamie grabbed a fork, shoveling food in as if he hadn't eaten in a week instead of less than sixteen hours.

Wade and Leland entered the room as Jamie said, "Heard about that scalawag getting loose. You stay close to Wade and Nolan. They'll keep you safe."

"What am I? Chopped liver?" Leland questioned with a grin.

"Damn, Leland, What you doin' here?"

Leland glanced at Wade then her. "Nolan isn't taking any chance with Abilene."

"He better not take any chances with my little girl."

Abilene stared at him. "Your *little* girl?" she asked, not sure she heard him correctly.

"My little girl," Jamie repeated, daring her to disagree.

Wade put a hand on Abilene's shoulder before saying, "You'd better spit it out, Jamie."

He put his fork down. He took Abilene's hand. "Nancy's back. You know her," he said, not looking at her.

He glanced at Wade and Leland, then back at her. Why was he talking about Nancy? She frowned, attempting to make sense of what he was saying. "Yes, she's back. I was shocked to see her. She worked for my grandmother while I was growing up."

"Nancy's my sister," Jamie imparted, his eyes going to Wade.

"The rest, Jamie," Wade commanded in a clam voice.

"You tell her. I can't."

"Tell me what?" she asked, her eyes going to Wade.

He took the chair facing her. "It's a bit of a story. What do you know about your mother?"

She searched Wade's face, then Jamie's. Jamie wouldn't look at her.

"I know she died when I was two from a rare cancer. She requested that my father take me to her mother to raise me, not wanting him to deal with a baby girl. I also know my grandmother insisted he give up all his rights to me before she would take me.

"Nancy, who knew my father, told me how he loved me as much as he did my mother. He cried when he left me there, but my father did it because he loved me enough to know Grandmother would do a lot better raising me than he would.

She also said he made Grandmother promise to keep him informed about what I was doing and to send pictures at least once a year. Grandmother did as he requested. She sent pictures and things I made while keeping him informed as to how I was doing, but she wouldn't let him contact me. Nancy said my grandmother didn't want me to be torn between two places and two sets of rules."

She waited for Wade to tell her what Jamie couldn't. A quick glance at the old him showed he still couldn't look at her.

Wade also glanced at Jamie before facing her. He took her hand, rubbing it with his thumb. She was afraid of what he would say.

"Part of the agreement of your father leaving you with your grandmother was that Nancy would be there with you. Nancy is your aunt. Jamie's your father."

She stared at him for a few seconds until the words made sense. Her eyes brightened as she took Jamie's hand and gave him a big smile.

"I know there had to be a reason you didn't complain about being in the house with me after they told me you didn't care for women."

"Couldn't let anyone else near my little girl," Jamie admitted.

Her smiled dimmed. "Why didn't you contact me when Grandmother died?"

"Started to. Didn't want to mess up your life."

"You could have told me at the house."

"Nope. Had to see if Wade would go after you like I did your mother."

She didn't know what else to say. Jamie reached out an touched her hair.

"You look like her. Pretty as a new born foal." Two tears tracked down his weathered cheeks as he studied her.

"Daddy, don't cry. I understand what you did and why. Nancy was there and took care of me for you, and Grandmother didn't say one bad thing about you."

"I love you, Abilene. Always have."

"I'm home now. It'll be alright."

Jamie cried as Abilene hugged him, kissing his cheek again. She handed him a tissue before giving him a stern glare.

"Now you have to promise me to be nice to the nurses who are taking care of you. They're only doing their job."

Wade said, "From what I was told, you should be able to come home tomorrow if everything looks good, with strict orders to take it easy."

"Why not today?"

"Because you lost a lot of blood and they need to make sure your blood counts are holding steady or increasing, that's why." Leland told him. "Pop, you really do need to take care of yourself if you want to spend time with Abby."

Want to go home."

He sounded like a stubborn child to Abilene. In her mother's voice, she said, "Tomorrow and not a minute sooner. I don't' want to bring you back here." She turned to Leland. "I take it you're my half-brother?"

He glanced at Jamie before saying, "Yes. My mother died of pneumonia when I was ten. She was Apache. I had the advantage of my mother's family being close by, so I learned from Pop and my mother's people."

"Did you know about me?" She hoped Jamie hadn't hidden her from them.

"Sure did. Your grandmother sent the best letters. We almost felt like we were there with you. She thought the world of Pop, but knew your mother wanted you to be with her because of how rough it was here."

It was a lot to grasp, but there was on things she admitted. "I which Grandmother would have allowed me to come and visit." Turning to Jamie, she told him, "She wouldn't talk about you or tell where you were. She wouldn't even tell me your last name. I knew Clifford was her name. She had mine changed so it made it easier for me in school."

Jamie proudly stated. "Name's James Theodore Boone."

Abilene smiled reciting, "J-T-B." Her hand went to her neck. She pulled a locket from under her shirt and showed it to him. "You sent this to me for my sixteenth birthday. Nance told me it was from you. It had a picture or you and Mama in it. She said it was my mother's."

"M-E-B. Mary Ellen Boone. Gave it to her or our first Christmas. Felt you needed it. Wasn't doing me no good."

Leland reached over and opened the old locket. He stared at the picture, then at the woman who was wearing it. "You do look a lot like your mother."

She smiled at him before turning back to Jamie. "Daddy, I want your promise to behave until you're released from here. No more yelling at the nurses, the housekeeper or the lab people."

"Yes, ma'am."

"I'll have them put this other container in the refrigerator. They'll heat it up for your supper. Don't you dare complain about the breakfast. You should be home for lunch."

"Yes, ma'am.

"We need to get home, I'll see you tomorrow." She patted his hand before she stood.

"Abilene," Jamie said, taking her hand to hold her in place.

She turned to him.

"You stay close to these two boys. You hear?"

"Not to worry. I promised Wade I wouldn't run away again, so I'll be close to them."

"Wade, Leland, don't you let nothin' happen to her."

Wade put his arm around her waist, smiling down at her. "You needn't fret. I have a vested interest in keeping her safe." He bent his head and gave her quick kiss.

She let her hand brush his face before leaning over to kiss Jamie cheek. "Behave," she said before leaving with Wade and Leland.

Leland waited until they were in the elevator before saying, "You do know you made him one happy man when you called him Daddy?"

"I dreamed of meeting him after I got this necklace. He's always been Daddy to me."

Yes, he was her Daddy. She was thrilled to finally meet the man who had loved her enough to give her a life her mother wanted for her. There was no question in her mine that he cared for her. He had shown that love during the time they had been together at the ranch. She now understood why he had wanted to be in the house with her, and it wasn't just to protect her.

Chapter 20

Nolan met them at the door when they returned from their visit to Jamie. He put his arm around her as they walked through the kitchen. She wondered what he was preparing her for now.

"There are some men here to see you. They're from the government, and believe it or not, they're here to help you," he said.

She followed him through the living room to the den where four men were sitting in comfort sipping drinks. The men stood, their eyes following her as she walked into the room to a chair where she would be able to see all of them. It was up to them to tell her what they wanted.

When no one spoke, she asked, "What do you need from me?"

One of the men lifted a manila folder from the coffee table and handed it to her. She took it but didn't open it.

"Tell me what it is," the man requested.

Abilene opened the folder. Her picture was attached to the first page. Lifting the picture, she noted it was a dossier on her. It was correct. The next page was a synopsis of her work. She flipped through the pages, scanning them. Someone had lifted her work, but he or she had changed it, adding things she had never written.

When done, she surveyed the men. "most of it's my work, but someone has changed it. If you read it. You can tell my work from theirs. My style is simple, written so schoolchildren can understand it. Every part mentioning the oil is done in technical terms. It would be incomprehensible to anyone but a geologist. I've no idea who changed it, but they did it to show I was working for the oil company."

"Do you have the original of your work?"

"Yes. It's on my computer."

"May we see it?"

She started to stand, but Wade stopped her with a hand on her shoulder. "I'll bring it to you."

She turned back to the men.

"We caught the differences in style right away," stated a man dressed in jeans and a plaid shirt. "We figured it was doctored."

She studied the speaker, brows drawn together. The man was familiar, but she couldn't place him and where she would have met him. He was studying her also with a partial smile on his lips. Who was he and how did he fit into this?"

Wade returned with her laptop, pulling her from studying the man. Once her computer booted up, she pulled up her research and set it on the coffee table, enabling all the men to see the screen. The men read through her paper. When they finished, they nodded to each other, smiling.

"You do wonderful work. This is what my youngest son was using for his science call. Do you mind if we look through the other files here?" the man in the plaid shirt asked.

"Feel free," Abilene said with a wave of her hand. She had gone through the files numerous times. There was nothing she had to hide which they could find.

The man worked at her computer, tapping keys, then studying the screen before typing again. A few minutes later, he turned the computer screen to face her.

"Is this one of your files?"

She studied the file, frowning, not sure what it was. "No. I've never seen that file before now. I've no idea of what it is."

"It so happens we do. It's how they've been tracking you and stealing your work. Most likely it was sent and automatically downloaded whenever you opened an e-mail it was attached to at the time."

A man dressed in a dark grey suit pulled a folder from a briefcase, handing it to her. "What we would like you to do, is to update your research with this. Put it in your words and make it believable."

She opened the folder and began reading. Before she had finished it, she was grinning. "Looks like a trap to me."

The man nodded, a smile tugging at his lips. "It won't be so blatant once you're finished with it. Tomorrow, Wade and Leland are going to take you to a place where you'll do what you normally do. When you get back, you'll add this to your paper. Make sure to use the coordinates for where you'll go tomorrow as we're certain they'll be watching you."

"Easy enough to do, but how can you be so sure Ron is still tracking me."

"He has his laptop. It has the other half to the tracking program on it. He'll be able to access what you're doing. His greed will pull him to where we want him."

She turned to Wade. "What do you think about this?"

"I believe you need to do it. Our friends here knew what to look for, and as you noticed, it took them less than ten minutes to find that tracking program. He'll only add a different tracker if we delete this one."

Abilene stared at the file in her hand, not sure what to do. If she did what they were asking, Ron would show up. If she didn't, she would need to hide until he was caught. Either way, there was going to be trouble.

"Wade, did you really mean what you said this morning?" She needed verification of how he felt about her before deciding on helping them. If he loved her, it would be worth all the trouble she knew would come to them once this plan was set into motion.

"Every word of it."

She stared at the computer for a few more seconds. "Alright, I'll do it." Facing the four men, she noticed the man in the plaid shirt still studying her, head tilted to the side. She wished she could place where she had met him.

"Good," the man said before breaking eye contact. He turned to Wade. "Have Leland get his group in place. We'll have backup close by also."

This may not be the correct thing to do, but there wasn't any other choice at the moment if she wanted to get her life back. Wade's love for her was crucial to her decision. Inside fear was zinging around. Maybe the secret she held could quietly fade into obscurity as the major players were taken out of what had become a game for them. She would have no safety until they were all out of action. The problem was the one man they didn't know about. No one had mentioned his name so far. It was a matter of time before he closed the net around her, entrapping her and everyone else with her.

The men stood to leave. The one in the plaid shirt turned to Wade. "You and Leland keep close to her. WE know most of the player, but there's no reason to take any chances at this point. Call us if there are any problems or questions."

"Don't worry. I'll make sure she stays save. We'll let you know if anything changes," Nolan answered for Wade.

The man smiled and nodded at Nolan, who returned the nod before the man followed the others out the door. There was a plan now, but she wasn't sure if it was going to work. None of them had any idea of what they were after. She knew, but it was a secret she couldn't share if she wanted to stay alive. Six months until she had the last piece.

Chapter 21

Wade and Leland took her to the area they planned to use. She took samples and pictures. They watched as she drew the rock formation and labeled the layers. She picked up a rock to study before staring at the good-sized vein of gold in the formation she'd been drawing.

"There really is a good amount of gold here, isn't there?" she asked, turning to the men.

"There is," Leland said. "There're minor veins all over the place out here, but there isn't enough in one spot to mine. It's in little pockets here, there and everywhere."

"Sneaky. He won't know that when he sees the vein on that outcropping since he has a clue about how the big veins are formed."

"That's what we're counting on. He'll believe it's a big vein and this is only tip of it." Leland winked at her before returning to watching the area for intruders.

Once she completed her drawings and exploration of the area, they returned to the house. While she was typing up the fake research from the plan she had been given by the four men from the night before, Wade and Nolan went to the hospital to get Jamie, leaving Leland with her. She was finishing when she heard the truck in the driveway. Closing her laptop to put it to sleep, she ran to the door, into her father's one-armed embrace. Jamie kissed her cheek, letting her fuss over him without complaint.

"The doctor said he needs to rest. That means saying in the house and not going to the barn, no giving order, no work," Nolan said, glaring at Jamie.

Abilene rand a hand over Jamie's head. "He'll behave or have to deal with one very irate daughter who has no intention of letting him do anything which will slow his recovery.

Jamie took her hand and kissed it. "Don't' have no reason to leave the house for now."

She led him to a comfortable chair, indicating he needed to sit. He was still pale, but other than that, he seemed to be recovering. Nancy entered the room, spying her brother. She put her hands on her hips as she warned him, "J.T., if you don't obey her, you'll have me on your back. She needs her father, not a corpse."

He reddened as his sister leaned over the chair and put her arms around him before kissing his cheek. "I'm glad you're home. Don't you go playing hero again."

"Couldn't let him shoot my baby."

"I know that, but once is enough old man."

"Who you callin' old?"

Nancy laughed before saying, "Lunch will be ready in fifteen minutes."

Abilene went back to her computer to finish what she had started. As she read it, she smiled. It was believable even to her. She was finishing when Nancy called them to eat. Abilene closed the laptop as she normally did when working before going to eat.

They were ready for Ron, but he didn't show up that evening as expected.

The next morning, Abilene found an e-mail from him. *"I'm coming for you, bitch"* was all it said. Fear washed over her, immobilizing her as she stared at the screen. Leaving the computer open, she ran outside to find Wade.

She located him in the barn, grooming the black stallion. "Wade, Ron is coming for me, not the gold," she rattled off, fear making her jumpy and shaky.

He stopped, frowning, "How do you know that?"

"He sent me an e-mail. He said he's coming after me."

Wade took out his phone and made a call, running his hand through his hair. "Trent, Ron is coming after Abby." He listened. "Alright. We'll see you in ten."

"Go back to the house, Abby. I'll be there in a few minutes."

Doing as instructed, she returned to her computer to stare at the message Ron had sent, fear trickling through her. He would find a way to get to her. There was no way she could run. There was no place to go where he couldn't find her.

Wade came up behind her. Leland joined him to look at what Ron had sent.

Leland glanced at Wade. "Looks like he isn't happy person right now. Trent will be here in a few minutes, right?"

Wade paced the room. For the first time since she had met him, he looked worried. It sent her fear into overdrive. If he was worried, things had to be seriously wrong.

Nolan ambled into the room. "What's the problem, son?"

Stopping his pacing, his eyes slid to her, then back to face his father. "Ron is coming after Abby. Trent's on his way. Dad, I can't figure out how he can get to her here, but he must know some way of getting in here, or he's planning on a way of getting her away from us."

Nolan glanced at her before concentrating on Wade. "I believe he's planning on getting us away from her. Let's see what Trent say and if he has any ideas."

Abilene wanted to break something. This wasn't fair! Life wasn't fair! How dare Ron make her life so miserable! She stared at the computer screen as the fear increased. Ron would do what ever he could to get to her. There was nothing she could do to stop what was to come. Those who were controlling Ron now wanted her dead. She shivered as the thought sent dread coursing through her. It meant they would kill everyone helping her. Every last one of them.

A car pulled into the drive. Several doors slammed. The four men from the night before filed into the room. They weren't smiling. She had a bad feeling about this setup.

"Trent, see if you can find out where he was when he sent the message," a man in a suit commanded.

The man who moved to her computer was the one who had been in the plaid shirt during their first meeting. Today he was in a dress shirt and slacks. She watched as he began typing. A flash of memory came to her. She knew this man. He was older, but there was no mistaking who he was.

He began typing, staring at the screen, then typed some more as they waited. After working for several more minutes, he said, "He was in town. I can't get it any closer than that."

"So he's here. Now what?" Wade asked, hands fisted, and voice strained.

"No sure. He must have a plan of some sort to get to her. My best advice is to make use of that safe house," one of the men proposed.

Wade took a seat on the arm of her chair, bending his head to see her face. "No. That would make her a sitting duck with little or no protection."

Nolan sat on the other arm of her chair. "What about her going with Leland to the tribe? They can make her disappear until he tips his hand."

Leland nodded in agreement. "That we can do. They would never find her where we would stash her."

There was a discussion for an against her going with Leland. She let the conversation whirl around her as she stared at Trent. Why was he here? Did he remember her?

Wade had listened without comment. He cut into the discussion, disrupting her focus on Trent. "She's not going anywhere without me." His words drew her back into the conversation they were have about keeping her safe.

"Wade, we're going to have to make it look like she's still here. If you aren't here, he'll know she's gone." Trent was emphatic in his statement.

"Stubbornly, Wade repeated, "She's not going anywhere without me."

The men sat in thought. Trent stared at the computer. A smile crossed his face.

"What about the high cabin? It's in a great defensive area. Chad and Leland can go with you. There's enough cover for Leland to place men so they can't be seen and we can keep the men around the gold site in case he goes there first.

"I like it. It's an area we know well, and he doesn't," Nolan said with a grin.

"I' like it, too," Wade said. "Chad will be here shortly. Maybe it'll work." Wade ran a hand over her hair. "Go pack a week's worth of clothes and something to read or keep yourself busy."

She didn't express an opinion as she went to do what Wade requested. It didn't matter where they took her. Ron would find her. It was him or her, and she knew it.

Returning to the room with a valise packed with enough things for a week, she set it on the floor by the door. Guessing it meant a horseback ride, she had changed into jean, a long-sleeved shirt, riding boots, and had a hat in her hand. Chad has arrived. He and Leland were talking. The stopped their discussion when she entered the room.,

"Let's go. The boys will be there long before us, so if Ron follows us, he won't see them," Leland said.

Trent added, "We'll have men there by morning. I've got the feeling he's after something more than Abby though." He focused on her as he spoke before turning away.

Abilene looked at her laptop. Should she tell them about what they were after? She glanced at Wade before scanning the men in the room. If she was going to die, Trent might as well have the information. Maybe he could still use it.

"He's after what's on that computer. There are some protected files on there and his bosses know it."

Trent turned and stared at her, his eyes boring into hers. "What's in them?"

Instead of telling him, she went to her computer and disconnected it from the Internet. She pulled up a file with a few keystrokes then opened it with a password before turning the computer for the men could see it. The one who seemed to be in charge glanced up at her then back at the computer, disbelief on his and the other's faces.

"We need a printer with plenty of paper and ink," Trent stated before he raised his head, staring at her with a frown.

She heard the stress in his voice. Unable to face them, she wandered to the window while they were setting up her computer to print the file, hoping she had done the correct thing. If she was wrong, she had wasted twenty years in keeping the files updated and hidden. Not only that, Steven's death would have been in vain, and all of her hiding, running and keeping the files safe were for nothing.

Wrapping her arms around her middle, she waited, staring out the window but not seeing the scenery. Instead or scenery, she was seeing her husband as he was in the morgue. It hadn't been a pretty sight.

Trent connected her computer to the printer. It started printing the file. When it was done, Abilene stopped him from disconnecting the computer. She closed the file which had printed and opened another one. Trent grinned and hit print.

"Any more?" he asked as the second file began to print.

"One more," she said. She opened the third file after the second one started to print. Trent gave it a quick scan and hit print.

My dear, you're a wonder. This explains why you're so valuable and they want you so bad. Your computer would be a bonus.

She turned from him, blinking rapidly. "If they try to open those files, they will disappear. A friend showed me how to set it up so it was fail-safe. They have to get the passwords exact and know which file get what password.

"Where do they go when they disappear?"

She pursed her lips and shrugged. "Never, Never Land."

"I'm asking if they can be retrieved if they disappear." Trent folded his arms and tilted his head to the side as he glared at her.

"You tell me. You're the technical expert."

She went to the keyboard and hid the file as Trent watched. His eyes sparkles in merriment as he saw what she did. With a quick smile, she hid the other two.

"Devious, my dear. I'm not sure I would ever find them where you put them. There's no way you would ever see them on the hard drive either. Whoever showed you that was good. Damn good."

"Yeah, he was. It was the reason they killed him."

She peeked at Wade, who had been watching them, then back to Trent who was studying her.

"Who are you talking about?" one of the men asked.

She lowered her head before saying, "My deceased husband, Steven Brown."

Trent grabbed her arm, causing her to arise her head and face him. "You did say Steven Brown, right?"

"Yes."

"What does her deceased husband have to do with all of this?" Wade asked, eyes going between her and Trent.

Trent smiled at her. "Her husband had some incriminating evidence against some very powerful people. I didn't connect Abby to him until she said his name. I haven't seen her in over twenty years. I wasn't sure if it was her or not." His gaze when to the other men. "We just hit the jackpot. All the pieces have fallen in place." He turned back to her. "Did he leave something with you?"

"Maybe," she evasively answered.

"He would have told you to give it to T.J."

She stared at him for a few seconds before she sighed, rotated and when to the room where her things were. She was gone for a good five minutes before returning with an envelope and a folder. The writing was faded on the old envelope. Superbly written in script were the letters, "T.J."

Abilene handed it to Trent. He took it, staring at the writing on the envelope, swallowing hard.

"Twenty years. Twenty long years I've been trying to find this envelope. I never in my wildest dreams even considered he had given it to you. Steven didn't die in vain. What's contained in here will bring some extremely powerful people down. These are people you never hear about."

Abilene glared at him, mouth in a grim line. "Why didn't you ask me if I had it at the funeral? You were there."

"Garvin. I couldn't with him there. When I went to talk to you a couple of weeks later, you were gone. I haven't been able to get close to you since without tipping our hand."

"And you think Ron doesn't know you're here?"

Trent grinned. "Oh, he knows we're here, but he doesn't know about this. His handlers wouldn't give him something to use against them. Besides, they probably believe it was destroyed a long time ago."

Abilene handed him the folder. She knew what it contained. It was the reason she had the three files on her computer. Trent flipped through the papers, scanning the pages. He raised his head, fear showing on his face. He mouth grim.

"Get her out of here. They'll kill her if they find her."

Wade moved behind her. His arms came around her and pulled her back against him. "What is that?"

"Her death sentence if they find out she had it all this time."

"That wasn't an answer," Wade grumped.

"This file contains names, dates, payoffs, profits, and links to everyone involved in all of this. It isn't just about the oil. It's about power and money. A lot of money and where it is, what companies are holding it and who has access."

"You talking Mafia?"

"Bigger. Wade, get her out of here now!"

Nolan took the file from Trent and glance through it. "Move it, Wade," he ordered, blanching under his tan.

Wade noticed the look on his father and Trent's faces. He took Abilene's arm, tugging her so she followed him. He scooped up her valise on the way out the door, heading the to already saddled horses. Even though he had no idea of what she had given Trent, whatever it was , his father was concerned enough to issue the unusual direct command which he expected to be obeyed without question.

Chapter 22

Abilene mounted Ghost as the others mounted their horses. Leland led them toward the mountains she had seen in the distance. From the speed they were going, it was going to be a long ride.

As they rode, she withdrew from them and ignored everything around her, concentrating on staying in the saddle while following Leland's lead. Wade and Chad brought up the rear. She knew what she had done. She had been a target, but now her death was their goal along with everyone with her if Trent and he men didn't act swiftly.

Steven told her the envelope contained the financial information of the people for whom he'd been working. They were involved in hiding money. A lot of money. He had planted a program they couldn't find. It would be transferred with any files they moved to a new computer. She only needed to download the information every five years, hiding it until T.J. contacted her. If he found her and identified himself, she needed to give it to him. If not, she was to send it to the Feds when she got the fourth download. At that time, she needed to disappear and not resurface.

The fourth download was due in two more months. With what she knew now, there was no way she could have stopped them from finding her. McGuire was the one tasked with keeping tabs on her. He was unaware of why they actually wanted her.

Because of what the Chapmans had done to stop McGuire and Gavin, they wanted her dead. Her only hope was that Wade and his family could keep her safe until the others where neutralized.

Even then she wasn't sure she would ever be able to live a normal life without looking over her shoulder. Yes, she had signed her own death warrant by given Trent the things she should have given him twenty years ago.

Steven hadn't known what the company was doing until he was give orders to do a yearly audit of the finances of the accounting company. He discovered what they were doing during that review. He was a good CPA—too good, and it had cost him his life. Now it appeared it would cost several more, including hers, before it was over.

The sun had set by the time they arrived at the cabin, the cool air heading to cold. She dismounted, took her valise, and put it in the cabin. She then went back out to care for Ghost. She took the saddle off and groomed him before turning him loose. She put the tack in the shed before returning to the cabin.

The three silent men turned to her as she entered the door. Without speaking, she took her valise and went to the smaller bedroom, curling up on the lower bunk. Her small pistol was slipped under the pillow. It was her out of things went bad and they couldn't hold the cabin.

The men began talking, but she ignored them. They didn't know what she had given Trent of what Steven had done. They had no idea of the danger they were in right now. She knew who the leaders were. They wouldn't rest until they had her in their clutches or she was dead. What they wanted was the information she had given Trent.

The door opened. Chad entered and sat on the edge of the bunk. The smell of food wafted through the room. The light touch of his hand on her shoulder brought home to her what she had one to this man. The brothers were willing to die for her and the secret she had given Trent.

"Abby, you need to eat."

"I don't want anything," she said, keeping her back to him, not wanting him to see her cry. She sniffed and dried her eyes with the pillowcase.

He set the plate on the floor before reaching over and turning her to face him. The handsome face showed his feelings as he wiped away the tears. She couldn't take the worry from him as there was no way to change things now. Lowering her eyes, she grieved for the man who would go to his death because he cared about her and his brother.

"It's going to be alright," Chad said before gathering her into his arms. "We'll come through this just fine."

She avoided facing him. "You don't know them like I do. They'll kill you and everyone else to get to me. I'm as good as dead."

Chad held her, letting her cry. She could feel his tears on her head. It would be her fault if he died with her. She felt when Wade entered the room. After disentangling herself from Chad's arms, she rolled so she was facing the wall. They both were as doomed like her.

"Wade?" Chad questioned, his voice carrying the concern he felt for her. She felt him stand, then heard him leave the room.

Wade motioned for Chad to leave before taking his place on the edge of the bunk bed. He put his hand on her hip.

"Abilene, we're going to need your help here."

'I can't help you. You shouldn't have come after me," She wanted to be alone. His being here with her made things that much worse. He and everyone else here would die.

"Do you know how to use a rifle?"

She sniffed. Why was he asking if she could shoot? "Yes." Her shooting a rifle wouldn't help them. Nothing would.

"Good. We'll need all the help we can get when they get here." Wade paused before asking, "Did you bring your pistol with you?"

She pulled the pillow back, showing him the gun under the pillow.

"Good. Save on bullet in case you need it."

Her back was still to him. "I know what to do. I refuse to go through a slow death like Steven. It took them four days to kill him. I won't allow them to do that to me."

Her words gave him more information than he had before about her husband's death. They would attempt to obtain information from her while making her death slow and painful, whether the did or didn't get what they wanted. These weren't normal people. He was worried, but she didn't need to know that. Not now.

"Will you eat something?"

"I'm not hungry." She turned to him, reaching up and cupping his face with her hand. She didn't try to stop the tears. "Wade, I'm sorry I got you and your family involved in this."

He blinked, unsure how to reassure her how she hadn't done anything to get him involved in her problems. It had been a conscious choice to help her after Jammie and his father explained what was happening and what they needed to do to help her. With her here before him, he knew he had made the correct choice in protecting and loving her.

She needed to know they were used to this type of thing. He wasn't sure, he was making the right decision, but if they all ended up dead, it wouldn't matter. If they managed to survive, she would know the truth about their second job. He hoped she'd be able to live with them taking risks to save innocent people.

"Honey, I want you to know I love you. No matter what happens, that won't change.

She sat up and put her arms around him, before whispering, "I love you, too."

He wrapped his arms around her, kissing her like it was their last kiss. He held her tight before telling what he felt she needed to know.

"What you don't know about us is that we do this type of thing often. You aren't the first person we've protected and helped to put the bad guys away.

"We've been tracking this group for close to twenty years with Trent's help. You happened to already be involved, but we weren't quite sure of where you fit into the whole mess. When McGuire stared his thing with you, we knew about it right from the start.

"Trent asked us to help him get you here with the hope of protecting you and making them tip their hand. He warned us you were involved with some extremely dangerous group, but we took it on anyway. When we met, I wasn't expecting to fall in love with you. I expected it to be another job of protecting an innocent person."

She pulled back and studied his face for what seemed like a long time. "How did you manage to get me here?"

A friend of ours made sure you found the ad for the house. WE knew you were looking for a place to hide, and Dad and Jamie wanted you to hide here. We were hoping to be able to protect you so we could work on how to get rid of those who were threatening you."

She hung he head. "I shouldn't have come back with you, but I didn't want to die. Not then. It was wrong of me to let my feelings put you all at risk of dying for me.

"Wrong. We're doing this because it's our job and we wanted to protect you. Jamie is my father's best friend and partner. He's been worried sick about you since he discovered McGuire was stalking you. Chad and I didn't know he was you father at the time."

She moved closer to him. "I've always wanted to meet Daddy. Now that I've found him, it looks like I won't be around to spend time with him. I don't want to die, but right now, if I was dead, they would be happy and let the rest of you go."

Wade shook his head. "You're wrong. They want us as much as they want you. This isn't our first run-in with them. What we didn't know was who all was involved. I'm sure Trent does now. This is really big, and you happened to get dragged into it through Steven. If we get through this, I want to talk about a future together."

She faced him. "I would like that."

Wade handed her the plate of food. "Eat. You can't use a rifle if you have no strength.

Abilene did as he requested. He was right. If she was going to be of any help, she needed to eat. The dread didn't leave her, but she could at least take a few of them with her. Preparing for death, she mechanically ate what Chad had brought her, not tasting it. When she was done, Wade took the plate from her.

"Try to get some sleep," He told her before leaving the room with the dirty dish.

She made herself comfortable before closing her eyes, shutting out the love she had seen on his face and in his eyes. The tears returned. She didn't want him to join her in death, but fate had set her on a course she couldn't change. Praying they would survive what was to come, exhausting pulled her into a restless slumber.

Chapter 23

It was still the in the early morning hours when Chad awakened her. There were no lights on in the cabin, and it was cold. They had let the fire die out, not wanting any light on the inside to show where they were inside.

Chad whispered, "Abby, we're going to need you. They're here."

Fear, dread, resignation fought for the upper hand at his words. Rubbing the sleep from her eyes, still tired, Abilene managed to wake enough to follow him into the main room. Chad pointed to the rifles lined up against the wall. After looking them over, she took one she knew she could handle. The .243 Winchester wouldn't knock her off her feet like the more powerful rifles. She took the four full magazines and two boxes of ammunition to the window she was assigned.

She returned to the bedroom to get her pistol. It had four filled magazines plus a box of shells. She pulled up a stool to use until they began to shoot.

The small .380 Glock rested on the table beside her. A quick glance to Wade revealed he had noticed the gun and knew why it was there. With a sigh, she sent a quick prayer heavenward, asking for help to survive this, yet holding little hope of ever leaving the cabin.

Wade handed her the night vision goggles she would need to see in the dark. No one spoke. After putting them on, she stared out the window. Leland and his crew were well hidden in the brush. Even with the goggles, they were difficult to pick out. They were all holding bows with arrows, ready to fire.

Farther down the hill, she could see several men facing their direction. All were dressed in fatigues, pistols on their hips and rifles in their hands. They appeared to be organized. Aligning the sites on one of the men, she waited patiently.

Several arrows flew toward the gathered force, striking two men. She continued to watch as the silent attack narrowed the opposition. It didn't take long for the men to formulate their attack, not willing to let themselves be picked off without fighting back. The main force began moving toward them, using the natural topography for cover. The command to fire at will came from Wade when the group advanced over the low rise below the Cabin. She fired. The man she had kept in the crosshairs went down. She moved to the next target and fired again, missing him when he moved to the side.

She pretended this was a video game and hitting the men and knocking them down would give her more points. It was the only way she could fire the gun. Like in a video game, she was methodical, not wasting ammunition if she didn't believe she could hit a target. As men came into her field, she picked off as many as she could, not hearing the other rifles firing due to her intense concentration on what she was doing.

Bullets zinged around her once the attackers were able to zero in on the flashes from the muzzle of her rifle. She shifted position when the bullets began getting to close. She began firing again, muttering curses when she missed. Several she missed moved away from her into an arrow. It probed how the old methods were effective at close range.

The men attacking hesitated when they were pinned down on the rise, unable to advance without major losses. They began to back down the rise into the hollow where they had stared. The initial assault was over. It was only a matter of time before they tried again using a new tactic.

When she couldn't see any more men, she held her fire, scanning the area. It had only been fifteen minutes, give or take a few minutes, for the skirmish to play out, but it felt like they had been firing for hours. Someone began to fill her empty magazines as they waited.

There was a group of men who moved slightly away from the rest of the men. Abilene recognized the contraption they were setting up. It was a grenade launcher. She took aim and fired four quick shots. Two of the four men fell as the other two moved to cover. She kept her eyes on the deadly launcher, determined to prevent them from using it.

It wasn't but a few minutes later that gunfire sounded from further down the hill. She could see the muzzle flashes as the two groups exchanged fire. Several bursts of a high-powered automatic weapon ended the exchange.

Silence. Three more bursts of rapid gunfire. Silence again. Muscles tense, she waited, expecting to have another assault on the cabin.

Leland's voice drifted to her. "I hope that automatic belonged to our reinforcements."

Silence reigned again until a man's voice broke the silence. *"Hanhepi wi wica."*

Leland answered, *"Sunkawakan."*

A large contingent of men materialized and started moving toward the cabin. She hoped they were friends when Leland went out to the porch, his rifle held at the ready position while staying in the shadows. Abilene joined Chad and Wade in the middle of the main room. The men were close to the cabin before Leland moved.

"Horse, I'm damn glad to see you." Leland greeted the lead man in fatigues as the other men remained in defensive mode, scanning the area for enemies they may have missed. Their weapons made a circle around them as they searched for threats.

"Man, I was beginning to think you guys were going to get them all before we could get into position," Horse stated with a chuckle. "I don't know who was firing from the side window, but I don't want them shooting at me."

Leland frowned. "What do you mean?"

"Whoever it was didn't waste much ammunition. They hit more than they missed."

Leland pivoted to see her standing with her rifle resting across her arm, leaning against a post on the porch. His white teeth flashed in the dim light as he grinned, pointing to her.

"There's your marksman. We put her on the side window figuring she could scare them off if she couldn't hit anything. Looks like she should have been in the front."

"Abilene descended the steps and walked toward the group. No one had asked her how well she could shoot.

"I've had some good training, plus I'm a skeet shooter. I like to hit what I'm aiming at and hate wasting ammo. How many did they send?"

"The first group we caught, which was the backup, had fifteen. Those who were attacking had twenty-five or so. We have a bunch of prisoners who are singing like divas. They know they're dead if they don't come back with you or proof you're dead."

"Yeah, well, they aren't going to get me alive, and dead won't get them what they want.

The leader grinned. "We want you alive." He turned to Leland. "Two more groups were apprehended before they could get situated at the canyon and the site which was in her paper. I swear they aren't the brightest people I've ever run into."

Abilene aske the question foremost in her thoughts. "Did you get McGuire?" She hoped they had as he wouldn't give up if he knew she was still alive.

"No and didn't expect to either. He sends others to do the dirty work, but he'll be running now. He'll be a target seeing as how he didn't kill or capture you."

When the men near her took several steps back from her, she wondered what was behind her. Rotating, a smile lit her face. She walked to Ghost who appeared ethereal in the faint light from the moon.

Ghost, what are you doing here?" she asked the big horse, putting an arm around his thick neck. The big horse put his head over her shoulder while she ran her hand along his neck in a caress.

One of the men, in a voice filled with surprise, said, "I thought I was seeing things. He really does look like a ghost."

"Oh, he's very real, but like a ghost. You can't see him until he wants to be seen," Wade said, stepping off the porch to join the men.

Horse said, "I now know what spooked the one group. The threw up their hands and surrendered without a fight."

With a chuckled, she patted Ghost. He had done as she guessed he would, scared the hell out of those who didn't know about him. Ghost stepped forward, knocking her off balance so she fell. He turned and ran off as the snap and splat of bullets hitting the cabin sounded almost simultaneous with the sound of a rifle firing nearby.

Having hung onto her rifle, she put four rounds blindly into the area, not sure if she was even close to the person or persons who had fired. The scream of a man rent the air, letting her know she had hit at least one of them. She rolled from where she was. Two bullets kicked up dirt where she had been. The men behind her fired within seconds of the flashed of the muzzles of the hidden shooters. Horse sent four of his men into the woods to find the snipers.

Abilene didn't move, not wanting to be seen, waiting until the threat was over. A few seconds later, four more men entered the woods. It wasn't long until the eight men returned with four men with them, two of whom were wounded.

"There's a dead man where we found these," the leader of the team from the woods said. "I've no idea of how that ghost horse knew they were there, but you need to give him a big treat."

Abby stood, aware one of them had made a noise to alert Ghost of their presence. According to Chad, he had been wild and still was to some extent which would explain his hearing the danger.

She glanced at the sky. The night was almost over. A faint light was beginning to show from the east and the myriad of stars in the dark sky were fading. A slight movement at the end of the cabin caught her attention. She aimed at the shadow which had moved and fired two shots. A man fell, his rifle falling from his hands as he hit the ground. Abilene move into the shadow of the cabin, hoping she was hidden.

Horse's men began a search of the immediate area as the sun peeked over the horizon. It made her feel safe enough to leave the shadows to go toward the front of the cabin. A shot rang out. A searing pain along the outside of her left arm had her letting out a squeak. Breaking into a run to the front door, she made it inside to the snap of four more bullet passing her as she ran.

Blood was running down her arm as she bent over, holding her elbow, the pain increasing with each second. "Fucking great. I get through the fire fight only to get hit by a fucking sniper," she swore, as tears of pain began.

Wade pushed her into the closest chair. With shaking fingers, he ripped the sleeve of her shirt, exposing he wound. A stifled scream was dragged from her when he probed the wound with his fingers. It was bleeding profusely. She clamped her teeth together, refusing to do more than grunt with the pain.

"It isn't too bad, but it's deep. I'm going to have to clean it and close it," he said, his eyes showed he wasn't as calm as he sounded.

"Whatever," she said tiredly, leaning back in the chair and closing her eyes. Her eyes popped open at a sound to her right. She pointed her rifle at the shadow in the doorway, finger on the trigger, ready to shoot.

"It's only me, Abby," Chad said. She lowered the rifle, beginning to shake. "I can see you're going to be fine."

"I almost shot you," she said, staring at him as the horror of what she had almost done washed over her.

Chad lifted the rifle from her hands and set it on floor. Ignoring Wade, who was holding the medical kit. He lifted her from the chair, carrying her to the bedroom. He placed her on the bed while she fought the fear of having come close to shooting him.

His gentle voice said, "Wade will fix you up, then you need to get some rest.

Her eyes met his. She reached up and tenderly touched his face. No, she hadn't been imagining what she had seen earlier. He cared for her, but was it as a brother or…

Teardrops ran downs the sides of her face. A sad smile formed on his lips. He ran a gentle hand over her face.

"It's okay, Abby. He loves you and I have Eve. She's everything I could wish for in a woman, but—" He hesitated then grinned at her. "I love her, so don't get all upset here. Besides, I like being the brother who can tease the hell out of you and play around without getting into trouble. It's okay. Really."

Wade stood at the door watching them. Chad glanced at him. He leaned over and kissed her cheek before standing. As he passed Wade, he warned, "You'd better take damn good care of her, or you'll have to answer to me."

Wade watched Chad as he left the cabin before taking a seat on the edge of the bunk. "You do know he cares for you."

"I know." She met his gaze. "I didn't encourage him."

Wade cleaned the wound on her arm, telling her about his agreement with Chad. "He stepped back when we first met you, saying I had dibs since I'd seen you first. He knows how I feel about you."

She didn't know what to say to make thing better. Her hope was that Chad had been telling the truth when he said he loved Eve more than her. There wasn't any other solution to this dilemma.

"How do I handle this? You are close to him. I can't avoid being around him."

Wade dried the wound as best he could before applying strips across it to hold the wound together before speaking.

"Treat him like you do Leland. As a brother. That's how he sees it. Unlike other brothers, we're quite open with each other and are good friends. Besides, he loves Eve more than he does you.

With a quick sigh, Abilene hoped he was correct. "Why do things always have to be so difficult for me?"

"Quite worrying. I've told you how I feel. You know how he feels, but he was honest with you."

She shook her head, her mouth twisted to the side. "It was somewhat of a shock. I really didn't know."

Wade kissed her upon finishing dressing her wound. "I understand. Now get some sleep. If things are quiet, we'll head back in a few hours."

He left her after coving the blood under her arm with several towel. In an attempt to relax, she closed her eyes. It would be a long ride back. Sleep would be good if for no other reason than to escape what she had seen in Chad's eyes, regardless of what he and Wade had said. It was another complication she didn't need.

Chapter 24

They made it back to the ranch as darkness settled over the landscape. Wade had insisted she ride in one of the ATVs Horse's group had used to get to them, not wanting her to use her arm for fear it would start bleeding again. The men left behind were guarding the prisoners until the federal marshals could collect them. They had passed the area where the bodies of those they had shot were laid out, covered with tarps. Horse told her she had shot over one third of those lying there and wounded that many if not more.

Wade helped her off the ATV when it stopped at the ranch. Chad, who had ridden beside it on the way back, joined them. He grinned as he put his arm across her shoulders. "You do know you are one remarkable lady."

"If you say so," she told him as she put her good arm around his waist.

"Wade's one lucky man."

Abilene assessed him. "Well, he has one wonderful brother."

"Yeah, but this wonderful brother will beat the living hell out him if he hurts you," Chad said, eyeing Wade.

She now understood he was letting her know he was there for her if she needed him. She took Wade's hand, unable to move her left arm without it hurting. "I don't want to come between you two."

Chad tugged the back of her hair. "You aren't and never will. Wade loves you and that's what makes it okay. I happen to love my big brother's taste in women. Besides, like I said before, I have Eveline. You did me a big favor in pointer her out. She's this wonderful lady, and lady is the key word."

Wade told him, without looking at him, "And little brother, if you hurt her, you'll have to deal with me, understood?"

Chad laughed heartily. Abilene's gaze flitted between the two brothers, not sure what was happening, but they both seemed protective of her and Eve. She was guessing it would all work out from Wade's statement and Chad's reaction.

Jamie and Nolan met them as the entered the house. Abilene went to her father and gave him a hug. His hand brushed against her injured arm. His face paled.

"You're hurt. What happened?" Jamie asked, examining her face.

"It's nothing but a flesh wound," she said, a reassuring smile on her face.

Jamie glared at Wade and Chad, guiding her to the sofa. "What happened?"

"A sniper. Nothing serious, Daddy. Honest. Wade dressed it and it'll only leave a slight scar. Nothing major," she repeated.

Jamie glared at Wade. "Well?"

"She told you the truth. It's nothing but a flesh wound."

Leland joined Wade. He crossed his arms and raised his brows. "What she didn't tell you is how she's a crack shot. She got over a third of those injured or killed according to Horse. And she shot two she couldn't see before she got hit."

"That's my girl," Jamie proudly exclaimed, hugging her to him with his good arm.

Leland laughed and shook his head. "Should have know sis wouldn't be a pushover with you for a father."

Everyone laughed. Jamie was tough. He had endured multiple injuries during his time at the ranch. He was also a good marksman and seldom missed a target. Yes, his daughter was much like him.

Trent and the three men entered the room with Horse and two of his men. She noted their faces were serious. It appeared there was more to come. The never-ending problems.

"What now?" she snapped, not really wanting to hear if it was more bad news.

"You want to tell her, or should I?" asked Trent, staring at Jamie.

"You," was his terse reply.

All eyes turned to Trent. He sat on the arm of the couch, putting a hand on her shoulder.

"Jamie looked over the things you gave us after you left. He filled in a lot of the blanks and added quite a bit to what you had given us. Based on what you had and what Jamie had, there's a massive roundup of members of this group worldwide. All their assets have been frozen. We confiscated a stash of weapons in four countries, including here. There are close to three hundred people in custody, including of the head honchos."

"What's he talking about? How did you know about this group?" Abilene glared at Jamie, crossing her arms.

Leland answered instead of Jamie. "Wade told you about our second job beyond the ranch. We gather a lot of information for the feds along with protecting possible witnesses. Dad and I have been gathering data on this group for years, aware you were involved somehow. What we didn't know was how you were involved.

"So you knew what was happening right from the git-go." It was a statement, not a question.

Leland glanced at Jamie. "Not everything, only bits and pieces. We knew when they stepped up the pressure on you. It's what made us get you here. There was no way we could have helped you if you disappeared on us. Pop and I weren't about to let anything happen to you. I wanted to meet that wonderful sister your grandmother wrote about."

It was unbelievable. Her knights, sans armor, had come in the nick of time. A few more months, a year at the most, was when they would have come for her. Garvin had warned her twenty years ago that he wouldn't play with her forever.

"What about McGuire? Did you catch him?"

"Not yet. He's gone underground along with two other who are somewhere close." He paused. His gaze went to Wade then back to her. "We have hearing tomorrow in federal court. You'll need to be there."

"Why?"

"You'll need to say where you got all this information. Without you, it'll all fall apart."

She lowered her lid to shield her eyes, staring at her hands. There wasn't a choice here. If she didn't testify, it would continue because they all would walk away scot-free. Letting out a deep breath, she said, "Okay." That is if she made it to the courtroom tomorrow to give that testimony.

Chapter 25

There was a contingent of guards around the house and ranch for the night courtesy of the US government. The hearing would be held at the county seat in the courthouse there. A federal judge came from the capital to hear the case thanks to Trent saying it wasn't safe for her to travel far from the ranch.

Jamie had awakened her before five. They left before dawn for the nine o'clock hearing. She was surrounded by guards in an armored Hummer with dark bulletproof glass. It pulled in behind the courthouse near a door which had armed guards in front of it. She was escorted into the building by Trent and thee other men dressed in full battle gear with automatic rifles head as if she was in imminent danger. Supposedly the courthouse was secure, but knowing who they were dealing with, Trent wasn't taking any chances.

One of the men led them down a long hall leading to a side door into the courtroom. They judge was already on the bench and court was in session when she was escorted into the room. From the judge's expression, they had been waiting on them.

The witness stand was raised with an old-fashioned wooden rail around it, enclosing her other than the entrance from the side. She was given the oath to tell the truth before taking a seat in the large wooden chair. A microphone was placed to pick up her voice, enabling the court reporter and the attorneys could hear her. The prosecutor nodded and smiled at her.

There were two men in fatigues stationed in the courtroom. One was slightly to her right with another to the left. Both were able to see all the onlookers in the courtroom. Trent wasn't taking any chances. The third man stood before the door where they had entered. Trent took a seat at the end of the row behind the prosecutor.

Surveying the room, Abilene's gaze stopped on two men she knew from a long time ago. They were to her left near the center aisle, two rows back in the observation seats. Fear slammed into her as she looked into the eyes of the one nearest the aisle.

She leaned forward to tell the guard on her left about the two men. Two loud pops sounded simultaneous with two holes appearing in the wall behinds her. If she hadn't leaned over, she would be dead.

She slipped to the floor, scrabbling behind the chair where she had been sitting as the guards subdues the shooter. She touched the man who had stepped in front of her to get his attention. He leaned down to hear what she had to say while keeping his eyes on the observers in the courtroom.

"The one to the left of him is with him. I know both of them," she told him, fear whizzing around inside of her.

The man spoke into the small microphone he was wearing, not moving from where he was standing, continuing to hide her from those in the courtroom. The two other men went into action and took the second man out of the room. She didn't move, not sure who else might be in the room working with those who wanted to kill her.

When the two men were in custody, Trent helped her stand. The judge returned to his seat from the floor behind the bench where he had dropped with the shots. He banged his gavel, saying, Order in the court. Everyone take your seats."

Again, she scanned the crowd, looking for more of the men who didn't want her to testify. She blanched when she located Ron, eyes hard and a sneer on his face. He was in the back left corner of the room, a pistol in his hand.

Grabbing the arm of the man beside her, she screamed, "Noooo!" diving out of the witness stand behind the guard as the loud report echoed in the room. Another hole appeared in the wall. The man by the door raised his rifle, sighted and squeezed the trigger. Ron's gun fired again as he fell backward into his set, blood spraying those close to him. Another hole appeared high on the wall.

The judge banged his gavel. "Order in the court," he loudly demanded before turning to the bailiff. His voice was controlled, but the anger hardened it. "I want everyone in this courtroom removed and searched. Every nook and cranny on this floor is to be searched for hidden weapons. There had better not be a weapon on any unauthorized person in this room when I return in an hour."

He banged his gavel, stood, then stalked out of the court room to his chambers. The people where ushered out of the room leaving Ron and his mess in the corner of the room.

As the courtroom cleared, Abilene, remained hidden, afraid to move. She was on the floor, curled into a ball hidden by the paneling around the witness box. Trent squatted beside her,

"Are you hurt?" His voice was calm, the hand he put on her arm gentle.

She shook her head, unable to speak, shifting further into the corner.

"The worst of over. You need to come with us."

She stared at him, unable to process what he wanted. He held out his hand. A trembling hand reached to him. He helped her to stand. With an arm around her, he walked her out the door where they had entered the room with the armed men surrounding them. He stopped at the end of the hall, holding her in an embrace until she stopped shaking.

His words brought back why she was hear. "Do you have a gun on you?"

She reached into her purse then handed him a small Glock. He checked it before handing it back to her with a smile.

"Keep it. You may need it. Since you didn't pull it, no one need to know you have it but us." Calming, she put it back into her purse.

"What now?" She leaned against the wall, needing the support for her rubbery legs. What else could happen?

"We'll go back into the courtroom and you'll testify. Once that's over, we'll take you back to the ranch."

His phone beeped. He checked the screen before answering. "Trent here. What's up?"

He listened, smiling at her. "Great. McGuire is out as are the two men who were planted to kill her." He listened again before saying, "I understand. She'll be on the stand in hopefully a few minutes. Once she's done, those in custody won't be able to get any type of bail. They'll have murder charges to deal with, so keep them out of the courts for at least another two hours." He listened again before disconnecting the call. "Well, my dear, it all hinges on getting hits hearing underway. You ready?"

"No, but I don't think that matters," she said, resigned to what was still to come. All she wanted was for it all to be over.

They were called back into the courtroom after what seemed like hours to her. She again took the stand. The judge warned, "Ms. Brown, you're still under oath." He turned to the lawyers. "Let's get this hearing underway."

There were fewer people in the courtroom. Her eyes locked onto the man behind the defense table. Fear threatened to paralyze her. If they missed any weapon on him, she would be leaving this courtroom as a corpse. Lowering her gaze to her clasped hands, she waited. There were more guards around her, but it appeared the questioning was about to start.

The Prosecutor stood behind the table before saying, "Please state your full name for the court."

"Abilene Ellen Brown."

The lawyer glanced at the legal pad on the table before asking his first question. She was afraid he would ask all the wrong things. Yes, he had the information, but he needed to ask the right questions to obtain what he had kept to herself for twenty years.

"Ms. Brown, you were married to a Steven Jerome Brown. Is that correct?"

"Yes."

"Where is Mr. Brown work?"

"For a company called Lowe, Brighton, and Weintraub Accounting."

"What was his position there?"

"He was a Certified Public Accountant."

"Did he do any types of audits for the company?"

"Yes." She met the lawyer's eyes. So far he was headed in the correct direction. He studied the legal pad on the table.

"Did he talk to you about what he had found during an audit on the company he did prior to his death?"

"No."

The man's head snapped up, eyes locked on her at her answer. He stared at her for a few seconds. "No?"

She didn't look away. "No, he didn't talk about it. He showed me what he found."

"I object. This is hearsay," the defense lawyer stated, having jumped to his feet.

"Overruled. Observation isn't hearsay. You may continue," the judge said, writing something on a pad.

"What did he show you?" the prosecutor said, resuming the line of questioning begun.

"He showed me an internal audit he did for the company he worked for which showed major discrepancies. There was money being put into shell companies which would then disappear. There was close to ten million in missing funds for that year."

"Is there a record of this audit he did?"

"Yes sir."

"Where is that record?"

"In a file he gave me to keep."

"There's more than one file, correct?"

"Yes. There's the initial audit in paper format, one in computer format and then three more files in computer format of follow-up audits."

"Did you show or give these records to anyone?"

"I gave them to Trent James."

"Will you point him out to the court, please?"

She pointed to Trent. "The man in the gray suit with the blue tie."

"Now, Ms. Brown, what did Trent do with those files you gave him?"

"He printed the ones from the computer and put them in the folder with the original audit I had given him."

"Would you recognize those files if you saw them again?"

"Yes I would."

There was no doubt in her mind she would recognize the files. She'd had twenty years of studying them. If asked, she could repeat the first file from memory if needed with few mistakes.

The lawyer pulled a folder filled with paper from the table. He handed it to her before leaning on the rail while she examined the contents of the folder.

The file folder was the one she had given Trent with Stevens writing on the tab. The original papers were there. The sheets had darkened with age and the writing had faded over time, but it was still legible. Steven's precise numbers telling the story. The others, to the best of her memory were the ones from her computer.

"This is the original audit Steven gave to me. The others are what Trent printed from my computer. There is another copy of the original, then an audit from five, ten and fifteen years."

"What does this original audit contain?"

"It the initial audit showing the discrepancies Steven found."

"You said there were more files, correct?"

"Yes."

"What do the other files contain?"

"One is the final version of the original audit. The other three are follow-up audits."

"Okay. How did you get audits from the company without your husband working there?"

"Steven planted a small program in their files. It grabbed every company audit and redid it, using the techniques he did when auditing a company. It did an internal audit yearly, compiling them into a complete report covering five years."

"Do you know what these five years audits showed?"

"Yes. Each internal audit showed more money being transferred to off shore companies. The companies' names changed, but they all had the same owners."

"How much money are we talking about, Ms. Brown?"

"In excess of three hundred million on the last audit for that five years." There was an audible gasp with the amount she quoted from the onlookers.

"Is there any indication in these audits where all this money came from?"

"Yes."

"What companies are implicated?"

She opened the file so she didn't make a mistake and began reading the list of names of the various companies funneling money out of the company. Half way through, she raised her head, reciting the names without looking at the sheet, giving the company and owners. There was silence other then the resulting of the paper in her shaking hand when she finished.

"Your Honor, we would like to have these files along with the computer where they were stored, submitted as exhibit A."

He handed the files, then her computer to the bailiff. There went her research. She didn't have the last entries backed up to a thumb drive. Maybe they would give it back to her after cloning it.

The prosecutor picked up pointed to three boxes on the floor. "We would also like these hard drives and servers from the Lowe, Brighton, and Weintraub Accounting as evidence as exhibit B. They back up what Ms. Brown has given in her testimony."

"Now, Ms. Brown, did your husband give you anything to hold for him before he was murdered."

"Objection. Irrelevant."

"Overruled. Answer the question, Ms. Brown."

She glanced at the judge. He was taking notes, but she caught the quick wink of his left eye.

"Yes," she answered refocusing on the lawyer before her.

"What did he give you?"

"The original of his initial audit and an envelope with the letters T. J. on it."

"Were there any instructions on what to do with them?"

"Yes."

"And those instructions were?"

"To give them to T.J., who would identify himself."

"Did this T.J. identify himself?"

"Yes."

"Who is T.J." The lawyer leaned on the railing, facing the courtroom, waiting on her answer.

"Trent James."

"So you gave him the envelope and file."

"Yes."

"Now, Ms. Brown, please tell the court what happened to your husband."

"Objection. Relevancy."

The judge turned to the lawyer who was leaning on the rail of the witness stand. "Mr. Weldon, would you explain this line of questioning for the court?"

"Certainly. The attack on Ms. Brown is related to her deceased husband and the audit he did for the company. What happened then is relevant to the attacks on her today."

"I'll allow you to proceed for now."

"Now, Ms. Brown, in your own words, please describe what happened to your husband."

Her eyes darted around the room, settling on Wade. She hoped he wouldn't end up like Steven. Lowering her eyes to her hands, the began the story.

"Mr. Brighton discovered Steven had uncovered the hidden transfers of money. After Steven showed me the computer file, he then hid it. He told me to transfer it, along with any newer files I uploaded to any new computer and to keep it hidden. He then instructed me how to download the audits from the program he planted in their files. It would analyze all company transactions, putting them into an ongoing audit while would be compiled at the time I accessed the program. It would put those ongoing audits into a compilation of the five years of data. I was to upload that information to my computer and hide it as he had the first one.

"He also showed me how to hide the envelope and paper audit file. At the time, he told me Brighton was onto him, but the others two didn't know what was happening. Everything with the offshore companies was under Brighton's audit."

She sucked in a breath and let it out, relieving that time as she spoke.

"A week later, Steven didn't come home from work. I filed a missing person report twenty-four hours later as the police requested." She stopped, taking another deep breath. The pain was intense, even after all this time. "They found him five days later. He had been tortured to death. They had skinned him alive, cut the muscles in his arms and legs. Scalded him with hot water then disemboweled him. According the to medical examiner, it had taken four to five days for him to die."

"Did anyone contact you or threaten you after his death?"

"Not right way. They searched my house several times and my car too. Over the years, I would find my things had been searched at various times."

"What happened recently which made you believe they were still looking for things related to your husband?"

"I discovered someone had accessed my computer. Then Garvin contacted me. He said I and my secrets belonged to him and no one would ever get close to me without dying." Her eyes flicked to Wade. That threat didn't end with Garvin's death.

"And after that?"

"I met Ronald McGuire. He questioned me about my research. It was then used to find oil. He stalked me for over five years, making it appear as if I was working for Garvin and his group."

"Did this McGuire ever threaten you?"

"Yes. Several times."

"Backing up, did you know Garvin prior to all this happening?"

"Yes. I dated him a couple of times in high school and in college before I met Steven."

Weldon turned and met her gaze. "Did Garvin ever threaten you?"

"Yes."

"When?"

"At my husband's funeral."

The defense attorney popped up. "Objection. Relevancy."

The judge pursed his lips before asking, "Mr. Weldon, I need to know where you're headed with this line of questioning."

"Mr. Garvin has direct ties to Brighton. The company he worked for was one of the companies which had been transferring money offshore into shell companies and had their accounts at Brighton's company. Ms. Brown's testimony will end up tying him to Brighton and the death of her husband."

"Objection overruled. You may continue."

"What did Mr. Garvin tell you?"

"He said no one would ever have me if he couldn't."

"Did he do anything to support that threat?"

"Yes. Twice. The first time he had the man I was dating at the time beaten. They almost killed him. Garvin called me and told me not to try dating anyone again. The second time, he attempted to kill me at the Chapman ranch."

"What happened?"

"He attempted to kill me. He shot my father, who pushed me out of the line of fire. He was shot and killed within seconds of his first shot."

"You mentioned Ronald McGuire, who as following you for over five years. Do you know if he was connected with these people?"

"He was working for Garvin, who was the one using my research for the oil and gas. Garvin was using him to keep track of me for himself and Brighton. They did their best to make it appear like I was working for them."

Weldon paused, then asked, "And what happened to Mr. McGuire?"

"He was killed in this courtroom earlier."

"You recently learned who killed your husband; is that correct?"

"Yes. Zeke, one of McGuire's men, told me Garvin had him killed."

"And when did he give you that information?" Weldon watched her frowning, not sure of her answer.

She didn't look up, staring at the knotted fingers of her hand. Several tear drops plopped onto her lap, remembering the night Jamie was shot.

"It was the night he came to take me to Garvin, but we stopped him." Her voice was so soft, Weldon had to lean in to hear her.

"Why did Garvin want you with him?"

Her hands twisted. A deep sadness filled her. The events of the past twenty years now made sense. Garvin was a key player, but she had discounted his involvement as a minor part at best. She couldn't have been more wrong.

"He wanted me, refusing to believe I didn't like him other than as a friend. I'm sure Brighton told him to get me away from the Chapmans due to what he knew I had from Steven."

"Objection!" the defending almost screamed. Supposition and hearsay."

"Sustained. Mr. Weldon, you need to keep to the facts of the case. The last answer will be struck from the record after the first sentence."

Weldon surprised her with the next question. "Do you expect another attempt on your life?"

"Yes."

"From whom?"

"Brighton."

"Why?"

"He found out Steven had backed up the files of the audit which he changed to hide what he was doing. He knew Garvin and I were acquainted when Steven and I attended a party at his house shortly after the audit. Garvin was there. Brighton told me at the time I would end up being with Garvin, not Steven, before long because I belong to him."

"Belonged to whom?"

Her lip quivered, the knuckles on both hand white. "Brighton."

"Please explain that answer to the court."

Weldon was staring at her when she peeked at him. "Brighton told me I was his, but Garvin would watch me or see me dead. He also told me that he knew Steven had given me something to hold and if I wanted to keep him, I needed to give it to him. I told Steven when we got home what Brighton said. It was then he hid everything and put the program on my computer."

Tears were falling, but she continued with what she was saying. "Steven told me he loved me and Kristen, our daughter, and to make sure I took good care of her. There was no way he could get the information to the authorities at the time since they were following him. It was the reason for the envelope addressed to T.J..

Trent was his contact and was supposed to meet with him the night he disappeared."

Weldon handed her a box of tissues. She took a couple to wipe her face and blow her nose. So many secrets for so long. Her eyes went to the man behind the defense table. He would see her dead if for no other reason than her testimony.

"Would you recognize Brighton if you wee to see him again."

"Yes."

"Is he here in this courtroom?"

Abilene began to cry again. "Yes."

"Will you point him out to us?"

Her shaking hand, finger out, aimed at him as she met his light blue eyes which were icy with hate and anger. "The man in the blue suit with the patterned blue-green tie."

Brighton bolted from his chair and screamed, You're dead, bitch! Dead!"

Abilene hunched down in the chair, attempting to make herself smaller. The judge banged his gavel.

"Bailiff, Mr. Brighton is to be placed under arrest. The complete charges will be handed down within the hour, to be amended as the evidence is gone through. For now, threatening to kill a federal witness will hold him without bail."

Weldon handed the judge a file. "In there are the names of all the people and companies Ms. Brown named. There are more in the other files. They're all under surveillance. We would like charges entered for embezzlement, money laundering, murder, conspiracy to commit murder, murder after the face and attempted murder along with extortion with warrant for their arrests."

The defense stood, his voice almost tired, "Objection. There's no proof of any of the people having committed murder."

"Overruled. The death of Mr. Brown was murder. Then there was the attempt to murder Ms. Brown here in this courtroom, which you can't deny because you were a witness to it as I was." He turned his attention back to Mr. Weldon. "You'll have your warrants due to the preponderance of the evidence. In scanning these files during the questioning, there's reasonable evidence to support their arrest. Continue the protection for Ms. Brown. Court is adjourned."

She couldn't believe. The defense wasn't given a chance to refute her testimony. It was only a matter of time before she would need to testify in a criminal court. Hopefully they would search everyone and the building to prevent what had happened here. The last thing she needed was someone trying to kill her again as she testified.

The tears hadn't stopped. The guard to her left, helped her to stand, then steadying her with a hand under her elbow. They surrounded her as she was escorted out of the courtroom to the secure hallway. When she saw Trent waiting for her, she broke, unable to control the sobs fueled by the past and fear of the future.

She noticed a man leave as Trent walked her down the hall to the outside door. No way did she want to go out that door. Trent didn't let her stop, his strong arm around her pulling her forward.

When the door opened, the Hummer was there with Wade waiting for them. Trent held her up, keeping her from crawling away to hide.

"They will now kill all of us," she said.

Wade remained calm. "It's almost over, Abilene. Let's go home,"

He reached out to her. Jerkily, she moved toward him, each step an effort. Wade wrapped her in an embrace before assisting her to the vehicle. He helped her up the steps then slid in beside her. He enfolded her in his arms, letting her cling to him. It wasn't over yet. Brighton and the others would send assassins to kill her and anyone close to her which meant all the Chapmans.

"Honey, it'll be alright." He waited, but she couldn't stop sobs. "Abby, you're going to make yourself sick if you keep crying like this."

All she could see was what had happened to Steven. What were they thinking in attempting to protect her? Didn't they understand? A tightness settled in her chest as the fear for the man holding her grew. She couldn't keep them safe since they wouldn't let her leave.

The frozen look of horror on Stevens face came back again. They had left his face alone to show what they had put him through. She couldn't let Wade go through that. There was one way. She remembered the gun in her purse. It was an out and was save them.

Wade reached over and took her purse. She grabbed for it. When he handed it to Trent, she sent a glare of pure malice in his direction.

"Abby, that isn't the answer," he said.

Her eye filled with tears of anger. "I can't let them kill you," she declared as she pushed away from him. His arms tightened around her, keeping her close to him.

"It's my choice to protect you, so get used to it," he told her as she attempted to get her purse from Trent.

"Where's her other gun?" Trent asked, removing her Glock from her purse.

"I'm not sure, but you'll need to search her room. We'll need to have an around-the-clock watch on her for now."

At his words, she quite fighting. It was no use. The idiots wanted to die with her. With her head resting on his shoulder, she didn't stop the tears as a sense of doom filled her. They weren't going to let her do anything to save them. She sagged, resigned to their fate. Taking a deep shaky breath, she closed her eyes as an all-encompassing fatigue seeped into her. There was no use in fighting. They were as good as dead.

Then they arrived at the rand, she let them guide her into the house. She let Wade place her in the large overstuffed chair Nolan generally used. Resigned to her fate, she curled her legs under her, laying her head on the arm of the chair. With closed eyes, she withdrew into herself, allowing the exhaustion to envelop her. She ignored the hand on her shoulder, her body feeling like it had not bones, too tired to open her eyes. Two tears seeped out as she gave up. It wasn't worth fighting any longer. Her fate was sealed.

Chapter 26

Abilene awoke slowly, not sure where she was. The tiredness still had a hold on her. She had no idea of how long she had been sleeping. There were flashes of memory of someone feeding her and long periods of crying. The intense hopelessness had dissipated but she was resigned to her fate.

Listlessly, she rolled over, needing to get up, but the weight of the lethargy kept her in place. Forcing her eyes open, she didn't recognize the room. A slight noise had her rotating her head. Wade, Leland and Jamie were watching her from comfortable chairs arranged around a table with coffee cups and the remains of a meal on it.

She scooted to the edge of the bed, studying the room. It was decorated for a female. The curtains were a soft white sprinkles with tiny violet. The canopy over the twin bed and coverlet were made of the same material. The multiple shelves were filled with dolls, books, games and other toys. Against the wall under the window was a vanity with a brush, comb and mirror with violets formed in the silver handles. The walls were a pale violet matching the flowers on the material.

Abilene frowned. The sense of dè ja vu was strong but she couldn't place it in her memory. If she had been here before, why couldn't she remember it?

When she stood, she made her way to the bathroom without hesitation, aware of exactly where it was, ignoring the men as she passed them. The bathroom door clicked shut and it was if that click restored the memories she had blocked from so long ago.

She was young. Around the age of four or five. This was her room. The man who was with her, was the handsome man in the locket. He was smiling as she pronounced how much she liked the room and how violets were her very best favorite flower.

The way he held her and told her how nothing was too good for his little girl came back. Her grandmother was there, smiling at them. The two people she cared the most about were here with her, so what was there not to like?

The force of the memory had her hanging on to the counter by the sink to keep from falling to the floor. More scenes and emotions flooded back into her consciousness, swirling about in her thoughts like a video of her past. She had been here and hadn't wanted to leave.

She pulled herself together, doing what she came in here to do before putting the housecoat on the back of the door and returning to the room. Yes, this had been her room while she had been here.

All three men were still there. She moved to where they sat and took a seat on the floor beside Jamie. With her hands on her knee, she stared up at him. Her memory filled in more details.

It was easy to remember him now along with how happy he had been to have her here. He had cried as he hugged and kissed her. Without hesitation at the time, she called him Daddy and how he had smiled before telling her how much he loved her and missed having her with him.

Abilene lowered her head to stare at her hands on his knee. "This was my room for the summer Grandmother brought me here to visit. I remember it now. I was so excited about coming here. She had told me a lot about your and the ranch."

No one broke the silence as she remembered the aftermath of her summer here. She had cried when she had to leave, begging for them to stay longer. Her gaze met Jamie's as she held back the pending tears at the memory.

"She wouldn't bring me back because I didn't want to go home. I wanted to stay with you." In her mind, she saw him as he had looked when she five. It had been so difficult to leave him. He was her father. He had loved her and her mother.

Jamie ran a hand through her hair. "Yes. Your room. She called me two weeks after you went home. Said she couldn't bring you back. Too hard on you. Had hoped you would look forward to coming back but was too heart broke when you had to leave.

It was one of Jamie's longer speeches since she had been here. She smiled up at him.

"I remember you telling me nothing was too good for your little girl when you showed me this room."

"Still the same."

"I love you, Daddy." She laid her head on his knee, wishing she was that innocent child again.

"I love you too, Abby. Good to have you home."

She was unable to speak. Hopefully his home wouldn't become a battleground because of her.

"Abby girl, you need to come and eat," Jamie said, patting her head.

"Not hungry." The weariness held her in place at his knee.

"Don't' matter. Time to eat."

His words made her smile at the memory of him saying them from a long time ago. When she was playing, she hadn't wanted to eat. Like now, he had remained calm and waited for her to join him. Even today, she couldn't refuse to do as he requested.

"Alright," she said, rising from the floor, pulling the housecoat around her, not sure if she even had clothes in the room. Jamie put his arm around her. As they walked, he said, "Abby girl, things are a rough right now. You need to keep being tough."

She glanced at his face. The eyes looking at her were filled with love for her. Hanging her head, she understood he was afraid for her. There was no way she could disappoint the man who had waited all the years for her to come home.

Pulling in a shaky breath, she admitted, "Daddy, I don't' know if I can keep fighting. It's like being on a treadmill; I keep running, but I get nowhere."

"Then don't run."

Her head popped up. He was smiling. She hugged the wise old man. He was right. There was no reason to run any longer. It was time to stay put in more ways than one.

The guards stayed at the ranch for the next month. Abilene kept to the house and barn unless someone was with her. Ghost had kept close to the house, following her around like a big dog when she went outside. She took to talking to the big horse, who seemed to listen to everything she said. It had been good therapy to express her fears to Ghost who appeared to understand. No response was needed, only a good listener. He had been that for her.

The lethargy gradually left as the days passed. Her smile and laughter returned. She played with the dogs, occasionally teasing Leland who was staying at the ranch to help guard her along with Wade and Chad.

One morning she was pestering Wade by asking innumerable questions to see how long he would put up with it. He warned her to stop, but her persisted, wanting to she what he would do. In exasperation, he stalked toward her. She took off running, giggling as the other laughed when he chased her. She ran into the barn. He caught her when she turned into a stall, missing the aisle to the door. As punishment, he kissed her until she melted into him.

He pulled away. "I believe we better stop while we can." He turned as if looking for an escape route, struggling to hold himself in check. She took a step closer to him, but he backed up one in response. "Enough. I'm not sure who's being punished here, me or you, but it's time to stop."

"And if I don't want to stop?" she queried, head tilted.

Wade shook his head. "Not yet, sweetheart. Not yet."

"When then?"

"When the times right. It isn't now. I need to get back to work."

He moved past her, striding back to the corral where he had left the horse he was training. She grinned. He wasn't immune to her so now she needed to find out when the time would be right.

She walked out of the barn into the sunlight to find Trent getting out of his car. A spike of fear stabbed her. He noticed her, and a grin lit his face. Changing direction, she headed to him, hoping he had good news this time.

Abilene, you look great. I was worried the last time I saw you."

"Yeah, well, I was in the midst of a meltdown from all the years of dealing with the crap. What's up?" she asked, glossing over her breakdown after the hearing.

"Have some new. Where's the rest of them family?"

"Wade's working with the horses. Jamie and Nolan are there with Chad and Leland."

The began walking to the corral. Wade was working with the big black stallion he's been training when she first came to the ranch. Chad saw them and said something to Wade. He dropped the reins and the horse stood, not moving as he left the corral. All eyes were on them as she let Trent guide her to the men who were not gathered, waiting on them.

The family greeted Trent as if he was one of them. He glanced at her. "Well, it looks like we have them all. No bonds, federal lockups for most of them and all but a few underlings have murder, conspiracy to commit murder, or attempted murder warrants against them. A couple even have accessory to murder before and after the fact.

"The data Steven left has been verified. All their assets have been frozen or taken, essentially shutting down all the companies. Zeke's goons have been singing like beautiful song birds. It all leads back to the top and Brighton."

"How many are we talking about here?" Nolan asked.

"Well, at last count somewhere around two hundred here and overseas. Interpol loved the data and has close to a hundred in custody. Our last collar was the hired gun who was assigned to kill Abilene. He decided he didn't want to take the fall for them and rolled. The word on the street if, if you want to keep working, you stay away from any contracts on our little lady. Even the cheap ones are baking away. They don't want to spend the rest of their lives in a federal lock up of have their lives cut short when they fail."

Trent was grinning. "I guess the big guys are going to have to accept that killing her isn't an option and would help anyway since we don't need her testimony any longer. It would be a revenge thing. They've come to believe it wouldn't be in their best interest if anything happened to her after a very understanding judge told them they would all be charged with first-degree murder and felony murder after the fact.

Unsure if she had understood him, Abilene asked, "So if anything happens to me, they all get another murder charge against them?"

"Right. It's in their best interest to ensure you have along, uneventful life."

Jamie put his arm around her. "Worked out," he said with a grin.

Her arms went around his waist as she relaxed in his embrace. Finally, she could have a life. It was over.

Trent turned to Nolan. "I want to thank you for all your help. You were right. She was the key, and it was worth all the hassles, even twenty years down the road."

Nolan smiled. "It was worth the hassles. Jamie was correct when he said his little girl was in big trouble and needed our help."

Abilene straightened up, frowning at her father. "How...how did you find out?"

His arm tightened around her. "A little bird."

"Who?" She waited. When he didn't answer, she leaned back, her voice hardened. "Who, Daddy?"

He tightened his arm around her. "Kristen."

With the name, she closed her eyes and stiffened. "I need an explanation."

Trent reached out and brushed a strand of hair off her face. "Her boyfriend is my son. He encouraged her to talk to Jamie and Nolan, who in turn called me. It's a small world, Abby."

She had to ask, "Daddy, how did you know it was me?"

"Mentioned your grandmother and her father."

"So you all knew before I got here what was happening and who I was."

"Yep. Had to protect my baby," Jamie said.

She kissed his cheek. "Thank you, Daddy."

Jamie held her closer as if he was afraid to let her go.

"Thanks, Trent," Jamie said.

"My pleasure. There's no way I can top this bust and I owe it to all of you and your help. Abilene, you're some woman. Your daughter had nothing but praise for the wonderful mother she has and wanted to protect you like you had her."

"She's sort of special. If her boyfriend is anything like his father, she's getting a good man."

Trent's grin widened. "You'll get to see if that's true. Russ called to say he asked her to marry him. She accepted. They should be here next week."

"You live near here?" she asked.

"You could say that." His eyes put her in mind of Chad when he was teasing her.

"Um, that wasn't an answer," Abilene said with folded arms, foot tapping.

"You tell her Wade," Trent said, leaning on the corral, a grin on his face.

"Why me?" Wade asked, glaring at Trent.

Trent shrugged. "She's your girl."

Nolan snapped. "Boys, enough. Trent is their brother. He's two years younger than Wade. I don't' know why you're making it such a big secret.

Abilene stared at Trent, lips pursed before nodding. "Yeah, you're your father in a younger, bigger version. Now all the pieces have fallen into place.

Trent studied the ground as he changed position against the corral, avoiding looking at her. "Steven was my best friend growing up. He asked me to look after you after he found the books were being cooked. Until Kristen told Russ what was happening, I sort of kept track of where you were and what you were doing. I couldn't do much more without putting you in greater danger than you already were. When she gave us the details of what they were doing to you, I had to get involved again."

He grinned at her. "Getting you here wasn't easy. You're one slippery eel when you want to be. Luckily, I work for the feds and this is a federal case, so I talked my supervisor into using the set up here to protect you and to attempt to solve Steven's murder. I wanted to bring them to justice.

"Until you handed me that envelope and gave me those files, I was beginning to think we were going to have to hide you in the middle of nowhere."

"Be glad I remembered you," she said, glaring at him. His grin was like Wade's. She twisted so she could see Wade. "What do you think of my girl?"

"Pretty like her mother and just as brave. Russ is going to have his hands full."

Abilene giggled. Her daughter was much like her. She was a strong woman and wouldn't back down. Russ would definitely have his hands full.

"Does this mean it's all over?" she asked Trent.

"For you, yes. For me, no. I have several long years of court dates to attend, thanks to you."

"Complaining or bragging?" Chad quipped with a grin.

"Complaining. Court is generally boring most of the time."

"If I never see the inside of another courtroom, I'll be perfectly happy," she stated.

"Can't figure out why," Chad joked as he moved out of her reach, a grin on his face when she glared at him.

Jamie held her in place when she made a move to attack Chad. "Better watch yourself, boy," was all he said, his eyes twinkling at her response.

She returned to leaning against him, his embrace calming her. It was good to be home with her father and a chance for a normal life.

Chapter 27

The day after Trent's visit, Wade saddled Ghost and the black stallion. Abilene watched him for a few minutes. "Going somewhere?" she asked.

"Yes, we're going somewhere." He glanced over at her.

"Got a mouse in your pocket?"

"Nope. Figured we ended some time away from the house." He gave her a quick glance and said, "You might want to put on some boots."

"Oh. I guess that means you're inviting me to go for a ride with you." She stood with crossed arms, brows lifted, glaring at him.

He rotated his head to her, an arm around the pommel of the saddle, studying her. "Yes, I'm inviting you to go for a ride with me."

Finally. He had gotten the hint. He needed to ask her to go with him, not just assume she would fall in with his plans. It was something she would need to keep reminding him of in gentle ways.

"In that case, I'll be right back." She grinned when he shook his head, continuing to saddle Ghost.

She pulled on her boots, smiling at how he hadn't bothered to ask if she wanted to go with him. He had some learning to do about her and women in general. When she rejoined him, she had her hat and sugar for Ghost and the other horse. Ghost nudged her after taking the sugar before turning so she could mount him. After settling in the saddle, she patted his neck.

Where are we off to?" she asked.

"It's a surprise," Wade said, evading answering her question.

They headed to the open range. Abilene followed his lead, waiting until he kicked his horse into a run. She held Ghost back, letting him get a good lead before nudging Ghost and giving him his head. She held on for what would be a great ride.

While leaning over Ghost's neck, she could see the distance between her and Wade decreasing until Ghost passed Wade and his horse, which was running at full speed. Ghost was running for fun, not expending much energy. Once past Wade, Ghost slowed to a comfortable lope.

Wade caught up to them, having slowed his horse when Ghost passed him. She laughed. "I can't believe Ghost caught up to pass you so quickly."

"I can. He's bred to run. The race is in two weeks. I entered him in it, but you'll need to ride him."

Her voice was sharp. "Not happening. I don't ride in races."

"This is one where you'll need to ride as he'll run for you."

With a glare, she said, "He likes you, You ride him."

"I can't. I'll be riding another horse. Before you say Chad can ride him, he can't. Only you and I can ride Ghost."

She twisted in the saddle, examining him, eyes wide. "You can't be serious. What do you mean only you and I can ride him?"

He gave her a crooked grin. "He's only half broke. Chad has tried to ride him, but Ghost won't let him. Leland and Dad tried. Ghost refused to let them get near him. Other than me, you're the only one he'll let ride him."

"Humph," she sounded, signaling her disbelief.

"Ask them yourself. If you notice, everyone gives hm a lot of room. You and I are the only ones who are able to touch him other than Jamie."

She took a few minutes to go over the past few weeks. He was right. Ghost would move away when Chad or Nolan came close to her. The same with the ranch hands. Jamie ignored the horse. Not one person had touched Ghost other than her, Wade and Jamie when he saddled him on occasion or when giving him and Spot a treat.

"Why are you and you dad so set on me riding him in this race?" The reasoning was important since it would affect Ghost, who didn't like being around people.

"Because we know he'll win. Plus, he runs better for you than me."

"I've no idea of how to ride in a race." She couldn't understand how they believed she could win, having never raced a horse. Her training had been with jumpers and show horses, not racing.

"You just ran a race. It's all straight over a mile and a half. All you need to do it stay in the saddle. He'll do the rest."

She would think about it. It wasn't something he wanted to do, but maybe once might be alright. If it was like the run they did, she could handle it, but if she did agree to do it, it would be a one-time occurrence.

Wade took the lead, and she followed him. Ghost showed his displeasure in the way he tossed his head and sidestepped as they entered a narrow canyon. The canyon was short. When they left the high walls, there was a large valley with a river flowing lazily down the middle. The open area was covered in long grass. She could smell the water as a flock of birds expressed their disproval of them being here.

Wade stopped and dismounted. He unsaddled his horse and let him run free. Abilene followed suit. The two horses ran, frolicking in the grass, moving toward the far end of the valley.

As they strolled toward the river and a grouping of trees, Wade put an arm around her. When they were closer to the trees, she noticed the rope swing. A memory of coming here to swim flashed through her mind. She remembered the four boys, her father and Nolan. There had been a woman there also. Leland had called her mother.

They splashed and played in the water, Wade protecting her from Trent, Chad and Leland's rough play. She remembered the eight-year-old boy who stayed with her and taught her to swim so she could have fun with the rest of them. The summer was so wonderful, full of fun and love, she had purposely forgotten it. When she had to leave, it had hurt so much, she pushed it deep inside of her, keeping it from tearing her apart.

"In the summer I was here, I remember coming here several times. This was the swimming hole where you taught me to swim. You spent the whole summer looking out for me, playing with me and generally being a great pal to a five-year-old pest."

"You were the farthest thing from a pest. Before you got here, Jamie asked me to protect you from the others who were rowdy. When I saw this little doll of a girl, I didn't mind. Your willingness to help and not being afraid of the horses was a big plus. On top of all that, you didn't once aske me to play with dolls, so it wasn't a chore. Even then you were a very determined person."

She chuckled at his version of her summer here. "I guess I was. I remember Trent daring me to climb that tree. I did and sat on a branch he couldn't reach and laughed at him. Daddy told me to come down, so I did. I guess I gave him a fright as I was way up in that tree there."

With a laugh, Wade said, "Yeah, you did give him a good scare. I got reamed out for letting you get so high. I told him you were like a monkey and I couldn't catch you."

"Bet I can still get higher than you in that old tree."

"No be," he said with a grin. "I don't doubt you could beat me up that tree like you did as a kid."

They had reached the river. Wade began to undress as she watched. He turned to her. "You going in fully dressed?"

"Uh, dear, I don't have a swimsuit with me and we aren't children any longer."

"What's wrong with your underthings?" he questioned, his face showing his repressed laughter.

"Nothing except they're underthings, not a swimsuit." Heat rose to her face as he continued to undress.

"There's only the two of us here, so what's the problem?"

There really wasn't a problem other than he was male and she was female. Her underthings weren't meant for swimming, especially the lacey demi-bra which covered less than many bikini tops. The looked down at what she had on. There was a way out of the dilemma.

With a grin, she sat to remove her boots and socks. Wade was entering the water in his undershorts which showed off a physique most younger men would envy. She removed the bra, leaving her shirt one, then slipped out of her jeans. The shirt was long and would hide her well enough. At least the panties he had on were decent and could pass for a swimsuit bottom.

Upon joining him in the water, she swam out to where he was treading water.

When she reached him, he said, "I see you decided to join me, but what's with the shirt?"

"It provides more coverage than the bra did. Besides, it dries quickly, so deal with it."

He reached moved so his feet were on the bottom before pulling her to him. Following where he eyes were focused, the realized her mistake. Ignoring his ogling, she pushed away from hm to swim off to shallower water. He came after her. When he go near, she splashed water at him, moving away while laughing as he tried to catch her. As he chased her, she splashed him them swam away until he finally caught her. Holding her in place, he kissed her, eliciting a response which had them both breathing hard.

"I do believe we need to quit while we're ahead," Wade said moving away from her.

"And if I don't want to?" she said, daring him to continue, not wanting to stop.

"Like I said before, when the time is right."

"And when will that be?" she asked again, frustrated at h is evasiveness.

Wade came back to her, grinning, and gave her a quick kiss before moving out of her grip. "Patience, my dear. Patience.

She moved to him, pushing backward in to the water as laughter came from under the tree. Abilene dipped into the water as Chad and Eveline ambled to the bank.

"Hey, hope you two don't mind company," Chad stated, beginning to undress. He glanced a Eveline. "Your call, darlin'. I see Abby made concessions. It's underlings or clothes of sitting on the bank."

It didn't take Chad long to be down to his undershorts. He ran and grabbed the rope to swing out with a yell before splashing into the middle of the river like he had as child. Eveline had stripped to silky dark blue underthings and joined them.

Abilene stuffed the jealousy of Eve's perfect figure and underclothes which looked like a bikini back down inside as she swam gracefully out to join Chad. There was nothing like a perfect size ten to make her feel like she was a frumpy overweight middle-aged old lady.

Wade swam to her. He pulled her back against him, his arms under her full breasts. He nibbled on her ear before saying, "You're much more to my liking. I prefer having a woman with more to hang onto."

She rotated in his arms to face him. "Is that so?"

"Yes. I love curves and you have them in all the places I like."

The way his eyes raked over her, she could see he wasn't saying it to make her feel better. He meant it. She gave him a kiss before saying, "You're good for my ego."

His hands ran up her back under her shirt. Smiling, he leaned over to give her one of his bone melting kisses as he held her close to him. "Soon," he said cryptically before swimming away.

She could only guess what he meant, but it was his call, not hers.

When it came time to leave the water, she decided what was showing wouldn't matter. She was wrong. Both men stared at her and Eveline as they joined them under the tree. It was Eveline who had her blushing.

"My word, Abby. I'd give anything to have a figure like yours," Eve said.

Abby looked down at the clinging shirt, noting how it left little to the imagination. With a wry grin, she said, "I feel so plump most of the time. I'd love to be as thing as you."

Eveline laughed. "Honey, men like curves. The more the better. Even Chad can't hide his admiration of your charms. You really need to quit hiding what you have."

And this from the shy woman she first met. The brother snickered, increasing the blush spreading from her chest to her face. She moved away from them to a rock in the sun. She had to accept she was exposed until her shirt dried. Eve joined her on the rock to allow her underthings to dry as much as possible before they left. A sparkle on her left hand caught Abby's attention. She picked up Eveline's hand to admire the beautiful ring Chad had given her.

"When did this happen?" Abilene asked, happy for Eve.

"Last night. He said he wasn't going to wait for someone else to try and steal me away." She as silent for a moment before adding, "He cares for you. I hope you know that."

Abilene couldn't face Eve. "Then why did you agree to marry him?"

"He was honest. He told me he knew you would never be anything but a sister to him. He loves me, but you...you're this unattainable perfect woman, like a character in a movie, only you're here, not on a screen. I can live with that since he'll have to deal with my love affair with James Brolin in various movies." Abby giggled. Eve grinned before sobering. "He won't ever act on his feelings because he loves his brother, and he is aware of how strongly wade feels about you."

"I never encourage Chad," Abilene said.

"I know, but you can't change how others feel. I love Chad. He's everything I could ever wish for in a man, including being totally honest. You don't them like that any longer."

"You're one lucky woman. He's a good man and a great father. I know he adores you to no end."

Eveline casually commented, "Wade will ask you to marry him. Just be patient."

She was patient. There was no choice but to be patient. The problem was how he hadn't ever talked about marriage, and only hinted at a future together. All they had done was kiss. Marriage? Maybe, but not anytime soon from the way he was acting.

When the sun slipped behind the trees, they dressed. Wade whistled for the horses to come to them. As soon as she saw Ghost, Eveline started toward him. The big horse moved out of her reach, not allowing her to touch him.

"He won't let you touch him," Abilene said when Ghost moved away from Chad.

"Why not?" Eveline asked, staring at the white horse which shone in the fading sun.

Wade answered her. "He's still half wild. Abilene and I are the only ones who can get near him most of the time. He's more her horse than mine since he follows her around like a love-sick puppy." Wade moved his head in the direction of the entrance to the valley. "Abby, you need to start for the entrance. He won't follow us as he's the alpha of the horses. These are all from his herd.

With Ghost at her side, she did as Wade instructed, going to where they had dropped the tack. As they walked, she talked to the horse who followed, his ears twitching as if he understood every word she said. He was so docile with her, no one would guess he was still wild.

By the time the others arrived, she had Ghost saddled. It appeared she would be leading them back. When they reached the flat area, Abilene again let the others get a good head start as Ghost pranced, ready to play the chase game with the running horses. She gave him a nudge. He took off, his long strides eating up the distance, closing in on the other horses.

Abilene let him choose his way around the other horses. Ghost let the others chase him, not slowing down. She let him run, not noticing how close they were to the house. When she noticed the fence, it was too late to slow the big horse. Gripping him with her knees, she was ready when he bunched for the leap over the fence. He didn't slow, clearing the fence with ease, continuing to run until they neared the out buildings. Ghost slowed to a walk as they entered the barnyard, gently blowing from the run.

She slipped from the big horse, patting his neck before leading him to the barn. She had the saddle off him and had hosed him down before beginning to brush him when the rest entered the barn.

"What were you thinking?" Chad scolded sharply as he stood back from her and Ghost.

Facing him, Abilene frowned. "What are you talking about?"

"Jumping that fence. What were you thinking/"

She chuckled, returning to brushing Ghost. "I've seen him take that fence both coming and going, so what's the problem?"

"Yes, he jumps it, but not with someone riding him."

She glanced at Chad and shook her head, running the brush over Ghosts' side. "He knew he could make it with me aboard. It isn't the first fence I've gone over on a horse. I used to ride jumpers. Pulling him in wasn't an option since we were too close before I saw the fence."

Chad ran a hand through his hair. He turned to Wade. "You talk to her. She doesn't see a problem with jumping a fence at a full run."

To Chad's surprise, Wade grinned. "She knows her horse and trusts him. He cleared it with room to spare. Damn, it was beautiful to watch as he sailed over it. I can't believe how easily he took it."

"You both are nuts," Chad said, stomping off to take care of his horse.

Wade watched her as she groomed Ghost. She glanced at him. "Am I nuts?"

"No. You knew he would make it as long as you didn't make him break stride." He moved to beside her. "Abby, we do need to talk."

"About what?" she asked, continuing what she was doing.

"A lot of things." He was being evasive again.

"Alright. Let me know when and where."

"Tonight. After supper."

"Fine," was her short response.

With out saying anything more, Wade left to care for his horse. When she had Ghost groomed, she patted him on the neck. Her eyes followed Wade as he walked to the house with Chad and Eveline. She sighed, not sure where her relationship with Wade was headed.

She looked up at Ghost who was watching her. "I wonder if he's finally going to talk about us or skirt around the bush. He should be more like you and just show me he loves me and wants to be with me."

Ghost nodded his head an gave a neigh as if agreeing with her. She let him loose in the barnyard to do what he wanted after making sure there were oats and alfalfa for him in his stall. She was unwilling to confine him in a stall or corral. She headed to the house to shower and dress for the evening.

Chapter 28

The talk that evening at supper concerned Chad's engagement. Nolan appeared happy with him marrying Eveline. Abilene could tell from his smile how much he liked Chad's choice. Meanwhile Eveline was glowing, and Chad was all smiles. Regardless of what Eveline had said at the river, Abilene noted Chad's gaze was one of love and happiness. She had nothing to worry about. He had found the woman he wanted and was marrying her.

When the meal was over, they moved to the den to toast the newly engaged couple. Nolan popped the cork on a magnum of champagne he had chilling.

"Do you have a date in mind?" he asked, filling the champagne flutes.

Chad glanced at Eve. "We were considering a date in a couple of months. It would give Eve time to get everything arranged." He faced Nolan. "We were planning on having it here as it won't be a large affair."

"I'll need to know the planned date. I have to be back in the capital for the vote on the reservation annexation around that time." He handed everyone a flute of champagne. "May your lives be filled with lasting love and happiness," Nolan said as he raised his glass to them.

Everyone took a sip of the bubbly drink. The conversation moved to the wedding plans. Abilene joined Jamie on the sofa as Chad and Eveline looked over Nolan's schedule to prevent their wedding from disrupting something he couldn't miss. Wad sat on a stool at the bar saying little, listening to his father, Chad and Eve. He didn't seem to be in any hurry for the promised talk they were to have this evening.

Jamie put his arm around her after she set her glass on the end table. He quietly listened to the plans, not missing a things which was said. His only comment was, "About time he settled down."

When the last of the champagne was finished, Wade came to her.

"Let's go for a walk," he invited, holding out his hand.

She took the offered hand and they left through the French doors into the cool night air. A full moon was sitting on the horizon, appearing larger than normal when seen in contrasts to the trees and mountains. The yard was bathed in a silvery light, giving ordinary objects and other worldly look. The smell of horses, hay and grass tickled her nose.

Ghost galloped toward her, his coat glowing in the moonlight, making him appear in substantial and unreal. He reared up, neighed, then ran off on the direction of the fence. The sound of his hooves echoed in the quiet of the night.

"He's off for some fun. We won't see him again for a day or two," Wade commented as they watched him jump the fence at a full run in the dark.

"Lucky him," Abilene quipped with a grin.

They strolled to a secluded spot at the side of the house where two flowering bushes sheltered a lone bench, creating and outdoor alcove unable to be seen from the house. The spicy scent of the flowers surrounded them. Wade joined her on the bench. They sat quietly, enjoying the night air. Abilene waited for him to say what he wanted to talk about.

Wade leaned forward, elbows on his knees and hands folded together. The tenseness in his hands was easily seen even in the dim light.

"What are your plans now that everything is over?"

It was a fair question. He needed to find out if she had concrete plan which couldn't be changed.

"I'm not sure. There are some areas around here I want to study. I do have a six-month lease on the house, so that means I'll be here for another three months."

"So you aren't going to take the teaching job?"

She hesitated, watching him as he worried his thumbs, head down.

"Not yet. I'm going to have to sooner or later, but I'm putting it off for as long as possible.

He stilled, then tensed again. Remaining patient, she waited to see where he would head with his next questions.

"Would you consider staying here?"

She smiled at his back. He apparently had something in mind and wanted to know what she planned on doing.

"I already have. Daddy wants me to stay. My problem is how I don't have the funds to support myself much longer without finding paying work. I won't life off him."

Wade was quiet. He didn't move for several minutes then sat back before asking, "So three months is the time you'll be here for sure?"

"Yes. I can't see any reason to leave until the least is up on the place. After that, I'm not sure what I'll do."

He faced her for a few seconds before gazing at the moon. "Do you want to leave?"

This was an important answer for both of them. Honesty was called for since he needed to hear the truth.

"No, I don't want to leave. I've found the father I knew I had and don't want to leave him. Then there's you. I'm not sure where our relationship is going but leaving you will be difficult at best."

He put his arm around her and eased her next to him. "Then don't leave."

She relaxed against him, her head resting on his shoulder. "I can't stay and live off my father. I already told you that. I need a paying job to stay beyond the three months."

"Would you live off your husband if you had one?"

She hoped she was reading him right in where he was headed with his questions. Again, she answered him with honesty. "Depends on the husband and what restrictions he would put on me for living off him."

"No restrictions."

"Then yes, I would. It wouldn't' mean I still wouldn't attempt to bring in an income, but it would enable me to not be desperate and forced into teaching."

"So, you wouldn't mind a husband who was willing to support you, let you continue your research and stay here in the little house."

"No, I wouldn't mind."

He relaxed. It appeared the talk was over having gotten the information he wanted. She hoped she had read him right, but then again, he hadn't asked her to marry him. It was going to be a wait and see what the next three months brought.

Chapter 29

The next day, a Friday, Abilene moved back to the Haskell ranch. Jamie came with her. He took the bedroom on the first floor again while she kept the one she liked upstairs. He was all smiles now that he was back in the house with her. Waldo and Arf came with them as a precaution.

She thought of the not-so-little house as home. It was the first real home she had lived in since Steven had died. The cabin was never meant as more than vacations. She loved it here with her father and the Chapmans and didn't want to contemplate leaving.

Kristen and Russ were scheduled to arrive late Monday afternoon or early evening. She prepared a room for her daughter, excited at the pending visit. Russell, her fiancé, would be staying with his father. The plan was for them to meet at the main ranch house daily where they would be under the watchful eye of Nolan and Nancy. Abby smiled at the thought of the two young people with chaperones. There was no question about them finding ways of escaping the watchful eyes of their elders.

On Saturday morning, Abilene finished straightening the house and putting everything back in place. Lunch was finished, and the dishes were done. The phone rang as she was searching in the freeze for something to fix for supper. She smiled when she picked up her cellphone and saw the number.

"Hi, Wade. What's up?" she asked, pulling out various packages, not sure what to fix.

"Would you go out with me tonight?" he questioned, getting her attention.

She put what she had in her hand back on the self, closing the freezer door. He was asking her out on a real date. "Sure. Casual or dress?"

"Dress. Cocktail dressy. Would six o'clock be good for you?"

"Six if fine."

"See you then."

She stared at the phone in her hand smiling. She had a date. For the first time in over fifteen years, she was going on a real date. Upon lifting her head, she noted Jamie leaning against the doorjamb watching her.

"Wade just asked me to go out with him this evening."

Jamie's response was a nod, his eyes remaining on her.

"You okay with the leftovers in the fridge?" she asked, hoping he wouldn't object to her date.

"Yep. Better go and make yourself pretty for him."

She gave him a hug and kiss on his cheek before heading to the stairs, hoping she had something dressy enough for a fancy place.

Wade arrived in a suit, relieving the fear she was overdressed, allowing her to relax. The dress she had chosen was a dark blue with embroidered peonies around the fitted bodice and lower hem of the full skirt. Matching heels and a small shoulder purse rounded out her ensemble. She had left her hair down to lay in waves and curls around her face and down her back. Wade's head-to-toe scan resulted in a nod and smile. He apparently liked the way she looked.

As the started out the door, Jamie said, "You have her back by a decent hour, you hear?"

"She'll be back before one. I have to work tomorrow."

Abilene wondered where he was taking her which would keep them out until such a late hour. Her eyes widened when she saw the Jaguar parked in the driveway. This wasn't going to be a simple night out.

During the ride, they discussed their day. Before they reached the next town, Wade pulled into a discreet building with a sign proclaiming it was the Villa Maria Restaurant and Lounge. He assisted her out of the low car, leaving it for a valet to park before guiding her into the building, a hand at her waist. Apparently he came here often enough to for the maître d' to know him. He had been greeted by name before they were escorted to a table for two in a quiet corner of the large room.

Once they were seated, Wade said, "I hope you don't mind, but I ordered ahead for us. I don't believe you'll find the meal objectionable."

This was a side of him she hadn't see. He was suave, debonair and confident. It was going to be an interesting evening with the cowboy who had become a man about town with a change of clothes and environment.

"As long as the meat it cooked, I'll not complain," she said with a smile.

Wade filled in the time before their meal arrived with small talk. He was charming, funny and a totally different man. She had no objections when the Chicken Cordon Bleu, asparagus and scalloped potatoes was placed before her. She relaxed and enjoyed the change I him, allowing him to draw her out of her shell. She didn't attend to the others in the restaurant since the man across from her held her attention.

A small ensemble moved to the stage near the wooden dance floor as they were finishing their dessert and wine. She scanned the room. Most of the tables had been cleared of all but coffee or drinks. When Wade didn't indicate he was ready to leave, she assumed he was waiting for the dancing to begin.

At the start of the first song, her assumption was validated. It was a slow song. Wade rose and held out his hand with a smile. They joined the other couples already dancing. Abilene moved into his open arms, enjoying the fell of them about he as he guided her through the steps of the dance. His gaze remained on her as the moved to the music.

When the band segued into a faster song, she expected him to leave the floor, but to her amazement he didn't. With glee, she followed his lead, loving the man who liked to dance to something other than country music. She relaxed, enjoying the exercise and fun of being out on a dancefloor with him. Considering he was a good partner, she wanted to dance for as long as she could, not knowing when she would have the chance again.

After almost a half hour, Abilene indicated her needed to sit down and rest for a few minutes. They returned to their table to find Chad and Eveline waiting for them. The couple had been provided with chairs and something to drink.

"It's about time you two returned. I was beginning to think you were going to do a marathon out there," Chad teased as she and Wade took their seats.

Wade drank half his glass of water before speaking. "No marathon. It's so hard to find a good partner. She's so darn good, I wanted to stay out there as long as possible."

"I get it. I find women have a tendency to trample my toes more than I do theirs," Chad said with a grin.

Eveline lightly punched his shoulder with a mock glare. "I only missed a step one time and stepped on your foot.:

Chad chuckled then kissed her. "I know, but I can't help teasing you about it. You're a great dancer. It was my fault anyway."

Wade leaned back I his chair. "What brings you two here?" I wasn't expecting you." Chad sheepishly lowered his head, sliding a glance to her. "Jamie."

Wade laughed. Abilene knew her face had turned red. "It seems your father doesn't trust me with his precious daughter."

Chad shook his head. "It isn't that. He was grumping about a one o'clock return time when he called dad. When he found out we were going out, he asked us to look you up and make sure you two got home safely at a decent hour."

"Uh, Chad, I do think we're a little over the age of needing a chaperone," Abilene said, attempting not to laugh.

"You and I know that, but you're his 'little' girl. He felt the hour Wade gave for your return was too late. Besides, it gives me a chance to bring Eveline here while interrupting Wade's date for a change."

"Little brother, you aren't interrupting us. Abilene, you ready for another round of dancing?"

He was grinning, not minding Chad and Eveline showing up in the least.

"See you two on the dance floor," she chirped, leading Wade to where the dancers were enjoying themselves.

It was close to one when they pulled into the driveway to the house. Wade walked her to the door, gave her a chaste kiss, opened the door and made sure she was safely inside with the door locked before leaving.

Jamie startled her. "Glad you're home. Did you enjoy yourself?" The small lamp by his chair was turned on and a book was on his lap. He had waited up for her as if she was a teen.

She strolled to where he was sitting and kissed his forehead, then took a seat of the arm of the chair. "Yes, I did. He took me to this place which servers wonderful meals and has dancing afterward so you can burn off all the calories you ate. Not only was he a gentleman, charming and a lot of fun, he's also a fantastic dancer who enjoys dancing."

"Good. Need to get to bed," Jamie said, closing his book.

Abilene fiddled with the strap on her purse. There was something she needed to tell him and there was no time like the present.

"You do know if thing don't work out with Wade, I'm going to need to leave to find a job?"

"Don't need to leave. Have enough to keep you."

"I'm a grown woman and don't need to be living off you," she gently but firmly told him.

"Don't see why not. It's yours."

"No Daddy, it's yours. You earned it."

"Nope. Been yours for a piece. Don't need to leave."

She smiled at him. "What did you do?"

"Been keeping it for you. Don't need it. It's yours."

"And how much are we talking about here?"

"Not sure." He gave a quick shrug, lowering his gaze to the book I his hands. "Couple of million give or take."

"Um, how much?" she asked, not sure she had heard him correctly.

"Couple of million. It's in a trust for you."

"But...I don't understand."

"Own part of the ranch. Take what I need. Put the rest in the bank. Don't do without, but don't need it all. Sort of pile up over the years. Gave it to you when you were a baby."

"Did Grandmother know about this?"

"Yes. Like me, didn't want to spoil you."

The swirling thoughts had her staring at him, attempting to comprehend the words. "Well, I've no idea of what to say to that." It was the truth. She didn't know what to say about finding out she was rich.

"That you'll stay?" Jamie questioned hopefully.

"I'll stay, but don't tell Wade or he'll put off asking me to marry him."

"Won't tell. Bed." He gently pushed her and pointed to the stairs.

"Goodnight, Daddy."

She gave him a hug and kiss before going up the stairs to follow his command, still unable to believe she didn't have to worry about finishing her research, or anything else for that matter.

Chapter 30

On Sunday after church, Wade aske Abilene out again. It was a double date for bowling with Chad and Eveline. Even thought she was the worst bowler of the group, it didn't matter. They laughed a lot and had good clean fun.

On Monday, he invited her to join him for an early lunch date with the promise she would be back in time to meet Kristen and Russ when they arrived. It turned out to be a picnic in a secluded area for the two of them. His excuse was how she might be too busy for it later in the week.

It had been romantic, but again, he stopped the progression of things by keeping to kisses. She wanted more. The man appeared to have an iron control over himself, leaving her totally frustrated with the failure of things to advance. For the first time in years, she wanted a physical relationship. Each time she indicated she wanted to continue, he would repeat, "When the time is right."

Kristen and Russ arrived late in the afternoon. After spending the evening with Abilene and Jamie, Kristen stayed for breakfast the next morning then hurried off to whatever she and Russ had planned for the day. Abby knew it would be the same for the rest of their stay, leaving her free to spend time with Wade. It was good to see her daughter after over a year apart, but Abby was glad Russ was keeping Kristen occupied. It prevented a lot of questions about Wade and their relationship which she couldn't adequately answer.

Over breakfast they would talk and catch up on what the other was doing and then they would only see each other if Abby went to the ranch and the kids were there. As a female, she understood and didn't complain. At this point in Kristen's life, Russ was more important then her mother. It was as it should be for a young adult.

On Wednesday, Wade invited Abby to go to a movie she had mentioned she'd like to see. He didn't even steal a kiss. An arm around her shoulders was the extent of his intimacy for the evening until he kissed her at the door before sending her into the house.

Jamie had her invite Wade over for supper on Friday evening giving the excuse of not having seen much of her during the week. She thought it was a good idea until the two men began talking about the races tomorrow. Both men began pressuring her to ride Ghost.

For some unknown reason they were determined to have her ride in the feature race. Abilene kept refusing, saying she didn't know how to race a horse. When that didn't work, she said Ghost wouldn't willingly participate in their scheme.

Jamie finally said, "Ghost will run and win if you ride him. He loves you. My little girl needs to show 'em up."

"Why is this so important?" Abilene asked. She needed to understand their reasoning for wanting her to ride Ghost in this race.

Wade shifted in his chair, his long fingers catching the drops of water on his glass of iced tea. He glanced at Jamie before speaking.

"There are bets among the local saying you can't control him, let alone win. Many are calling you a city girl who has no idea of how to ride, let along win a race. We know better, but they don't. You need to prove you belong here with us."

Rotating her head, she faced Jamie. "This proving I belong is important to you, isn't it Daddy?"

"Yep."

Other than never ridding in a real race, she didn't have a valid excuse for not participating. It would be interesting to see how Ghost would handle being somewhere with a lot of people. It would also be fun to see if he would really show what he could do in a race. Besides, she didn't believe there was a horse in the state who could beat him, not matter who rode him.

"Alright. I'll do it. Hopefully there's a horse or two how can challenge him. I'd like to see what he can do. So far he hasn't even been trying hard to beat the others."

"What do you mean?" Wade asked, becoming alert.

She chuckled. "You don't know him like I do. I can tell from that question. He's been toying with the other horses. He's only been running for fun and isn't pushing himself to pass the others. He's like jogging while the others are running full out."

"If that's true, he'll win for the fun of being in the lead." Wade leaned back in his chair, a big grin on his face.

Abilene quirked an eyebrow. "You do realize I've been giving you all a big lead then let him catch up to you. He 'laughs' as he passes you, not nothing more than a simple, easy run. Like I said, it's like he's jogging past the other horses who are doing everything they can to stay ahead of him."

"You'll win," Jamie said with a nod.

"Yeah. I hope it won't be by a mile or they'll claim it's because she's light than the rest," Wade said with a smirk.

She stared at him for a few seconds, attempting to figure out where he got that idea, then shook her head. "I'm sure there will be several riders who are heck of a lot lighter than I am. I'm not model thin in case you haven't noticed."

Wade ogled her with eye showing what he was thinking. "Oh, I've noticed."

She laughed while Jamie glared at him. Wade had definitely noticed she wasn't thin and had mentioned on more than once occasion how he liked her weight and resulting curves. It wasn't that she was fat, but at five eight, she wore a size twelve with her weight normally between one forty and one forty-five. She had a lot of muscle but did have what she called "fluff" spread around her torso and thighs. As long as she stayed a size twelve, she didn't get too concerned.

Once she agreed to ride in the race, the men discussed the other races and the chances of their horses winning based on the other horses entered and the person riding. Nolan, Wade, Chad and Leland were all riding in various races. Wade was taking Jamie's normal place in the lineup since he was unable to ride yet because of his shoulder.

They would be taking six horses and were expecting all six of them to win their particular race based on the other entries. Abby hoped they were right. It would be fun to win every race they entered. She knew Ghost would win his race if he didn't get disqualified because of her.

Chapter 31

Saturday morning arrived before Abilene was ready. She loaded Ghost onto the trailer with Domingo, the black stallion Wade had been training. Jamie already had the tack in the trailer for both horses and was waiting for them to leave.

Leland joined Jamie, Wade and her for the trip to the flats where the races were to be held. Chad, Eveline and Nolan were the in the second truck pulling a trailer with four more horses for the races they had entered. Trent, Russ and Kristen would me them there. They were coming later in the day since they had planned a trip to see one of Russ's friends in the morning, not aware of the races.

Wade had informed Abilene prior to his father's arrival that they couldn't use the big trailer, which would have easily handled the six horses. Ghost wouldn't get into it. Besides, they had to take a second vehicle anyway because there wasn't enough room for everyone in one truck.

When they arrived at the race grounds, there were multiple of people unloading and setting up for the day. Abby wondered if there were any people left to watch the races with the numerous cowboys in the barns and corrals. Nolan had reserved their area on the outer edge of the corrals to avoid heavy traffic and excessive noise. It was the corral and shed they normally used when participation in the races. Their horses, unlike most of the others, weren't used to all the hustle and bustle of large gatherings.

Ghost docilely walked into the large corral when he came off the trailer. He looked around before standing still, ignoring everything around him. If people didn't know him, they would have thought he was an old horse sleeping with is head down, one leg bent with his hoof barely touching the ground. His back was swayed as the lounged in the middle of the corral.

The other five horses hilled about giving him protection. It was all Abilene could do not to laugh when several men came by to greet they family and see what horses they had brought with them. They couldn't imagine the white horse running, let alone winning. Like Wade, she let them make their own assessments, not commenting on their take on Ghost and his abilities. She ever heard one man saying how he couldn't understand by Nolan allowed them to bring an old nag to race.

The race she was to ride in was the last one of the day. It was the feature race, scheduled for around three in the afternoon. She had chosen to stay at the corral with the horses while the others went about their business. She didn't know enough people in the area to make it worth wandering around the grounds. One of the men returned to saddle a horse for a race then leave within a few minutes. They would talk as they worked but didn't stay long. She didn't mind, enjoying her time with the horses.

The corral where they were was reasonably quiet one everybody was set up for the day. She passed the time reading. So far, Nolan, Chad and Wade had each taken a horse to ride in various races. At lunchtime, Jaime, Wade and Nolan joined her, bringing food with them. Because she was hungry, she didn't complain about the food which was mostly fried.

Ghost hadn't moved much during the day. He still appeared to be a has-been to anyone who didn't know him. The only sign he was paying attention to things was the way his ears twitched, and his head moved.

"You still think he'll run?" Nolan asked, eyeing the docile horse with concern.

"Yes. He's avoiding the people. He doesn't like it here but he's tolerating it for me," Abilene answered.

What she didn't tell him was how she had gone into the corral to spend time with the unhappy horse. He would do what she wanted, trusting her as she did him. The way he shook his head and crowded her told her more than anything how much he disliked being this close to so many people.

She frowned and said, "I hope you know I won't agree to this again. It isn't fair to Ghost. He doesn't like it here with all the people."

"Once is enough," Jamie concurred with a nod.

With their lunch done, the men again left her alone. Wade had given her a quick kiss and said he would be back before the last race to take her to the track. Then he hurried off toward the stands.

At two o'clock, Abilene brought Ghost into the shed to get him ready for the race. When he tossed his head and pawed the floor, she looked around to see who was behind her. It was a man about six feet tall and lanky with a hawkish face under a worn Stetson. This was someone she had never met. He was staring at her and Ghost from the hitching rail located about ten feet in front of the shed.

"May I help you?" she asked, holding the saddle blanket.

"When he moved closer, Abilene got between him and Ghost, not sure what he wanted.

"Name's Sam. I'm ridin' against this horse. Just wanted to see him after all the talk I've been a hearin'. Take it you're riding' him.?"

"Yes. I'm Abby. I wish you luck in the race."

Same ran his eyes over Ghost before saying, "He don't look too happy."

She glanced back at Ghost. Sam was correct. Ghost wasn't exactly happy with being here. "He isn't, but he'll be fine."

"I take it he don't like strangers."

"Correct. I'd not advise anyone to get to close to him while on foot."

Sam didn't come any closer with her warning. "He don't look like much," Sam commented, studying the horse behind her.

When Abilene glanced back over her shoulder, Ghost was standing as he had been in the corral. It was how he had spent most of his day when there were people around he didn't know. She bit her lower lip to keep from grinning. "Maybe not, but he isn't too bad once you get him moving."

Sam chuckled, shaking his head. "Good luck on getting him to move."

He left, grinning and shaking his head, discounting Ghost as a contender. Ghost's head came up. He nuzzled her and nickered which Abilene characterized as his laugh. She guessed he knew what was happening and was having fun pretending he was a nag. She wondered if he had learned to look broken down by watching which horses the men kept versus the ones they returned to the wild. If so, it was a great tactic to get returned to freedom.

Leland was leaning against the post at the outer portion of the shed, having walked up as Sam left. Abby glanced at him before returning to preparing Ghost for the race. With pursed lips and creased eye, she could see he was holding back a laugh as he assessed her and Ghost.

"You teach him how to look like he was ready for the glue factory?"

Abilene laughed, tightening the cinch on the saddle who had played with the competition. "No, I didn't teach him that. I swear he's been playing a game all day."

"I hope you know Sam will have someone on foot to try to get close to him if he looks like he's going to win the race." Leland tilted his head, watching her as he waited for her response.

"I sort of figured that out. It won't work, but it's wroth a try for them, I guess." She continued getting Ghost ready.

"Now how do you know that?" Leland asked, moving closer.

"I've seen what he does. He'll avoid them if he can. If they get in his way, he'll just know them over. No big deal." She shrugged, replacing the halter with a bridle without a bit over Ghost's head when he lowered it for her.

Ghost turned and eyed Leland, who ran his hand down the big horse's neck. Abilene stared at him before saying, "I didn't think anyone but Wade, Daddy and I could get near him, let alone touch him."

Leland winked at her. "Yeah, well Ghost and I are old friends. I can't ride him, but he'll let me take care of him."

"Why?" she asked, curious about Leland's friendship with the untamed stallion.

Leland smiled, patting Ghost, who nipped at his shoulder. "It's sort of a long story, but I'll shorten it. Our tribe has been in this area for hundreds of years. They have always been fond of horses. For generations we've been exceptionally good at breaking and training them in a gently way.

When the Chapmans came here, they made friends with us. They agreed to work with us on keeping the herds hidden while giving us protection from the other settlers. In return, we taught them what we knew about training the horses without breaking their spirit, aware they wouldn't decimate the wild herds.

"I found Ghost up in the high country while I was looking for some missing cattle. His right rear hoof had split, and he could hardly walk. He has been left behind, not able to keep up with the herd. At the time, he couldn't have been but a year old, if that. I got him to trust me in order to treat and feed him. I kept him in a makeshift corral to stop him from walking on the hoof before it healed.

"When he got better, I turned him loose because he was too young to train. Once he was free, he would come back around every few days. I'd give him some oats and brush him, take care of his hooves and that type of thing.

"On day, I attempted to get him to accept a rope halter. He refused and backed way from me. When I put it down, he came back over to me. I tired several times during that visit with the same results. I never attempted to but a halter on him after that day.

"When he walked into the pen with the herd and stayed, I was surprised. It was the last things I had ever expected him to do. Ghost would let me touch him, but he only allowed Wade to put a halter on him and ride him. He seemed to know Wade would never attempt to fully break him.

"Long story short, Wade didn't have the heart to pen him up, saying he needed to be free, so Ghost does as he pleases. Now he loves you because you seem instinctively to understand him. He'll be your horse as long as you don't try to take away his freedom."

She rubbed Ghost's nose. "I'd never do that. It would be the worst cruelty anyone could ever do to him." She stared off into the distance before bringing her focus back to Leland. She needed to know where she stood in their little family. Now was as good a time as any to ask her questions. "I take it you'll inherit Jamie's portion of the ranch."

Leland played with Ghost's mane as if thinking before answering. "I'll inherit, but I have to split the profits with you. Pop said it was only fair."

She shook her head. "I don't need it. Daddy already has saved enough for more than a lifetime for me."

Leland's brows rose with her statement. He faced her. "Abby, what Pop has for you is a drop in the bucket. This ranch and the secondary jobs pay really good. Just wait. You'll see."

She changed the subject, not wanting to argue with him about money at this time. "I take it from the way you use a bow and arrow that you've spent a lot of time with your mother's family."

"Yes, but that doesn't mean anything. My friends and I actually began to learn the old ways for fun from several of the elders in the tribe. Those of us who use the bow an arrows are competitors in various competitions. We're the top team in the nation for bow and arrow, crossbow and rifle. We wanted to show the white men we're still a force to be reckoned with, even if we are on a rez." His grin showed his pride in their accomplishments.

"So you learned the old way to stay ahead of the game, so to speak."

"Yep. Comes in handy in protecting people. No one expects arrows. Learning to blend in with our environment has paid off big time. I can thank my grandfather and his friends for teaching us the old ways and language. I've taught my children what I've learned, too. Two of them were there with us at the cabin."

She blinked, her mouth agape. He had to be only a couple of years younger than her even though he looked like he was in his late twenties or early thirties. It was hard to envision him with grown children.

"I'd like to meet them sometime," she managed to say.

Leland nodded. "You'll get to meet them soon. Nolan is having a party to celebrate the signing of the canyon property over to the tribe as an official part of the reservation. We'll all be there including Maya, my wife, and our three boys and two girls."

"Great. I can hardly wait."

Leland glanced back over his shoulder to see if anyone was around before saying, "Good luck."

She smiled at him before turning back to Ghost. "Thanks."

He gave Ghost another pat. "You had better win, big guy. I've got a big bet on you."

Ghost nudged him as he chuckled. He returned to the corral and lead a horse which hadn't raced to the saddling shed. It looked like there was still one race to run before the feature race. Leland had the horse ready in minutes before leading him way, leaving her to think over that he had told her.

She still couldn't imagine him with children, let along grown children. If she remembered correctly, he was only two years younger than she was. His oldest would be close to the age of

Kristen, who was twenty-four. Yes, he could easily have two children over twenty-one.

Chapter 32

It was close to a half hour before Wade came to walk her to the holding area for the race. The last race had just finished. Leland has won and was leaving the winner's circle. As they waited, Ghose kept up his act of being a dispirited horse. Abilene noticed he was watching and listening to everything about him. The horse was cagey. It explained why he was the leader of the wild herd. He hadn't only beaten them in a fight, but he also had outsmarted a lot of the competition.

They were called to the starting line. Wade gave her a kiss for luck, then helped her in to the saddle before leaning them to the starting position. He kept his hand on Ghost's bridle since he was the only one who could be near enough to hold him as required. Wade had already cleared it so Ghost didn't need a bit to race, preventing disqualification for not using one.

Abilene scanned the competition. They wouldn't be able to claim she was too light either. There were several riders the size of jockeys with racing saddles to lighten the weight. She patted Ghost's neck, letting him know she was there with him. His head came up, ears twitching.

Wade winked at her when the big horse turned his head to look at the other horses. Ghost shook his head, snorted and twitched his ears again. It was the only sign he gave to indicate he was ready to run unless one of the others who had visited their corral recognized he was no long swaybacked.

After blowing out a big breath to calm down, Abilene studied the racecourse. The rock outcropping which marked the end of the race was barely visible. She was aware it was a short distance for Ghost to run. He could do double the distance and then some if not pushed hard. The only question was: would he run the race as required? If he did, she knew he would win for the fun of being in the lead.

When a man with a bullhorn began to give the instructions for the race, she listened closely, not want to be disqualified. When he was finished, the men who had been holding the horses stepped away. Ghost raised his head, shook it, then snorted again. She could feel the tenseness in him, telling her he was ready to run.

The gun went off, signaling the start of the race. Several horses jumped off the starting line ahead of the group. Ghost waited for her to nudge him into action. It put him in the middle of the pack. He started with an easy run, quickly overtaking the slower horses with his long ground-eating stride, enjoying running in the pack.

Abilene let him find his way through the other racers, leaning over his neck, reveling in the feel of power Ghost exuded. He wasn't racing. As he came even with the other horses, he would let them run beside him for a few strides before easily passing them to catch the next horse or horses. It was as if he was checking on how good each horse was before moving to the next ones.

Before they were halfway through the race, Ghose was behind the leader. Abilene knew he wasn't pushing to pass the big roan horse with a white blaze on his nose. It was almost as if he was gaging the stamina of his competitor. She recognized Same, who was hitting his horse to make him go faster when he noticed Ghose on his tail.

As the finish line came into view, Abilene nudged Ghost gently, not wanting to wait until the last minute to get ahead. He responded with a slight increase in speed, but he was still running for fun, not racing like the other horse. Pulling even with Sam, Ghost ran with the other horse for several strides before easily moving ahead of him, increasing the distance with each long stride. The big white horse was only running fast enough to remain ahead of the others as they streaked down the last portion of the track, showing the other horses who the leader was.

A man stepped out from the crowd when they were close to the finish line. An involuntary gasp left her mouth, but she didn't attempt to exert control, letting Ghost decide to brush past, never wavering in his stride. They crossed the line well ahead of Sam, who was the closest to them. After running for a short distance past the finish, Ghost slowed to a lope and tossed his head.

For the first time since she had been riding him, Ghost was breathing hard, but he wasn't bellowing. He was prancing about as the others passed over the finish line. By the time the last horse came in, he had recovered and was breathing normally.

With his tail swishing, he was playful and full of energy, ready to run again as the other horses were being walked to cool them down. Ghost hadn't run enough for the day and was showing his displeasure at being stopped so quickly by tossing his head and attempting to take off for the grassland.

Not dismounting, Abilene let things settled down before maneuvering Ghost to where Same was standing with his horse. She overheard him growling about how his horse was the best and Ghost's win was only a fluke. She knew better. Ghost was far better than Sam's horse would ever be. Ghost had the advantage of being able to run whenever he wanted and for how long he wanted. Sam's horse, on the other hand, was kept in a corral or small pasture and couldn't exercise as needed to develop the stamina for the big white horse.

"Want to race back?" she asked with a big grin, her eyebrows raised. She was challenging him to prove it was a fluke as he said.

"There's no way that horse can race back after running that distance," Sam stated. He stared at her as if she had lost her mind.

"Race you back," she challenged again, the big grin not leaving her face.

Sam studied her. A sly grin crossed his face before saying, "Only if I can change horses."

"Go for it," Abilene said with a shrug as Ghost moved away from the man who was too close to him.

She watched as Sam requested a horse which hadn't been raced today which he felt could be Ghost. He was confident he would win, not believing Ghost would be able to repeat his run. She had watched the bets being exchanged with most of them being placed on Sam. She patted Ghost, who was pawing the ground, ready to run again.

"Be prepared to scrape him off the ground," Sam gloated, astride a small gray filly.

With a laugh, Abilene moved Ghost to the finish line. Sam had made a huge mistake. There was no way Ghost would let a filly win a race here or on the plains, that is unless it was so he could mate with her. It proved how little Sam knew about horses in general.

Sam, or those with him, had apparently made it known Abilene was challenging him to a race back to the starting line. Once they had lined up, a man with a handkerchief held high in his hand stood on the line where both riders could see him. When he decided they were ready to race, he dropped the handkerchief. The two of them took off, racking back to the starting line.

Sam got the filly off the starting line in the lead. Ghost ran easily behind the other horse for the first half of the course. He then pulled even with the filly. Again he didn't expend much energy, enjoying the run while challenging the filly to keep up with him. She felt him slowly speeding up as the filly did its best to outrun him.

As they neared the starting line, Abilene didn't have to nudge him forward. He knew to go faster. She felt the change as he sped up, easily leading the other horse by three lengths as the crossed the starting line.

Ghost slowed then circled back to greet the other horse. The two horses nosed each other, Ghost was barely breathing hard while the other horse was fighting for breath. Ghost could have easily run a third race, but she wasn't going to push him. She had proven she could handle the big stallion without a problem.

Meanwhile, Ghost has shown them what he could do, and that was enough for one day. There wasn't another horse there who could keep up with him and she knew it. His running in the wild had given him a lot of stamina for the long races. As Wade has stated, he was bred to run and run he did, every chance he got.

Sam dismounted before facing her. It was easy to see he was seeing dollar signs as he stared at Ghost. "I don't know where you go that horse, but I'll take him off your hands for whatever you want for him."

With a quirked eyebrow, Abilene said, "He isn't for sale. Besides, you wouldn't be able to ride him even if he was. He's a one-person horse."

"I can't believe he just ran three miles and is barely winded. He must keep you busy running him all the time."

"He's a leader," she said, leaving him to figure out what she meant.

Without getting down, she walked Ghost back to the paddock where Wade was waiting. He helped her form the saddle, held her close then gave her a quick kiss.

"Girl, you do realize I just made a bundle on you and that nag as they were calling him."

"Really? On which trip?" she quipped with an impish grin, remaining in his embrace.

"Both. They didn't believe he would make it back, let alone in the lead."

"So glad I could increase your coffers." She gave him a kiss on the cheek before heading to the shed with Ghost following her.

Wade put a hand on her arm, stopping her before she got halfway to the shed. He handed her a wad of cash. She looked at it, then back to him. "What's this?"

"Your half. You did all the work."

She sifted through the money. Most of it was hundred dollar bills. Unbale to comprehend betting more than a couple of dollars on a race, it was difficult to believe he had handed her several thousand dollars.

"You won all of this?"

"Yes, sweetheart. We have some friends who like to bet big, and this time I was willing to take them on at their price. A couple still owe me money, so you'll get some more."

She stuffed the money into her pocket and shrugged. It meant she wouldn't have to hip up her savings for the rest of her stay. There was no way she was going to turn down free money.

"You all are nuts," she said, unsaddling Ghost.

Wade watched as she sprayed the horse with the hose then began to brush him as he stood docilely for her.

"I may be nuts," he said, "but that crazy return ride was what got me the big money. I was hoping you knew what you were doing."

She kept brushing Ghost, not looking back at Wade. "He can run up to five miles if you don't push him too hard. Three was a fun jaunt for him, especially on the flat ground."

"Now how do you know that?" Wade moved to where she was working to better hear her answer.

"Daddy. He followed him one night to see where he was headed. He ran in an easy run for over five miles to get to the herd. When he got there, he wasn't even winded. He did his thing and then ran back to the ranch where he was waiting for Daddy to get back."

Wade didn't speak for several minutes before chuckling. "Foxy. His nag routine and you knowing what he's capable of doing blew them out of the water. I now know how you survived all these years."

"And here you thought I was only a dumb broad," Abilene snidely retorted, barely holding in her laughter.

He chuckled. "A broad you may be, but never dumb."

She threw the wet rag she was holding at him. He caught it with a laugh. Giving him a shove, he reached out and captured her. The kiss had her melting against him.

"Abby girl, you're one of a kind."

"I know and don't you forget it."

"Alright you two. Enough play. I'd like to get home before midnight," Nolan stated, startling them.

Wade moved away from her. "Working on it, Dad."

"Didn't look like it to me," Nolan commented as he walked off, grinning.

Wade got busy putting the tack in the trailer, his face read as Abilene snickered. She returned to grooming Ghost as the others joined them to pack up and leave. It was hard to believe how his father's simple teasing embarrassed her tough cowboy.

Chapter 33

Over the next month, Wade spent more time with Abilene than he did at home in the evenings. He took her out at least once a week. Jamie insisted on her being home at midnight after one night when they didn't get back until close to two in the morning. He didn't mind if she didn't come in right away, but he wanted her home. Each date, he would wait for her to come in prior to going to bed. To her, it showed how much he cared about her, even though she was forty-six years old.

Abilene looked forward to the time she spent with Wade. It had gotten so she didn't want him to leave. On the days he worked, she would go to the ranch on a frequent basis. She and Nancy visited as she watched the men working. Wade and Leland were the best with the horses with Nolan and Chad not far behind. They understood the horses and were gentle in their handling of them. All of them enjoyed working with the horses.

All too soon, she realized her lease would be up in a month. She could stay. Money was no longer an issue. It was a difficult decision, but she decided if Wade wasn't going to marry her, she couldn't remain here. Jamie had understood when she explained it to him even though he didn't want her to leave.

She started going for memories, instead of expecting permanence, during their time together. Jamie knew what she was doing. He only comment had been, "He'll come after you."

Two weeks before she planned to leave, she decided to go to the place she wanted to explore when she had first arrived at the ranch. She might as well get back to work. There was no time like the present. Besides, it was a beautiful day for a ride.

She packed a lunch, saddled Ghost, and left a note on the table which gave Jamie where she was going to be. She knew Jamie would be worried if she wasn't there when he got back to the house. Things had been quiet, so she wasn't afraid of going off on her own. She always took her hip pistol with her in case she ran into an aggressive animal, be it one of two legs or four.

Ghost was happy with the trip, running as she headed to the large rock formation several miles from the house. When they got there, Abilene couldn't believe her luck. It was perfect. She began to work as Ghost stayed close to her, grazing on the grass in the area. She was drawing when she heard someone coming into the area where she was working.

Pivoting on the rock she was using as a seat, she saw Wade on Domingo coming toward the formation. She returned to her drawing, continuing what she was doing. He dismounted and came up behind her. When he didn't speak, she ignored him, focusing on what she was doing.

"You shouldn't be out here alone," Wade said, his voice holding controlled anger.

"Why? Trent said I was safe. I need to get back to work."

"Jamie is back at the house, cussing up a storm with you being out here by yourself."

"He'll get over it." Her voice was cold, preparing herself for leaving.

Wade moved to stand before her, blocking her view of the rock she was recording.

"Will you please move. I'd like to get this done while the sun is hitting the rocks."

"What's going on, Abilene?"

"I'm leaving in two weeks. What do you think is going on?" Her voice was sharp, peering up at him with a frown.

"I won't let you leave," he stated.

"I can't stay."

"Why not?"

With a glare she snapped, "Figure it out. Now move!"

He moved. She continued with her drawing. When finished, she gathered her things and packed them on Ghost. Before she could mount, Wade's voice stopped her.

"Abby, do you love me?"

She kept her back to him. "Yes. I love you." It was because she loved him she couldn't stay, but he didn't seem to know it.

"Then why do you want to leave?"

Leaning her head against the saddle, she let the tears which had welled fall. "I didn't say I wanted to leave. I said I had to leave."

"Why?"

This was the crux of the problem. He didn't understand why.

"Figure it out, Wade," she repeated. Straightening, she mounted Ghost and left, leaving him standing there staring after her.

She wasn't going to beg him to marry her, and she wouldn't stay if he didn't. It hurt too much to be so close without the commitment she needed from him.

When they hit the level area, she gave Ghost his head and let him run, wanting to get as far away as she could from the man who was tearing her apart. Ghost suddenly veered from the ranch. She let him go, not knowing what the problem was until she noted a group of men chasing her. Leaning low over the running horse, she let him choose where to go.

He ran down a couple of small canyons before her sharply turned into the narrow opening, almost unseating her. It was filled with torturous turns along with several openings going off on both sides, all barely big enough for a horse to get through. Ghost took a quick right into one of the small canyons.

When they exited the canyon, she saw it had taken them to where she could see the ranch. Ghost took off at a full run. A second group of men were chasing her. He took the fence in a giant leap and kept on running until he was at the barn. When Ghost stopped, he was breathing hard, having run at top speed. She slipped from his back.

Nolan ran out of the barn. "Get in the house. Now!"

She ignored him, unsaddling Ghost and pulling off his bridle. The big horse trotted into the barn. Nolan picked up the saddle and put it on the corral rail.

"Abilene, go to the house," Nolan commanded in a voice which didn't allow room for argument. He had a rifle in his hand, eyes hard and mouth grim.

She obeyed, running to the kitchen door. Jamie was there waiting for her as were Trent and Chad.

"What's going on?" she asked.

"Not now," Trent said as he picked up a high-powered rifle and went out the door, followed by Chad who also had a rifle. They took aim at the riders who were close to the ranch. Trent squeezed off two rounds. Nolan and Leland, who had appeared in the yard, joined him as they fired methodically at the group of men, slowing them down. They weren't trying to hurt them. The purpose was to stop them from getting too close.

Abilene paled when she remembered Wade. He was alone out there with two groups of men who seemed bent on catching her. She checked her pistol. It was ready with an extra full magazine on her belt. Moving to the window, she watched as the men kept coming, but slower than when they had been chasing her.

Wade's voice came to her. She began to run out the door only to have Jamie hold her in place

"Let them handle it," Jamie said, pulling her back from the door.

Not bothering to fight the inevitable, she let him lead her away from the men firing at the riders until they stopped and milled around at the fence line of the main compound. The men seemed to know what was happening, but she had no clue, and no one was talking to her.

A helicopter flew overhead, circling the compound. It wasn't long until the yard was filled with flashing light. Resigned to being kept in the living room with Jamie, she curled up on the sofa, despondent at the turn of events. Wade was lost to her and her safety was gone again.

The helplessness at the situation, she waited for someone to tell her what was happening. As the time wore on, she laid her head on the arm of the couch, closing her eyes as she attempted to calm herself. In the quiet of the room, she slid into a light doze, exhausted from being out in the sun and the tension of the current situation.

In her dream, a gentle hand brushed her cheek, making her smile at the feelings it elicited. In the dream she reached out to the man. Her eyes popped open when she realized she was touching the arm flesh of a live person.

Wade's face was even with hers as he squatted by the couch. His eyes were worried but held something else she couldn't place. He leaned over on kissed her. "I figured it out."

It took her a second to understand what he was referring to at first.

"Oh?" she questioned, hoping he had it right.

"What do you think about us moving into the Haskell spread after we're married?" he questioned, his eyes boring into hers.

"Are you asking me to marry you?" she asked. The way he phrased it, she wasn't sure if he was or if he was asking questions as he had the night of Chad's engagement to Eve.

"Yes."

"I'd love to stay there," she responded.

He bit his lower lip before taking a deep breath. "Are you saying you'll marry me?"

"Yes," she answered, her hand caressing his cheek. At that moment she realized what she had seen in his eyes. It was fear.

"I won't leave without you. Promise," she swore him as she watched the fear recede to be replaced by the tenderness and love she knew he had for her.

His mouth tilted in a grin. "It wouldn't matter. I'd come after you."

She returned him grin. "I know, but there isn't any reason to chase me all over the globe when you could just come with me."

He gave her another kiss. "I love you, Abby. I'm not letting you go."

She met him gaze. "You'd better not. I don't believe I could survive if you did."

His face creased in a smile. "You're a sly one. Come on. It's suppertime and I'm hungry, but we can't eat until this mess is settled. The deputy needs to talk to you."

He helped her up from the couch, guiding her through the doorway into the kitchen. There were multiple people sitting or standing waiting for her. She stopped short, surveying the gathered men, not sure what they wanted.

"It's about time you decided to join us," a state trooper commented with a smile.

"What now?" she asked, not sure she wanted to know.

"Well, there a small matter of a charge of horse theft against you," a deputy said with a grin.

His words had her staring at him. "Really? And what horse am I being accused of stealing?"

"A big white stallion. Says here the horse's name is Star."

With a frown, tapping her foot and arms crossed, she said, "No horse by that name here. Who's accusing me of stealing this horse?"

"A man named Samuel Langley."

It all made sense now. He had noticed Ghost has no brand and decided if she wasn't willing to sell him, he would get him another way. "If he believes we have his horse, it should have his brand on it."

"He said the horse wasn't branded," the trooper imparted with raised brows.

"Humph. If he thinks I have his horse, then let him come and ride him out of here," said with sarcasm not missed by the trooper.

"Ma'am, are you sure about that?" the deputy asked, worry on his face.

With a glare, well aware Sam wouldn't get near enough to put a bridle on him, she said, "I'm positive. If the white horse I have is his, he should be able to ride him out of here without problem, agreed?"

"I agree," Nolan said with a grin.

"Any objection for anyone?" the officer questioned, scanning their faces.

"No objections," Trent said. "But he has *ride* him out of here. We'll give him ten minutes to get on him and leave."

"And if he doesn't?" the trooper asked. His grin showed he knew there was a catch to what they were saying.

"Then you arrest him for attempted horse theft and filing a false claim against Abilene," Nolan stated.

"Oookay," the deputy drawled, his face showing he wasn't sure of what to expect.

"I'll turn him loose in the paddock," Abilene volunteered. "no roping allowed. If this is his horse, he should be able to walk up to him and saddle him."

The officer didn't respond. He followed her out of the house. She found Ghost standing in the barn waiting for her. She led him to they paddock, a hand on his shoulder. Ghost moved to the middle of the paddock, eyeing the people who were sitting on the rails. She walked away, smiling at Sam.

"Go ahead. You say he's your horse, now prove it."

Sam picked up the halter he had with a bit on it, moving toward Ghost. "It's okay, Star," he crooned.

Ghost moved out of his reach. Sam continued to talk to the horse while Ghost continued to move away out of his reach.

Everyone watched as Sam kept attempting to get near to the horse he claimed was his. He eventually backed Ghost into a corner, believing he could put the bridle on him at that point. When Ghost reared, his hooves beating the air, Sam stumbled back, falling on his buttocks, scrabbling to get out of the way of the deadly hooves above him. His feet scrabbled for purchase in the dirt in his haste to move back from Ghost.

Ghost returned to all fours, trotting past him, back to the center of the big paddock. He turned to face Sam who picked himself up off the ground. Abilene giggled. There was no way Sam would ever get that bridle on Ghost, even if he could touch him.

The state trooper put a stop to the farce. "I've seen enough. Missy, go and put your horse back in the barn."

She slid off the fence. As she passed Same, she said loud enough for all the others to hear, "You can't use a bit on him. He doesn't like them." Scooping a halter off the post, Ghost lower his head, allowing her to put it on him. He then followed her to the barn without her touching him like a well-trained dog.

Ghost stood in an open stall, eating the oats she gave him. He had received an extra portion as a reward for not hurting Sam.

Sam glared at her as she passed him, his hands in cuffs. "Same, I liked you until you tried this stunt. You know damn well that just because he doesn't have a brand, he isn't your horse. Wade trained him, but even he can't fully control him. He's my horse. I told you he didn't like people. I hope you believe me now."

"How did you get away from the posse?" Sam asked, his eyes on her face.

"That's my secret," she said with a wink at Wade, who was holding in a laugh.

One of the men on the fence commented, "Yeah, like on minute you're there and the next you're gone. Poof. Like a ghost."

She crossed her arms, facing the men, daring them to guess how she had disappeared. "My secret on how to go poof."

Another man added, "She goes poof for you and disappears then for us, poof and she appeared out of nowhere."

She grinned and left the paddock. Wade's grin and merry eyes told her he knew what had happened. He had seen Ghost disappear before when chasing him.

"Do you believe in ghosts?" she asked Wade, who had joined her.

"You bet I do. I saw you go poof and wondered where you would end up. I do have to say, I'm going to have to keep Domingo. He outran the posse with room to spare."

Wade held her as he listened to the officer read Sam his rights. His arms tightened around her when the officer led him away. Wade bent his head, planting a light kiss on her lips.

"When are we getting married?" he asked, surprising her with the question.

She giggled, "Is tomorrow too soon?"

He didn't answer for a few seconds then chuckled. "I believe so. Dad would have a fit."

"Then I'm lucky. I believe Daddy would be relieved."

"Let's see what we can set up while Kristen and Russ are here. It would save them a trip back."

She asked, "Do you know when they are planning on leaving? Kristen has said anything to me."

"Two more weeks."

She paused, going over the plans for a simple wedding, calculating how long it would take to get everything arranged. "Ten days from now is the date."

"Then I guess I'd better give this to you now." Wade slipped a ring onto her finger. She stared at what she thought was the perfect ring. He raised her hand to his lips. "You're mine, Abilene."

She chuckled. "I've been yours since you said excuse me in the store as you reached around me for dish soap."

His face reddened as she laughed. He shook his head, gathering her close to him. "I can see live with you will always be full of surprises."

"Of course. Can't have you getting bored with me too quickly," was her muffled reply as she continued to giggle.

He tugged her hair. "I won't get bored with you. Well, maybe in thirty or forty years, but not anytime soon."

She leaned back in his arms grinning. "I'll make you chase me if you get too bored."

He broke into laughter. She joined in his merriment, well aware life with him wouldn't ever be dull.

The End